P9-DDN-876

Praise for the Flower Shop Mysteries

A Rose from the Dead

"The tale is wrapped around the wonderful hallmarks of this series: a spirited heroine surrounded by zany characters, humor, and irreverence." —*Romantic Times*

Acts of Violets

"Abby's sharp observations bring laughs while the intriguing, tightly plotted mystery keeps you guessing." —*Romantic Times*

"A delightful, lighthearted cozy." —The Best Reviews

Snipped in the Bud

"Lighthearted and fast-paced, Collins's new book is an entertaining read." —*Romantic Times*

Dearly Depotted

"Abby is truly a hilarious heroine. . . . Don't miss this fresh-as-a-daisy read." —*Rendezvous*

"Ms. Collins's writing style is crisp, her characters fun . . . and her stories are well thought-out and engaging." —Fresh Fiction

continued . . .

Slay It with Flowers

"Upbeat, jocular . . . an uplifting, amusing, and feel-good amateur sleuth tale."
—The Best Reviews

"What a delight! Ms. Collins has a flair for engaging characters and witty dialogue."
—Fresh Fiction

"You can't help but laugh . . . an enormously entertaining read."
—*Rendezvous*

"Collins has created a delightful amateur sleuth."
—*Romantic Times*

Mum's the Word

"Kate Collins plants all the right seeds to grow a fertile garden of mystery. . . . Abby Knight is an Indiana florist who cannot keep her nose out of other people's business. She's rash, brash, and audacious. Move over, Stephanie Plum. Abby Knight has come to town."
—Denise Swanson, author of the Scumble River Mysteries

"An engaging debut planted with a spirited sleuth, quirky sidekicks, and page-turning action . . . delightfully addictive . . . a charming addition to the cozy subgenre. Here's hoping we see more of intrepid florist Abby Knight and sexy restaurateur Marco Salvare."
—Nancy J. Cohen, author of the Bad Hair Day Mysteries

Other Flower Shop Mysteries

Shoots to Kill

A Flower Shop Mystery

Kate Collins

AN OBSIDIAN MYSTERY

OBSIDIAN
Published by New American Library, a division of
Penguin Group (USA) Inc., 375 Hudson Street,
New York, New York 10014, USA
Penguin Group (Canada), 90 Eglinton Avenue East, Suite 700, Toronto,
Ontario M4P 2Y3, Canada (a division of Pearson Penguin Canada Inc.)
Penguin Books Ltd., 80 Strand, London WC2R 0RL, England
Penguin Ireland, 25 St. Stephen's Green, Dublin 2,
Ireland (a division of Penguin Books Ltd.)
Penguin Group (Australia), 250 Camberwell Road, Camberwell, Victoria 3124,
Australia (a division of Pearson Australia Group Pty. Ltd.)
Penguin Books India Pvt. Ltd., 11 Community Centre, Panchsheel Park,
New Delhi - 110 017, India
Penguin Group (NZ), 67 Apollo Drive, Rosedale, North Shore 0632,
New Zealand (a division of Pearson New Zealand Ltd.)
Penguin Books (South Africa) (Pty.) Ltd., 24 Sturdee Avenue,
Rosebank, Johannesburg 2196, South Africa

Penguin Books Ltd., Registered Offices:
80 Strand, London WC2R 0RL, England

First published by Obsidian, an imprint of New American Library,
a division of Penguin Group (USA) Inc.

First Printing, August 2008
10 9 8 7 6 5 4 3 2 1

Copyright © Linda Tsoutsouris, 2008
All rights reserved

PUBLISHER'S NOTE
This is a work of fiction. Names, characters, places, and incidents either are the product
of the author's imagination or are used fictitiously, and any resemblance to actual persons,
living or dead, business establishments, events, or locales is entirely coincidental.
    The publisher does not have any control over and does not assume any responsibil-
ity for author or third-party Web sites or their content.

To my great big, wonderful, extended and cojoined family, and dear friends, without whom my life would have little meaning.

ACKNOWLEDGMENTS

The idea for this book originated in the creative mind of one of my offspring, who thought a story on identity theft to the max would be a horrible situation for Abby to be in, but a terrific mystery for her to solve. You were right, Jason. Thank you so much for inspiring the story and helping me come up with its unusual twists.

The accuracy of the procedural and legal matters can be attributed to (or blamed on) my husband, Jim, who has amazingly vast quantities of information, advice, and wisdom to share, and who never complained about having to read the same scene over until I got it right.

The critiquing fell to my sister, Nancy, who was willing to brainstorm with me whenever I needed her, and who spent hours poring over my chapters, offering her perspective on the unusual situations in which Abby finds herself.

The integrity of the characters and plot stayed on course under the guidance of my editor, Ellen Edwards, whose opinion I trust and value.

The encouragement and support came from my family and dear friends, near and far, as always. You are the true jewels in my life.

The grunt work I did all by myself.

A big thanks to Pam and Emaly Leak, of Autumn Hill Llamas (www.autumnhillllamas.com), the actual owners of Catastrophe. Pam and Emaly were kind enough to give me a lesson on the care and feeding of these sweet, gentle animals. It didn't take long for me to understand why the Leaks are so fond of them.

PROLOGUE

As far as I knew, being a five-foot-two-inch green-eyed redhead wasn't a crime.

"Matron? Can you hear me? There's been a mistake."

Yet there I was, jailed for being a five-foot-two-inch green-eyed redhead. At least that was what the state trooper had told me when he yanked me out of my beloved old Corvette, slapped handcuffs on my wrists, and stuffed me into the backseat of his squad car.

"Hello? Is anyone out there?" I pressed my ear between the steel bars, listening for a reply. With all that clanging metal and cacophony of female voices ping-ponging against cement-block walls, it was a little hard to hear.

"I need to talk to you," I shouted up the hallway. At least a dozen women responded with comments that weren't helpful, but *were* pretty colorful.

"Baby, you're wastin' your breath," came an easy voice from behind me. "You got to wait till breakfast is over. They eatin' now."

"Someone has to be up there," I muttered. "They wouldn't leave the post unattended."

"Post?" Hearty laughter followed. "Baby, this ain't no army base. This is lockup."

Lockup. I clasped my fingers around the bars and held on as a shudder shook me. I'd seen the lockup once before, but from the other side, during one of my dad's "educational outings," designed to scare the bejeepers out of my brothers and me. It was part of my father's ongoing effort to keep us on the straight and narrow. He'd been a cop in the police department of New Chapel, Indiana, at the time. It had worked well. None of us had ever been on the inside—until now.

"Hey!" I called up the hallway again. "I need to speak to Sergeant Sean Reilly. Tell him Abby needs to see him right away. He's a good friend of mine. Seriously. He'll want to talk to me."

"Will you shut up?" someone behind me snarled. "You're making my head pound."

"Matron, please?" I called softly. I waited another few minutes, then leaned my aching forehead against one cold, thick bar. Damn it, where was Dave? I'd used my only phone call on my former boss—now my soon-to-be attorney—and had gotten his voice mail. Didn't he check his messages?

Then I remembered that Dave had gone out of town last week for a legal conference and wasn't due home until later today. And Marco, my hunky knight in shining black leather jacket, the guy who was always there for me . . . wasn't there anymore. He and I were history. *Finito.* My eyes filled with tears. The shock of losing him was so new and raw that I hadn't fully absorbed it.

Quickly I blinked back the tears so my cell mates wouldn't think I was some wimpy little girl. I couldn't think about Marco now. I had much bigger problems on my plate. I glanced around at my dismal surroundings—the long, narrow room, the stainless steel sink in the corner with the short partition beside it that hid the stinky toilet, the high, barred window on the back wall, the six bunks on a side wall, stacked two high, jutting from the cement blocks, the single lightbulb overhead. . . . I was actually *incarcerated*. Me, a harmless florist.

I glanced down at the putrid orange prison jumpsuit I had been forced to put on, then shut my eyes as the walls began to close in on me. Sweat broke out on my forehead and my hands grew clammy as my claustrophobia clawed its way to the surface. My only hope was that word of my arrest would quickly reach Sergeant Reilly's ears, because if I didn't get out of there soon, I was going to have a serious meltdown.

"Baby, those bars ain't gonna bend. You might as well stop pullin' on 'em and have a seat. 'Sides, they ain't gonna let you out until you been arraigned."

"I know how it works," I muttered weakly. "I went to law school."

"You did? You a lawyer then? Well, that's a whole 'nother situation. You hear that, girls? We got ourselves a bona fide—"

"I'm not a lawyer," I said, cutting off the sudden excited chatter. "I didn't make it."

"You run outta money, or what?"

"Brains." Like I needed to be reminded of that particular failure *now*. "If you don't mind, I'd rather not go into it."

"So, what are you in for?"

Her questions weren't helping my glum mood. "No one would tell me. All I know is that I didn't do anything wrong."

"Sugar, that's what everyone says."

"I don't care what everyone says," I snapped. "I'm innocent."

"Well, *someone's* got herself some attitude."

There were snickers at her comment.

"And someone's got *herself* too many nosy questions," I retorted.

Silence.

Ticking off an inmate probably wasn't the smartest thing to do, considering I had nowhere to hide, so I loosened my grip on the bars and turned to apologize. There were five women in with me, each on her own bunk. One was a pasty-skinned, emaciated middle-aged white woman who was so blotto that her eyes kept crossing. She was lying on a second-tier bunk, one arm hanging limply off the side. On another bunk was a young Latina with long, dark hair, who looked like she was barely in high school.

On a lower bunk was a woman who desperately needed a good bath and possibly a delousing. Beyond her lay a woman displaying multihued tattoos on her arms and neck. One bunk farther was an attractive black woman sporting an ugly purple bruise on her jaw and another around one eye. She was giving me a scowl. Clearly, this was the woman I'd offended.

"Sorry," I said to the scowler. "I'm getting some major claustrophobia here and it makes me extremely edgy."

Her expression softened. "Yep, this place'll surely do that to you."

"I tried to explain my condition to the state trooper, but he didn't care."

"Did you think he would?"

Well, actually, I had, but I didn't want to admit it now for fear of showing my naïveté. I'd even pulled out my ace in the hole, telling the trooper that my dad was a twenty-year veteran of the New Chapel police force, but he'd just ignored me. He'd laughed out loud when I said I hadn't done anything wrong. The only thing he seemed to give a rip about was whether I understood my Miranda rights. I told him what he could do with those rights. It hadn't improved my situation.

"You'd better sit down, honey," the woman called. "Come on over here. I won't bite."

I peered up the hallway again, but it was still empty. Taking a deep breath, I made it across the narrow room in three strides and plunked down on the edge of her bunk, resting my head against the chilly cement wall behind me. I hoped the bunk would hold both our weights. My cell mate was a good-sized woman and I wasn't exactly anorexic myself.

The woman stuck out a beautifully manicured hand, where each nail had its own personality. "Lavender Beals."

"Abby Knight." I shook her hand, then gave a start at a loud clang, hoping it meant someone had heard my calls for help. But no one appeared, so I sank back against the wall. "Will the matron come by when she's done eating?"

"You never been here before, have you?"

"Once, when I was ten, on a field trip."

"I was eighteen my first time, but it wasn't for no field trip. This is my third visit, all told, and each time it's been because of that bastard I married. I got rid of him this time, though—for good. He done slugged me for the last time."

I eyed her warily. "You got *rid* of him?"

"I didn't kill him, baby, just kicked his booty right out."

"If he hit you, why are *you* in jail?"

"I took a baseball bat to his windshield, just to show him I meant business. Now I get to cool my heels here until Thursday."

"For hitting his windshield? Why so long?"

"'Cause I don't have the money to hire a lawyer, so the court appointed me one, and now I got to wait until the next hearing date, and that's Thursday."

"Can't you get someone to post bail money for you?"

"Baby, what you been sniffing? Nobody I know's got that kind of money."

"How long have you been in here?"

"Six days now."

"Six days, plus another three . . ." I could feel my indignation rising. "Do you realize that you'll probably get less jail time than that for smashing the windshield?"

"'Course I realize it. What am I gonna do about it?" Lavender nudged the underside of one of the bunks above us. "This here's Maria. She's sixteen—shouldn't even be in here—but she was with two boys who TP'd and egged her neighbor's house."

"What?" I stood up so I could see the girl. My claustrophobia was receding as fast as my outrage was growing. "You're in the adult lockup for throwing toilet paper and eggs?"

Maria shook her head, her eyes huge in a tiny face. "I

didn't throw the eggs. I just tossed rolls of paper into the trees."

"And you were *jailed* for that?"

"See, sugar, it's all about having political connections," Lavender explained. "That fatheaded neighbor of hers wasn't about to let some little punks get away with pranking him, so he raised a stink with a councilman he knows and got the kids waived to adult court to prove how important he is. If he gets his way, Maria will have a criminal record. Ruin her life in the process. Won't that make him feel important?"

"How long have you been here?" I asked Maria.

"Four days."

"And you have to wait until Thursday, too?"

She nodded and started to cry. "I'll flunk my classes. I just want to go home."

Boy, was my blood boiling. "Even if you had damaged his property, Maria, you should have been taken to the juvenile-detention center, not here. And then you probably wouldn't get any jail time, only probation. What they've done to you is outrageous and totally unfair."

"You tell her, girlfriend," a woman in the cell across the hallway called. I glanced around and saw a dozen women in two cells standing at the bars, listening avidly.

Lavender snorted. "It's the system, baby. Money talks. Nothin' fair about it." She pointed to another woman. "That there is Cherry. She's bipolar and can't afford her meds, let alone a lawyer. She's been here seven days."

"Sitting in here isn't going to help her get better," I said, pointing out the obvious.

Lavender shrugged. "Does anyone care?"

"I care. Someone else has to care, too."

"Hey, Abby," a woman across the aisle shouted. "I been here five days. They got me on a public intox charge."

Having clerked in Dave Hammond's law office, I knew a public intoxication charge would probably merit her a weekend in jail. She'd done more than enough time already.

"I been here a week," one of her cell mates called.

"Where's the justice in that?" I asked. "What happened to a person's right to a speedy trial? There has to be some way to stop this insanity."

Lavender laughed.

I stood up and began to pace, which meant going a few feet in either direction. No way could I let this pass. I hated injustice. "We have to raise public awareness of the problem."

Women in the other two holding cells were starting to discuss their own situations and the injustices therein, their voices growing louder and more irate.

"Okay, here's what I'm going to do," I said to Lavender. Instantly, the others stopped chatting. "I'm going to contact a reporter at the *New Chapel News* to talk him into doing a piece on this. Maybe if people are aware of the problem, they'll demand a solution."

"Yeah!" a woman across the hall responded. "We want a solution!"

"We can get our families to picket in front of the courthouse," someone else called. "Justice for all, not just for the rich!"

Another voice repeated the phrase, and then the call moved through the entire cellblock. Within moments the halls echoed with their cries. Someone else began to shout, "Abby! Abby!" and they all took that up, but somehow it changed to, "Attica! Attica!" and then they began to run metal cups along the bars and stamp their feet, until the noise was deafening.

It was, in fact, a small riot—and I was in the middle of it.

Somewhere down the hallway a door clanged open. I heard the sound of many heavy boots thundering toward us. Because my cell mates were clamoring at the bars, there was no way I could see what was going on.

"Stand back!" the guards were shouting, striking the steel with their clubs.

As my cell mates fell back, allowing me my first glimpse of the hallway, the jail matron strode forward. But this wasn't Matron Patty, the petite, gum-snapping ball of fire my dad had introduced me to years before. This was a thickset, no-nonsense woman who bore a striking resemblance to a pug. "What's going on here?" she demanded.

The five women in front of me all swung around to gaze at me, waiting for me to speak up. Then someone from across the hallway pointed at me and said, "She says we're not supposed to be held here so long, and *she* knows the law."

The matron's piercing gaze zeroed in on me. "Is that so?"

My cheeks immediately began to burn. "Well, you see, I attended law school and—"

"Name?"

"New Chapel University School of—"

"*Your* name!" she barked, making me jump.

"Abby Knight." It came out in an embarrassing squeak.

She glared at me as she inserted a key into the lock and slid back the cell door. "Your lawyer's here. You're free to leave."

Instantly, the mood inside that cell turned from red-hot to icy cold, and I could feel the wrathful glare of every woman there. I broke out into a sweat, afraid to make a move. "Thank you," I whispered.

At once, like a messenger from heaven, a tall, familiar cop stepped inside the cell. "Let's go, Abby."

I blinked up at him in surprise, so happy to see my old buddy Sergeant Reilly that I could have kissed him. However, he didn't seem all that pleased to see me. He was giving me a look that said, *I should have known I'd find you at the center of this.*

I paused to say to Lavender, "I'm going to find a way to help." Then, sticking close to my bodyguard, I walked through the open door, leaving my impoverished sisters behind me.

In a tiny cubicle just inside the main security door, I stripped off the ugly jumpsuit and donned my own clothes, never fully appreciating just how much I liked them until that moment. I checked my purse to make sure everything was there, then headed outside, where I gazed up at the blue sky and breathed in the crisp November air. Ah, the glorious smell of freedom.

From out of nowhere two photographers and three reporters rushed me, firing questions and snapping pictures. Before I could open my mouth, I was whisked off to Reilly's squad car parked at the curb, one arm firmly in his grasp and one held by a slightly paunchy, balding man in a gray suit and white shirt, red tie loosened at the collar—Dave Hammond.

"My client has no comment," Dave said to the reporters as we ducked into the backseat.

"Dave, you're back!" I cried in relief. "And just in time, too. It was getting a little dicey in that jail cell."

"Ask her why it was dicey," Reilly said from the front seat.

Dave gave me a skeptical glance. "Do I really want to know?"

"It was nothing," I said. "A little disturbance."

Reilly snorted. "It was a riot, and guess who started it?"

"Just a tiny riot," I countered, "but there was a very good reason for it, which I will go into later. Right now, I want someone to please tell me why I was arrested."

"Let's go back to my office to talk," Dave said as photographers continued to snap photos through the windows.

"At least tell me why the trooper picked me up."

"You have to promise to stay calm," Dave said.

"Look at me, Dave. I'm the very picture of calm."

"Uncurl your fists."

"Done."

He studied me for a moment. "I think we'll wait."

"Good call," Reilly said. He circled the courthouse and stopped in front of the old brick building that housed Dave's law office. "I'll catch you both later. I've got to get back to my beat. By the way, Abby, Marco text-messaged me from Chicago a little while ago. He heard the news about your arrest and wanted further details when I got them."

My heart soared—Marco asked about me!—then immediately sank. "I was on the *news*?"

"Just the local radio station. You haven't made the TV airwaves yet. You'll probably be hearing from Marco soon. In fact, I'll bet there's a phone message waiting for you now."

Not likely. Not the way things stood between us. I didn't say that to Reilly, of course, because he didn't know about Marco and me. The only person who knew was my best friend and roommate, Nikki, in whom I confided everything. Still, I had to check.

I turned on my cell phone, anxiously waiting for the screen to light up. There were seventeen messages from my mom, three from my dad, and five from Bloomers, but just as I'd thought, there weren't any messages from Marco.

Dave's office, and my flower shop, were located on streets surrounding the courthouse in the heart of New Chapel, Indiana. Bloomers Flower Shop was on Franklin Street, on the east side of the courthouse, and Dave's office was on Lincoln, above a tavern on the north side. As we stepped inside the door and climbed the lopsided stairs that led to Dave's second-floor law office, I phoned Bloomers to let my assistants know where I was and what had happened, promising to give them the details when I got back. My only request was that if my mother or father called, they were to be told I was out on a delivery and would get back to them soon. With any luck, they wouldn't hear the news until I'd had a chance to prepare them.

With a brief hello to Dave's secretary, we headed straight for his office, a room with forest green carpeting and peach walls that screamed 1980s. I sat in one of the two leather club chairs in front of his desk and Dave settled into his creaky, high-backed brown leather chair, slid his briefcase across the top, and leaned back with a sigh. "Coffee?"

"I could really use some water." I glanced at my hands

and thought of those grimy steel bars. "And maybe some disinfectant."

Minutes later Martha bustled in with a cup of coffee for Dave and a bottle of water for me, promising to return with sanitizing lotion. She was always on top of things. She reminded me of my own assistant Grace, who used to work for Dave. In fact, I'd met her in this very office when I'd clerked for him—back in the days when I thought I had a chance in law school.

Dave had thought so, too, apparently, or he wouldn't have hired me. But after I flunked out and found a new home at Bloomers, where I'd blossomed, so to speak, he agreed that flowers were my true calling. He just hadn't realized that they weren't my only calling. I was developing quite a little sideline solving puzzles, usually involving some very bad people.

"End my misery, Dave," I said, opening the screw-top water bottle. "What did the trooper think I'd done?"

"It's nothing to worry about, Abby, a case of mistaken identity."

I nearly spilled the water. *Mistaken identity?* A suspicion began to form in my mind.

"The trooper was responding to an APB. He happened to be passing by the public parking lot as you were getting out of your car, and reacted instinctively. He's a rookie, and right now a very embarrassed one."

"He ought to be. But you still haven't told me what my alleged crime was."

Dave gazed at me from under lowered brows. "Are you calm?"

I put the bottle on his desk and showed him my unclenched fists. "Absolutely."

"Murder."

Not calm now. My fingers curled into my palms as my eyes narrowed in fury.

"Are you okay?" Dave asked.

"Not so much. Who was the victim?"

He scanned the typed page in front of him. "No information on that yet."

"And this person the trooper thought was me, is her name Elizabeth Blume?"

"Yes. Do you know her?"

With a groan, I buried my face in my hands. "She's my evil twin."

"Your *what*?"

"My doppelgänger, my deadly double—whatever you want to call her. You're probably the only one on the square who hasn't met her. She's a young woman I used to babysit, and for the past three weeks she's been slowly making her life over into a perfect copy of mine. I knew she was planning something. I just never expected a murder."

At that thought I sat forward, my whole body tensing. "Have I been cleared as a suspect?"

"Your arrest was a mistake, Abby. You're not a suspect."

"I will be, Dave. Trust me. It's all part of her plan."

"You'd better enlighten me." He took a hearty swallow of coffee and, thus fortified, pulled his yellow legal pad closer and readied his pen.

CHAPTER ONE

Three weeks earlier

"Don't worry about a thing, Mrs. Salvare," I said into my cell phone, hurrying up the street as the mid-October wind whipped my hair into a red froth. "The shower centerpiece and table decorations will be there first thing Sunday morning. I have it all under control."

The woman on the other end, Francesca Salvare, my boyfriend's mother, said, "*Bene, bambina.* We'll see you then, eh?"

"I'm looking forward to it." Like a tooth pulling.

I slid my phone into my purse and pulled my scarf tighter around my neck. The only reason I'd agreed to furnish the flowers for Marco's sister's baby shower was to make points with his family. I hadn't realized what an ordeal it would be—all because of his sister Gina.

I hate gerberas, she'd told me when I sat down with her to make flower recommendations. *And don't even think about using cockscomb. Ew. Scabiosa? Isn't that a disease? Anemone? Aren't those sea creatures? I absolutely have to have baby's breath in the centerpiece. It's bad luck not to have baby's breath at a baby shower. Artichokes? Seriously?*

I'd nearly shredded my tongue that afternoon, trying to keep my cool. I was fairly certain that Gina was being difficult because she didn't want me dating her brother. She was determined that he should find a woman who wanted to get married and have lots of kids right away, and that just wasn't me—or Marco, for that matter. Although we'd been dating each other exclusively for four and a half months and were very close, neither one of us felt ready for that walk down the aisle. For me it was a matter of maturity. I was only twenty-six, after all, and trying to establish my new career. And although Marco was thirty, he didn't feel the need to rush things, either.

I turned the corner onto Franklin, wondering if I could send over the flowers and skip the shower. Trip on the curb and sprain my ankle, perhaps? Ouch. Too painful. Color my freckles red and claim I had measles? Um, no. The health inspector might shut me down.

You can handle a baby shower, Abby, that little voice of reason said. *Just clear your Saturday calendar so you'll have a full day to concentrate on making those centerpieces the most awesome they've ever seen.*

I eyed the curb in front of my shop, wondering just *how* painful a sprain would be.

"Hey, Sunshine. Why the frown?"

When I heard that low sexy voice, my frown was history. I turned to see Marco getting out of his dark green Prius, a surprise since his bar didn't open until eleven o'clock.

Marco Salvare owned the Down the Hatch Bar and Grill, located two doors up the block from my flower shop. He was an ex–Army Ranger and ex-cop, and had a nice sideline going as a private investigator. He and I had clicked the moment he'd first set foot inside Bloomers. With his dark hair, bedroom eyes framed by dark, expressive eyebrows, nose that was strong and just a tad bit askew, expressive mouth, and sexy grin, he'd set off bells inside my head that were still chiming. Add to that a black leather motorcycle jacket, tight-fitting blue denims, and polished-to-a-sheen black boots, and how could I have resisted?

He came sauntering toward me, looking hot and dangerously yummy, as always—maybe even more so than usual because of that serious five-o'clock shadow he had going on. "I've been up all night on a stakeout."

"Which case? Missing uncle, or rich wife-cheating husband?"

"Rich wife-cheating husband."

"Poor baby." I stroked his stubbly cheek, knowing how much he hated that kind of case. In Marco's opinion, either you trusted someone or you didn't. If you didn't, then forget trying to prove an infidelity. Just get out of the marriage. "I'd volunteer to tuck you into bed for a nap," I said, lifting one eyebrow suggestively, "but I've got a jammed schedule today."

"Me, too. Besides, my mother is staying with me until after the shower." He sighed miserably. "I'll be so happy once that damn thing is over."

"Make that two of us. I just got off the phone with her. She needed more reassurance that the centerpieces would be ready on time."

"She called you again? I'm sorry." He picked up my

hands and rubbed them between his warm ones. "I'll make it up to you."

I leaned into him. "Want to give me a little preview?"

He glanced around to make sure no one was coming up the sidewalk. Then he dipped his head toward mine for a kiss.

"Abby? Abby Knight?"

I turned to see a young woman approaching us from the courthouse square across the street. She was my height, with long, gleaming, pale blond hair topped by a stylish tam. She was wearing a white wool trench coat and silver boots, carrying a shopping bag in one hand and a silver-hued woven leather purse in the other.

"Who's she?" Marco asked.

A strong gust of wind carried her to the curb, bringing her close enough for me to recognize. "Oh, my God," I whispered. "That's Elizabeth Blume, a girl I used to babysit."

"Abby!" she squealed. She dropped the shopping bag and, with a childlike cry of delight, ran toward me with open arms. It was Elizabeth all right.

She squeezed me tightly, then leaned back to smile. "It's *so* good to see you. I was hoping I'd run into you this morning."

Hearing Marco clear his throat—as if I could forget he was there—I said, "Elizabeth, I want you to meet Marco Salvare. Marco, this is Elizabeth Blume—"

"There's no need for introductions," she said, giving Marco a fey grin. "I'd know this gorgeous guy anywhere. I've heard all about you, Mr. PI Salvare."

Marco darted me a questioning look, but since I hadn't told her anything—I hadn't spoken to Elizabeth in eight years—all I could do was shrug.

She held out her hand and he shook it. "Please call me Libby. Elizabeth is too formal." Then she turned to loop her arm through mine, drawing me to her side. "Abby was my babysitter, but she was really more like a big sister to me. I was eleven and she was fifteen, and I thought she was wonderful—as I still do. We had oodles of fun back then, didn't we, Abby?"

That wasn't how I remembered it. "So, are you home on a college break?"

"I graduated," she said, seeming surprised that I hadn't known. "I came home to launch my career." She turned to look at Bloomers. "So, this is your shop. Oh, Abby, you must be so proud. Look at that lovely old-fashioned door. I'm not surprised it's yellow. I remember how much you love that color. Is that a genuine beveled-glass center? And that charming redbrick facade, those two big bay windows . . . I mean, it's perfect, isn't it? I'll bet the inside is just as nice as I've imagined it to be."

I watched Libby hurry to the nearer bay window and cup her hands to the glass to peer inside. "Will you give me a tour? I'm free all morning."

She caught me off guard. "Gee, I'd love to, Elizabe—er, Libby, but Bloomers opens at nine, and my assistants and I have a lot to get ready before then."

"Then I'll just have to come back." She retrieved her shopping bag from where she'd dropped it, then aimed a high-beam smile at Marco. "It was such an honor to meet you, Mr. Salvare. I'll see you around town soon, I'm sure." With a little wave at me, she headed back the way she'd come, moving at a brisk pace.

"Why didn't you show her inside?" Marco asked. "It wouldn't have taken long."

"Are you kidding? The last thing I want to do is encourage her."

"Why? She's a cute kid, and she seems harmless enough."

"That's what I thought when I first met her." I turned to gaze across the square, where Libby was getting into a white Mercedes SL. "She's always been able to fool people."

"Libby seems to have done well for herself," Marco commented, eyeing her car.

"It's not her money. Her mother is an extremely wealthy woman—also a tyrant. Think Meryl Streep in *The Devil Wears Prada*. When I babysat for her, I hated going over to the Blume house. The woman scared me, so I usually babysat at my house, which turned out to be a big mistake. Boy, I sure hope Elizabeth doesn't come back."

"You mean Libby."

I wrinkled my nose. "*Libby* sounds so juvenile."

"I like it. It reminds me of your name." Marco drew me close, gazing down at me with those dark, sexy eyes. "And that reminds me of this evening. So what do you say we meet at the bar after work for a little dinner?"

"This dinner," I asked in a sultry voice, "does it include dessert?"

"You name it."

"In that case, I'm thinking of something Italian—last initial *S*."

"Spumoni it is."

"Good morning, dear," my assistant Grace called in her crisp British accent as a pile of dried leaves blew through the doorway with me. Grace was in the coffee-

and-tea-parlor side of the shop placing red roses in bud vases on the white wrought-iron tables. I knew by the heavenly aroma that greeted me that she'd already brewed her gourmet coffee.

As always, I felt a renewed burst of pride as I took in my surroundings—the Victorian-themed tea parlor; the glass-fronted display cooler stocked with a rainbow of fresh daisies, mums, orchids, roses, carnations, and lilies; the sales counter with its old-fashioned cash register; the antique tables and armoires filled with silk-flower arrangements, candlesticks, and other gift items; and the decorated wreaths, sconces, and mirrors of varying shapes and sizes hanging on the walls. It was my personal paradise.

Through the curtained doorway at the back of the shop came the sounds of my other assistant, Lottie, humming a Willie Nelson song, and as I walked farther into the shop, I could smell toasted bread and eggs fried in butter. Monday morning breakfast was a tradition that Lottie had started years ago.

"I'm heading toward the kitchen, Grace," I called. "Let's eat."

"I'll join you momentarily. By the way, Abby, sixteen orders came in over the wire yesterday."

"Sixteen! Wow. We're off to a good start."

"Also, dear, one of the walk-in coolers is acting up."

"Figures. As soon as we get a little extra money, it's gone."

"And there are two messages for you on the spindle."

I stopped short. "From my mom?"

"No, love. Had that been the case, I would have prepared you."

I breathed a sigh of relief. Monday was traditionally the day my mother dropped off her latest work of art—although the word *art* applied loosely in her case. She thought displaying her work at Bloomers would increase my sales, but about the only thing that *had* increased was the pile of unsold Maureen Knight originals in our basement.

"Thanks, Grace," I said, and again started toward the kitchen.

"However," she called, "I do want to prepare you for one message. There's a problem with your order of *Gypsophila paniculata*."

I froze. Not the *baby's breath*!

"It's a mold issue apparently," Grace explained. "I've placed a few calls to other suppliers and hopefully we'll hear back later this morning."

"I've got to have that gypsophila by Saturday, Grace."

"I understand the importance, dear. We'll have it by then."

What would I ever do without Grace?

Grace Bingham was a well-read, charming sixty-something widow who'd had many careers before coming to Bloomers, all of which enabled her to perform the many tasks I heaped on her, including running the tea parlor, answering the phone, waiting on customers, and even handling my mom. Grace loved her job, luckily, because there was nothing lovable about the salary I could afford to pay her.

I walked through the purple curtain at the back of the shop into our workroom, detouring up the left side of the big table in the center to grab the messages from the spindle on my desk. I continued past a long counter and a wall of shelving filled with plant containers, buckets of silk flowers, and various other supplies, through a doorway in back that led to the galley kitchen, where Lottie was stirring scrambled eggs. A stack of toast and a jar of orange marmalade sat nearby.

"Here you go, sweetie," Lottie said, dishing out a heap of fluffy eggs onto a plate.

Lottie Dombowski was a friendly, hearty, forty-five-year-old mother of four who hailed from Kentucky. She had owned Bloomers until her husband's health got so bad and the medical bills got so high that she had to sell. It nearly broke her heart to lose the charming but not very profitable shop, but with having to care for her beloved Herman, not to mention raising her quadruplet teenage sons, she'd had no choice.

That was where I entered the picture. Having been ejected from (a) law school and (b) my then fiancé Pryce Osborne's life, I was desperate to do something that justified my existence. Still holding the remnants of my farmer grandpa's trust money, and having worked as Lottie's delivery girl, where I discovered my talent for floral artistry, I plunked down the last of Gramps's money, got a *ginormous* mortgage, and never looked back.

I pulled up a stool, read the first message about the moldy baby's breath, then scrunched it up and tossed it into the trash can in the corner. Grace was already on it. I glanced at the second slip of paper just as Grace came in with a tray holding three cups of coffee.

" 'Elizabeth Blume is in town. Please call,' " Lottie read over my shoulder. "Now, there's a name from the past." She put the skillet back on the range and sat down beside me.

"Who's Elizabeth Blume?" Grace asked, delivering

our cups. Mine was made just the way I liked it, with a healthy shot of half-and-half.

"Just a kid I used to babysit when I was in high school. Lottie, did Grace tell you about the mold issue with the gypso—"

"*Just* a kid you babysat?" Lottie snorted, as though I'd somehow belittled Libby. "Gracie, do you remember Delphi, the famous cover model?"

"It doesn't ring a bell," Grace said, sitting down on another stool.

"You have to remember Delphi. Her trademark look was her pale blond hair cut in a pixie do, big brown doe eyes, red, bow-shaped lips, enormous"—she held her hands way out in front of her breasts—"and long legs. She was the swimsuit model who first appeared in a magazine with a belly button ring. They called her the Belly Button Babe. She and her family were always in the tabloids. Well, anyway, Elizabeth is her daughter."

Grace took a sip of coffee. She wouldn't read a tabloid if her life depended on it.

"Delphi's real name is Delphinia Haskell," Lottie continued, determined to prod Grace's memory. "Delphi's first husband had a big bank account and a weak heart. She had a son with him, Oliver, and inherited a fortune. Hubby number two was a foot shorter than her, owned a minor-league baseball team, and was Elizabeth's daddy. Delphi kept his moniker as her professional name.

"Then there was number three, who gave her a huge divorce settlement. She used that to open a talent agency here in town for all those little angels whose mommies want to turn them into TV stars." Lottie stuck out her tongue, leaving no doubt as to her opinion on the subject.

"So, getting back to the gypsophila," I said.

My words floated off into space unnoticed, because Lottie's comment had induced Grace to weigh in with her perspective, which she usually imparted in the form of a quotation.

"As Stanislaus cleverly observed," Grace began, " 'What is fame? The advantage of being known by people of whom you yourself know nothing, and for whom you care as little.' "

"This Stanislaus," Lottie said, "has he ever been in *People* magazine?"

Grace carefully placed a napkin across her lap. "You, of all people, should know who Stanislaus is, Lottie Dombowski."

Lottie put down her cup. "Why is that?"

"Wouldn't it be best to research it, and find out for yourself?" Grace teased.

"Why would I waste my time researching when we have you?" Lottie gave me a wink.

"In the words of William Hazlitt," Grace volleyed back, " 'Learning is its own exceeding great reward.' "

"In the words of my wise old granny," Lottie said, and we held our breath, waiting for the slang to start flying, " 'A learned man is an idler who kills time by study.' "

Grace and I looked at each other in bewilderment. "That wasn't your granny who said that," Grace said. "That was George Bernard Shaw."

"Shaw . . . Granny. I knew it was one of them. And just so you know, Abby, Stanislaus was the patron saint of Poland." With a sly smile, Lottie took her plate to the sink.

I tossed Libby's message into the trash and finished eating.

After breakfast, we headed our separate ways, Lottie to take inventory, Grace to freshen the supply of cut flowers for the showroom, and me to prioritize the orders and gather the tools and supplies I would need.

The first order was for a kitchen-table centerpiece. The client wanted something earthy and spicy, appropriate for a fall display. I turned to gaze at the containers on a top shelf. Earthy and spicy. I'd seen an idea using cinnamon sticks, and had ordered a supply to keep on hand. I pulled those now, along with a ribbed papier-mâché pot. Then I got out my glue gun and began gluing the sticks around the pot like fence posts, giving it a rustic feel.

Next I gathered the flowers, pods, vegetables, and berries, all in shades of yellow, gold, rust, and green—miniature callas, gloriosas, hypericum berries, cockscomb, artichokes, scabiosa pods, persimmons, sneezeweed, and my favorite, chocolate cosmos. Humming happily, I cut the wet foam, lined the container with it, and began to arrange my flowers. This was where true artistry came in. Plus it kept my mind off Gina's shower.

At nine o'clock Grace called into the workroom that she was going to open the shop. Almost at once, the bell over the door jingled, and a moment later, Grace stuck her head through the curtain. "Abby, Libby Blume is here to see you."

Feeling a wrinkle of annoyance crease the space between my eyebrows, I put down my floral knife, wiped my hands, and headed for the curtain. I'd just have to give Libby a quick tour and shuffle her out the door.

But Grace had already seated Libby at a table in the parlor.

"Abby!" Libby exclaimed, jumping up to give me a

hug, "Grace was just telling me how she came to work here. I've been wondering how you were so lucky to find her. And I just love her accent. It's divine. Grace, you sound just like Dame Judi Dench." She focused her admiring gaze on Grace, who wasn't usually swayed by compliments. This time, however, Grace beamed.

"My goodness," Grace exclaimed, glancing from me to Libby, "but for your hair and eye color, you could be sisters."

Libby's big brown eyes opened in amazement. "Honestly?"

"Honestly." Grace smiled at her just like she always smiled at me—fondly. Honestly! She didn't even know the girl.

"Coffee?" Grace asked her.

Libby turned her gaze on me. "Do you have time?"

"Well," I said, glancing at my watch, "Mondays are kind of hectic. . . ."

"Don't give it a second thought," Grace said. "I'll mind the shop while you two have a nice chat. Now, what do you take in your coffee, love?"

Love? Libby took off her white coat and laid it carefully over the chair. "The same as Abby, please."

She knew how I drank my coffee? I hadn't even taken up the caffeine habit until after I'd gone away to college.

"Bloomers is amazing," Libby told me, gazing around in delight as Grace brought over two cups of coffee. "How I adore these high tin ceilings and the creaky wood floors, and I love what you've done with the brick walls. Look at these darling ice-cream tables. And of course there are no words for your gorgeous flower arrangements.

Honestly, Abby, walking into Bloomers is like stepping into a fantasy world." She sighed dreamily.

"Your cream is on the table, dear," Grace said to Libby as she brought over two cups.

Libby reached for the little pitcher and doused her java with a generous helping. I refrained just out of spite, then could hardly drink my coffee.

"I have something for you," Libby told me. She pulled a large albumlike book out of her bag, set it aside, then reached in for a small silver box tied with a gold ribbon. "It's a welcome-home gift."

A welcome-home gift? But I wasn't the one who'd come home. I glanced at Grace to see if she caught it, but she was already bustling off toward the shop. Libby thrust the box at me, then watched eagerly as I untied the ribbon and lifted the lid. Inside was a sterling-silver "Best Friends Forever" locket—a jagged half of a heart on a silver chain.

"You shouldn't have," I said, trying to hide my dismay.

"Look, I'm wearing the matching half." She tugged on a chain hidden inside her shirt and out came the other half.

I thanked her and started to put the locket back in the box, but Libby snatched it out of my hands. "Here, let me fasten it around your neck."

Moments later, wearing my new BFF locket, I put the cup of coffee to my lips to hide my annoyance. This was going to be a long five minutes.

"Now," Libby said, scooting her chair close to mine, "I have to show you the scrapbook I made." She flipped to the first page of the album, onto which she had pasted a newspaper article about Bloomers' grand reopening.

From the *New Chapel News*, the headline read: NEW FLOWER-SHOP OWNER BLOSSOMS ON SQUARE. Beneath it was a grainy black-and-white photo of me in front of Bloomers, with a pot of mums in my arms. I noticed that Libby had hand-painted a trellis around the photo and decorated it with tiny roses.

Libby smoothed out a wrinkle in the photo, gazing at my flower shop as if it were her own. "Such a pretty building, isn't it?"

"I've always thought so," I said, glancing at her askance.

Glowing with pride, she continued through the album, showing me pages filled with every article in which I'd ever been mentioned, even those about my involvement in helping to solve local murders. Each clipping had been meticulously decorated with a border of leaves, vines, or various types of flowers. Clearly, she'd spent a lot of time on the scrapbook. When she'd finally exhausted her supply of articles, she closed the book and sat back with a sigh of satisfaction. "So?"

"I'm blown away, Libby. I can't believe you went to all this effort for me. Thanks!"

"Oh," she said in surprise, gathering the album to her chest. "It's not for you. It's my keepsake. To be honest, I came to ask if I could work for you."

CHAPTER TWO

It took me a few seconds to absorb her request, and even then I didn't believe it. Libby turned to gaze around her. "I just have to be a part of this. You understand that feeling, don't you?"

Maybe I was wrong to let the past influence me, but there was no way I wanted Libby near me every day. Luckily, I had the perfect excuse. "The thing is, Libby, I'm not in a financial position to hire any more help."

"Oh, that." She waved away my concern. "You don't have to pay me. I'll be your intern."

My hand shook, rattling the cup as I set it on the saucer. My *intern*?

"Just imagine me at your side, soaking up everything there is to know about flowers. Plus, I can take orders, clean up the workroom at the end of the day, pick up sandwiches for lunch—whatever you need. I'll even make deliveries. Honestly, doesn't that sound perfect?"

Perfectly appalling. Trying to be gracious, I said, "I'll have to get back to you on that."

She tilted her head as though she didn't know how to interpret my answer. Then, as it sank in that I wasn't leaping at her offer, a fiery blush stained her cheeks. She removed a business card from her purse and tossed it onto the table. "Here's my phone number." She rose, slipped into her coat, gathered her purse and shopping bag, and walked out of the parlor.

Feeling like a heel, I tucked her card into my pants pocket and followed her to the front door. Wearing the expression of a heartbroken child, Libby said good-bye to Grace, gave me solemn air kisses on both cheeks, then left, her boots crunching the leaves as she hurried away. I felt Grace's inquisitive gaze upon me as I shut the door.

Lottie came hurrying through the curtain and glanced around. "Did I miss her? Does she look like her mom?"

"A little," I said, and returned to the parlor to clean off the table.

"Didn't you think we could use the extra hand, dear?" Grace asked from the doorway.

"Extra hand at what?" Lottie asked.

"Libby Blume volunteered her services as an intern," Grace explained.

"We can always use another pair of hands around here," Lottie said, "especially when they come free."

"As you're always fond of saying, Grace," I said, "there is no such thing as free help. Besides, we're not busy enough to have an intern."

"Certainly, it's your choice, dear," Grace said as I headed for the workroom, "but—"

"Let me tell you about Libby," I said. "She was a giant

pain in the ass when I sat for her, and I don't want her to become one to me again."

"Come on, sweetie, she was just a kid when you knew her," Lottie argued. "All kids are pests. She's a mature young woman now."

"Mature? Look at this!" I unclasped the locket and handed it to Lottie. "Do you know what it is? A Best Friends Forever necklace, the kind middle-school girls exchange. She gave it to me as a welcome-home gift. A *welcome-home* gift, Lottie. I didn't come home—she did!"

Lottie let it dangle from her fingers so Grace could examine it. "It's kinda sweet."

"It's juvenile!" I took the locket, marched into the workroom, and tossed it into a desk drawer. "I don't want Libby Blume here. Period."

They didn't argue. I knew they thought I was being unreasonable, but my gut feeling was very strong. Having Libby around would be nothing but trouble.

Trouble with a capital *D* walked through the door just before closing time. I was in the back, finishing an arrangement of tropical flowers for a Hawaiian luau, when Lottie poked her head through the curtain and said in a whisper, "Delphi Blume is here to see you." Lottie's eyes were stretched wide—she was apparently suffering from a bad case of awe.

I put the bird-of-paradise stem in water and followed her to the front, where Libby's famous ex-model mother waited, tapping the toe of a black patent, spike-heeled boot against my tile floor. I'd forgotten what a striking woman Delphi was. She was wearing a belted Burberry plaid coat and those killer boots, with a black patent leather purse the size of a travel bag over one wrist. Her pale blond hair was still styled in its famous pixie cut, her eyes were still brown and doelike, though with a few wrinkles now, and her lips were still red and bow-shaped, although they looked a little plumper than I remembered. Also a bit on the lumpy side.

"Hello, Abby," she said in a frosty tone, fixing me with an equally frosty glare.

"Mrs. Blume," I said with a nod. "Nice to see you again."

"Just Delphi, if you please. I'd like a word with you."

I led her into the parlor, passing Lottie—who was having trouble closing her mouth—to a table in front of the bay window. Grace had been at the coffee counter in the back, cleaning the machines, but immediately came to take our orders.

"Would you care for coffee or tea?" Grace asked her, not the least bit awestruck.

"Nothing, thank you." Delphi's words came out clipped. Angry.

Grace quietly returned to her duties, though I knew she and Lottie would be listening in. I took a deep breath, feeling suddenly anxious. The negative vibes Delphi emitted were powerful. Putting on a smile, I said, "What can I do for you?"

"Why did you tell my daughter she couldn't be your intern?"

Nothing like getting right to the point. "I don't need another employee at this time."

"You don't think she's capable of working *here*?" Delphi's nose wrinkled as though she'd detected something rotten in the room.

"Her capabilities had nothing to do with my decision.

I just don't need another employee right now. Maybe in the future . . ."

"She needs to work"—Delphi tapped a long, dark fin gernail on the table—"now."

"I'm sure there are other shops in town that are hiring."

"She wants to work with *you*. She admires you—for some reason."

Ouch. "I appreciate that, but as I said—"

Delphi leaned toward me, emphasizing each statement with a tap of her fingernail. "She's an art major. She ranked at the top of her class. She has a minor in business. She's loyal. She has a winning personality. She'd be an asset to you. I don't understand your problem."

At that moment, my problem was sitting across from me. I sat back and folded my arms. There was no way I was going to let her bully me into taking on her daughter. Bullies really pushed my buttons. "I don't need the help. Maybe some other time."

Her doe eyes narrowed into feral slits, but I didn't give her time to reply. I stood up and glanced at my watch. "I'm sorry, but the shop is closing now and I have a dinner date."

Her eyes widened in disbelief, as if to say, *You're dismissing me? Do you know whom you're talking to?* She pushed back her chair, put her bag over her arm (it probably would have crushed her shoulder), and marched out of the parlor, through the shop, and out the door.

I locked it behind her. There went one more reason why I wasn't going to have Libby in my life. Who needed another pushy mother around? I started to pull back the curtain to walk into the workroom, but paused when I heard Lottie and Grace discussing the situation.

"Poor girl, having to put up with a mom like that," Lottie said.

"The child really could use our influence, couldn't she?" Grace said.

"Not gonna happen," I said, breezing through the curtain. I grabbed my coat and purse and waited for them to do likewise. We left the shop without another word on the subject.

Down the Hatch Bar and Grill was the town square's local watering hole. Marco had bought the bar about the same time I bought Bloomers. Like my shop, it was housed in an old brick building, but unlike my shop, its old-fashioned charm had been buried beneath dark wood paneling and suspended ceilings typical of the 1960s. The decor wasn't much better—a fake carp mounted above the long, dark wood bar, a bright blue plastic anchor on the wall above the row of booths opposite the bar, and a fisherman's net hanging from the beamed ceiling.

When my eyes adjusted to the dim lighting, I spotted Marco at the last booth, "our" booth, as I thought of it. I slid in across from him and sighed wearily.

Marco slid a frosty mug of beer toward me. "Bad day?"

"Weird day." I took a long pull of beer, licking foam off my upper lip.

"Want to tell me about it?"

"Food first. Details to follow. What are the specials tonight? I'm starving."

Over a meal of hearty veal stew, thick with carrots and potatoes, onions and peas, simmered in a tomato broth, and a mixed green salad and crusty bread, I told Marco about Libby's strange gift, her even stranger scrapbook, and her offer to intern, topping that with her mother's annoying visit. Marco found the whole situation humorous and told me not to worry. So I took his advice, enjoyed the food and his company, and was rewarded for it.

"What would you say about working with me on the cheating-husband case?" he asked.

It was the first time he'd ever asked for my help on one of his private investigations, and I was supremely flattered. "I'd love to."

"It'll require some evening surveillance, not always in the same vehicle as me."

"That's not a problem."

He sat back. "Great. Can you start tonight?" I nodded. "You take my car and I'll use a rental. So go home, put on dark clothes, park your Vette down the street, and meet me back here in an hour."

I was out the door before he could blink and back in forty minutes. Wearing a black jacket, jeans, and boots, with a black knit cap wadded in my pocket, I parked under a streetlight a block from Down the Hatch and got out of the car. At once, a car door closed nearby and footsteps hurried up behind me. Thinking I was about to be mugged, I spun around with my hands balled protectively, my keys jutting out from between my fingers, ready to do some serious gouging.

"Libby!" I cried with relief. "You nearly gave me a heart attack."

"Sorry, Abby. I didn't recognize you. I thought someone was trying to steal your car. Why are you dressed in black? Are you working on a murder investigation?"

At that moment, a tall, thin figure in a long, olive drab

trench coat and camouflage pants came slinking toward us. I wasn't sure whether to ignore him or run, but then Libby said, "Here you are, Oliver" as her brother halted beside her. His hair was short beneath his army cap, and his eyes were deep and hollow looking.

I remembered Oliver as a strange, skinny adolescent who loved to play war games in the woods with his friends. He was two years older than me, so I'd had little contact with him in school and none after, yet there was one incident I'd never forgotten: He and several friends had broken into the high school and destroyed the computer lab. Someone had snitched on him, and the conviction had prevented him from being accepted into the army. Judging by the way he was dressed, he hadn't gotten over that rejection.

Libby looped her arm through mine. "Oliver, you remember Abby Knight. She owns Bloomers Flower Shop."

He put two fingers to his forehead in a salute. "Ma'am, pleased to meet you, ma'am."

"Oliver and I are having dinner at Down the Hatch," Libby told me. "Mummy is busy this evening, so it's just the two of us out on the town. I hear they serve great casual meals there. Are you meeting Marco? Well, of course you are. You're working on a case together, right?"

I shrugged. "I really can't say. It's confidential."

Oliver glanced around as if checking for spies, then held his hand to the side of his mouth and whispered, "The coast is clear."

"I still can't discuss it," I said.

He gave me a nod. "I understand, ma'am. Carry on, then."

How about moving on? "Well, I should be going. Nice to see you. Enjoy your dinner."

"But we're going to the same place, aren't we?" Libby called as I hurried away from her.

No way did I want to walk into the bar with those two. I took the side street to the back alley to reach the bar, where I had to be admitted by a puzzled cook. Marco wasn't in his office, so I went up front, only to spot him pouring tall beers for Libby and Oliver. I flagged a waitress and told her to let Marco know I was waiting in back. Then I went to his office and sat down.

Ten long minutes later, he showed up. "Have a nice visit with the Blumes?" I asked.

He slouched into his black leather chair, propped his feet on the black metal desk, and shook his head, as though amused. "That Libby is something else. She said she wants to learn the PI business. She asked to be my intern."

CHAPTER THREE

I sat forward, my hands clutching the arms of the chair. "Your *intern*?"

Marco reached for the shiny black coffee mug on his desk. "She's interested in learning the investigation business."

"That's not why she wants to be your intern, Marco. Think about it. First she asks to be *my* intern, because she just *has* to be a part of Bloomers. Then I turn her down and she asks to be *yours*? Trust me. Libby doesn't care about PI work. This is merely a way to get even with me."

"By learning how to be a private investigator?"

"No, by working with you. By taking your time away from me."

"Do you really think she'd go to all that trouble just to get even with you?"

"It sounds crazy, but I know Libby."

"You *knew* Libby."

"A leopard can't change its spots, Marco. Let me tell

you something about Libby Blume. I babysat her at my house after school, and whenever she got there before me, she'd go up to my room, paw through my drawers, read my diary, and eat my private stash of Hershey's Special Dark—and never bother to hide what she'd done, as if she saw nothing wrong with it."

"So far she sounds like one of my kid sisters."

"Just wait. She started tagging after me everywhere I went, and wanted to be included in all my activities. After a while she even began showing up at our house on weekends and holidays, hanging around all day, even when we had company. Then she had her hair styled like mine and bought clothes like mine, too. She figured out my locker combination and left me notes in it. She even called up my friends, pretending to be *me*. I felt like I had a stalker, and that's what I don't want to happen again."

I leaned forward, bracing my hands on his desk. "Do you understand why you have to turn her down? Because we have to nip this in the bud."

"Take it easy, Sunshine. I told her no."

I sank back in relief. "Thank you. But just so you know, you might be in for a visit from her mother, the Enforcer. After I told Libby she couldn't work for me, Delphi showed up and tried to bully me into changing my mind. I almost threw her out on her famous ass."

Marco grinned that enchanting, quirky grin of his as he came around to raise me to my feet. No one intimidated him, least of all an aging model. He traced a fingertip down my nose. "You're cute when your Irish temper is up."

I leaned into him, sliding my arms around his waist. "How cute?"

His arms came around me, and I knew we were seconds away from a kiss, but then he pulled back with a sigh. "Let's save that for an evening when we don't have to go anywhere."

"We don't *have* to go anywhere now, do we?"

"Yes, we do have to go somewhere now. I have to get this case wrapped up."

Damn. I pulled out my knit cap and tugged it on over my hair, tucking in stray strands. "Then let's do it."

Marco showed me photos of the target he was tailing—a hefty, forty-year-old man in a navy parka with a Bears logo on it. Marco had photographed him getting out of a black Camry. Now he needed proof that the guy was visiting a woman on the other side of town. He picked up two thermoses of coffee from the kitchen and gave me instructions as he walked me out to his car. I was to keep the front of an apartment building under surveillance and Marco was going to watch the back. I had one of his specially designed cameras that could shoot photos in the dark without a flash, and he had another. We would communicate via cell phone.

I drove to the designated street and found a curbside parking space where I would have a good view of the building. I was glad I'd worn warm clothes. The temperature had dropped into the thirties, and I didn't want to run the motor all evening. I settled in as comfortably as possible, the camera in my lap, then reached for the thermos.

A loud rap on my window jolted me upright. A face peered in at me—Libby, smiling cheerfully from beneath the brim of a black hat. She waved a black-gloved hand. "Hi, Abby."

I had to start the engine to roll down the window. "What are you doing here?"

"I came to keep you company. Look, I wore black." She stepped back so I could see her outfit. "Unlock the other side. I'll sit with you for a while."

Obviously Libby had tailed me there, still trying to worm her way into my life. "That's not a good idea, Libby. I have to focus."

"I'll be quiet."

"You'll still break my concentration." I shrugged. "Sorry."

Libby pushed out her lower lip. "I just didn't want you to be lonely. Here. I brought you a snack." She pulled a zip-top bag filled with Rice Krispies Treats from her purse.

I couldn't turn her down twice, so I thanked her and stuck my hand through the open window to take the bag. At that instant, a car door slammed close by, then an engine started, and before I could get a clear view, a car pulled past, giving me a quick glimpse of a man inside. Oh, no! Was that my target? Libby had blocked my view, and now it was too late to tell.

I rested my forehead against the steering wheel. "I think I just missed the person I was supposed to watch."

"Want me to take the camera and run after him?"

I sighed. "No, Libby. That would defeat the purpose of working undercover."

She slapped herself on the forehead. "Oh, right. Silly me."

Had she really not realized that, or had she wanted to sabotage the job for me?

"I'll let you get back to work now. Have a good evening." With another wave she left.

My cell phone vibrated and I saw on the screen that it was Marco checking in. What could I tell him that wouldn't sound like I'd screwed up? This was my first official case with him. I didn't want him to think I'd missed the target—even if it wasn't my fault.

"Hi, Marco, what's up?"

"Hey, Sunshine, good news. The target just snuck out the back entrance and I got some great shots of him. We can head home now."

I ended the call and sagged against the back of the seat. Damn Libby for following me. Somehow I was going to have to get the message to her to leave me alone.

Between working at Bloomers during the day, helping Marco with surveillance in the evenings, and fretting about Gina's baby shower at night, I was able to push aside my worries about Libby. Since I hadn't seen her after that first night on the case, I was hoping she'd forgotten about me, too—until I showed up at the country club for the Friday evening Knight family dinner and found her seated in my chair.

My dad was in his wheelchair at one end of the long table, with my mom at his right and Libby at his left, which was where I always sat. My brother Jordan and his wife, Kathy, were seated beside Mom. Opposite Kathy was my brother Jonathan and my other sister-in-law, Portia.

My mother spotted me first and jumped up, hurrying

over to greet me. "Abigail, look who's back in town. It's little Elizabeth Blume!"

"What is she doing here?" I asked, trying to unclench my teeth.

"I ran into her downtown the other day and she asked if we were still having our Friday night dinners at Greek's Pizzeria—remember when we used to have them there?—so I explained how we had moved to the country club when your brothers became members, and then it just seemed polite to invite her to join us. It's like old times, isn't it?"

Too much like old times. Mom was playing right into her hands, just like she did when Libby was eleven. "You didn't have to give her my seat," I whispered angrily.

Mom pulled back to look at me. "It's just a chair, Abigail. How old are you? Five?"

Twenty-six going on twenty-seven, to be exact, but at that moment I *felt* like a five-year-old. "If it's just a chair, why didn't you give her *your* chair? Or Jonathan's or Jordan's chair? Or let her sit in the empty chair at the opposite end of the table?"

"Come sit down and have some of your favorite crab cakes. They're Libby's favorite appetizer, too. And for heaven's sake, smile or everyone will think something's wrong."

Something *was* wrong, but I seemed to be the only one who recognized it. So I sat—in the empty chair at the end of the table, where I glared at Libby throughout the meal, although she didn't notice because she was too busy impressing my family. How dare she usurp me!

To make matters worse, I was forced to watch picky Portia spend the entire hour nibbling six string beans, a mound of peas, and a bowl of edamame. It was so unappetizing I could barely face the chocolate volcano I'd ordered for dessert, but somehow I managed.

Libby was in my face again the very next day, Saturday, when I showed up at First Impressions Beauty Salon for my early-morning haircut and found my stylist trimming Libby's long, ash-blond locks into a new sleek, blunt, shoulder-length bob—just like mine.

I turned around and walked out. Time to find a new hair salon.

Then at noon, when I went down to the deli to grab a quick turkey sandwich, I found my annoying cousin Jillian seated at a table with Libby, the two of them whispering and giggling together like a pair of teenagers.

"Get some food and join us," Jillian called when she saw me. "We can go shopping together afterward."

"It'll be oodles of fun," Libby added. "You can help me choose my winter wardrobe."

I tried to look properly dejected. "I have to work today. Sorry."

Jillian shrugged her shoulders and they resumed their conversation, heads bent together like they'd been friends forever. Vexed, I paid for my sandwich and left. Sure, Jillian was an annoyance, but she was *my* annoyance. I was more convinced than ever that Libby was trying to pay me back. Maybe she couldn't work for Marco or me, but she *could* hijack my family.

Sunday was Gina's shower—my day of reckoning. Luckily, I had managed to find a snappy tan corduroy fitted jacket to wear with a navy and tan print shirt and a denim skirt, which Marco said made me look hot and which gave me a big boost of self-confidence, since the Salvare women were stylish dressers.

Marco's mother had decorated his bar with blue, pink, and yellow balloons and streamers, and my mother had furnished the shower favors, but the hit of the afternoon was my floral centerpiece, made with pink 'Stargazer' lilies and alstroemeria, blue delphinium, yellow solidago, and a fresh supply of baby's breath. It was so awesome that Mrs. Salvare hugged me twice. Even Gina complimented my artistry. It seemed the Salvares were finally finding me acceptable, even if I had mistakenly called a Salvare aunt an uncle. She had a mustache and short hair and wore men's trousers. It was an innocent mistake.

The only hitch in my wonderful day occurred that evening, after Marco and I had settled onto the sofa in my apartment with a bowl of popcorn and a rented movie. Nikki was working the evening shift at the hospital, so we had the place to ourselves.

"Guess who called me this afternoon," Marco said, grabbing a handful of the buttery kernels. "Libby. She wants to meet with me Wednesday about handling a PI case for her."

I made a *pffft* sound and reached for the popcorn.

He put his arm around me and leaned his ear against mine. "I hear the wheels grinding. What's going on in there?"

"Libby doesn't have a case, Marco. She's got an ulterior motive."

He pulled back to look at me. "Come on, Sunshine, she's not that devious."

"Oh, no? Shall I remind you that she got my mom to invite her to our family dinner, took over my chair there, appropriated my hairdresser, got her hair cut like mine, and cozied up to Jillian? Now she suddenly wants to hire you and you think it's innocent? No way. It's a ruse."

"Relax. I can tell within the first five minutes of meeting someone whether he or she is making it up. If Libby is making this up, I'll tell her to hit the bricks."

"Can we shake on that?"

His mouth curved up at one corner. "We can do better than that." Then he leaned me back against the sofa to prove it.

My suspicions about Libby's intentions to get even with me were confirmed on Monday morning, when I noticed a lot of activity on the west side of the square. In front of an old hardware store that had been empty for months, huge crates were being unloaded from a semi-trailer, and a large crew in painter's coveralls was carrying in buckets and supplies.

Grace, Lottie, and I stepped outside of Bloomers to watch a big crane hoist a new sign onto the front of the two-story brown brick building. On a creamy white background, big gold letters spelled out BLUME'S ART SHOP. Beneath that, in smaller letters: LIBBY BLUME, PROP.

My mouth fell open. I immediately spun around to gaze up at my sign. On a creamy white background, big gold letters spelled out BLOOMERS FLOWER SHOP. Beneath that, in smaller letters: ABBY KNIGHT, PROP. "She copied my flower-shop sign!"

"As the saying goes, dear," Grace said, "imitation is the sincerest form of flattery."

"That's not flattery, Grace. That's Libby getting even with me."

Grace and Lottie glanced at each other. Then Grace said, "Wouldn't it be impractical, not to mention expensive, to lease a shop, stock it with art, and hire staff merely to get even?"

"For a normal person, yes," I said. "Libby isn't normal."

"As my boys say, define normal," Lottie said.

I was about to say, *Look at us! We're normal.* But then I glanced at Lottie, with her white socks and pink penny loafers, her size 14 body squeezed into size 12 white jeans, her husband's oversized Chicago Bulls sweatshirt, her brassy dyed-orange curls in a Shirley Temple hairstyle, with pink bow barrettes fastened above each ear, and I paused.

Then there was Grace, who had been a nurse in the British Army stationed overseas in Germany at the same time Elvis Presley was there, who had since devoted an entire room in her home to Elvis memorabilia, and who, deep down, believed Graceland was named after her.

I dropped the subject. I'd just have to ignore Libby *and* her shop.

But on Tuesday morning, that proved impossible, because the first thing I saw when I came around the corner onto Franklin and glanced across the square was the newly painted door of Blume's Art Shop—bright yellow with a beveled-glass center.

"There has to be some way to keep her from copying me," I told Lottie and Grace. "I'll have to call Dave Hammond and ask him if he'll submit a petition for a cease and desist order."

"Dave will be in federal court all week," Grace said. "Martha told me yesterday."

"Can a cease and desist order be issued for storefronts anyway?" Lottie asked.

"I'll have to get out my law books and see what I can find. . . . Oh, wait. I burned them."

"If I remember correctly," Grace said, "one must have a patent on one's design, logo, or sign before legal action can be initiated."

"Damn," I grumbled. "There has to be something I can do to stop her."

Lottie put her hands on my shoulders. "It's just a door, sweetie."

"Just a door. Just a sign. Just a haircut. Just a chair at the table. Next it'll be just my life."

They were gazing at me as if *I* were crazy. "Abby, you simply can't go on this way," Grace said. "It's not healthy."

"You're absolutely right," I replied, heading for the door. "I've got to put an end to it."

CHAPTER FOUR

When I stepped inside Blume's Art Shop, Libby was standing amid drop cloths and tall stepladders, watching quietly as her mother fired off a list of instructions to a team of painters who were applying pastel colors to her walls. More drop cloths covered display furniture that had been grouped together in the center of the room.

"Watch that trim," Delphi ordered. "It must be pristine white. If you spill one drop of green on it, you'll have to repaint the whole length. Oliver? Where's Oliver? Did he leave again?"

"Abby!" Libby called in delight, catching sight of me. "What a wonderful surprise. Mummy, look who came to visit."

At once, Delphi spun around, a vicious look on her face. She was sporting a pair of enormous gold hoop earrings, a cowl-neck angora sweater in powder blue, a pair of white skinny jeans, and gold ballet flats. She gave me a fierce scowl, then stalked across the room and disappeared through a doorway in the back, yelling, "Oliver! Didn't you hear me calling you?"

"Isn't this exciting?" Libby asked, squeezing my hand as she gazed around her new shop. "My very own art gallery, and it's just across the square from Bloomers."

Her childlike delight made it hard to be angry. "Speaking of that," I said, slipping my hand from her grasp, "there's something I need to discuss with you."

"Okay." She pressed her palms together as though she couldn't wait to hear it.

I scratched my ear, feeling suddenly petty. "It's about your sign."

"Don't you just love it?"

"Well, see, I do, but that's because it looks like *my* sign."

"It does?" She looked perplexed for a moment. Then her face cleared. "You know what probably happened? I was picturing your sign when I talked to the man from the sign company."

"Were you also picturing my yellow door when you talked to the painter?"

"Isn't it fun? We're the two bright spots on the square—like golden bookends. Maybe some of the other shop owners will take the hint and paint their doors bright colors, too."

"You're missing my point, Libby. I opened a flower shop on the town square named Bloomers, and you opened an art shop on the square named Blume's. I have a yellow door with a glass center, and you do, too. Even our signs are identical. You could have called it Libby's Art Gallery, but you didn't. Do you see what I'm getting at?"

"Honestly, Abby, it's not what you think. I opened an

art shop because I majored in art. It's what I know and, more importantly, what I love, other than flowers, and I'd certainly never open a flower shop and hurt your business. I didn't want to call it a gallery because that sounds too uppity for New Chapel. *Blume's* reminds me of flowers and *Art Shop* has a cozy sound to it.

"The location was purely a business decision, too. My uncle owns the building, and Mummy leased it as a surprise for me. My color scheme, as you can see, is pastel green, ice blue, orange sherbet, and bright yellow, and of those, I thought the yellow would work best on the door. I'm really sorry if you thought I was copying you. I would never purposely offend you."

Libby's answers sounded so rational that I began to think maybe I was being overly sensitive. "Well, then, thank you for clearing that up."

A loud crash from the back room made both of us jump. "Oliver!" Delphi screeched. "That's not how you carry framed art. Now look what you've done!"

"Poor Mummy," Libby said. "She's determined to make this shop a success for me."

Oliver strode out of the back room wearing green and tan camouflage pants, a crisply ironed tan shirt with brown tie, and army boots. He saluted me, then did a neat pivot to face Libby. "Ma'am, you have been summoned to command headquarters, ma'am."

"Oh, Oliver, honestly," Libby said, rolling her eyes. "Sorry, Abby. I have to go. We're opening Friday and there's a lot to do. You'll come to our grand opening, won't you?"

"I, um, well, the thing is . . ." I rubbed my nose, trying to think of a reason to decline.

She gave me a little girl's pout, with big sad eyes. "Please?"

I hated that look. It reminded me of babysitting for her. "Well . . . I'll try."

"Thanks, Abby." Libby hugged me and sped away. Oliver saluted, then pivoted and marched after her. I glanced up at the painters on their tall ladders, who had paused, paintbrushes in hand, to watch Oliver. As I left the shop, I could hear them snickering.

I was creating a birthday bouquet in the workroom after lunch, and Grace was delivering a cup of tea to me, when Lottie came rushing in with a tabloid journal she'd picked up at the grocery store. Breathlessly, she tapped the front cover. "See why I read these things? This is how I know what's going on."

I stopped snipping thorns off a 'Red France' rose to glance at the headline: WOMAN GIVES BIRTH TO TWO-HEADED CALF. "Wouldn't it be shocking enough for a woman to give birth to a calf with one head?" I asked.

"Not that. This one—about Delphi." Lottie tapped a tiny corner photo with a small caption that read: FORMER BELLY MODEL GOES BELLY-UP.

Now, *that* was interesting. I turned to page 14 and read the article to myself while Lottie summarized it for Grace. "Listen to this, Gracie. About four years back one of Delphi's clients filed a suit against her talent agency. So that she-devil Delphi hired a Chicago lawyer to fight it, but when the jury sided with the client and awarded the girl a huge amount of money, Delphi filed for bankruptcy so she wouldn't have to pay the poor kid her settlement. Then she opened her agency under a new name." Lottie pointed to the paper. "It's all here, the whole sordid story."

I stopped reading to say to Lottie, "Isn't this she-devil the woman you were so awed by a few days ago?"

"That was then, this is now. As far as I'm concerned, anyone who cheats a kid can take a long walk off a short pier. Did you get to the part about the surgery yet?"

"I'm trying."

"What happened was this," Lottie continued. "The young girl, Kayla Olin, was sixteen years old when she signed up with Delphi's agency. Delphi told her she had real potential—if she got a nose job and chin augmentation. Well, there was no way Kayla's folks could pay for that, so Delphi arranged for it to be done by a surgeon she knew—on the cheap, know what I mean? The surgery was botched, the girl's face is a nightmare, her career is ruined, her dad has died in the meantime, and now, four years later, she can't even collect on the judgment because that she-devil declared bankruptcy!"

Grace shook her head sadly. "As Shakespeare wrote in *Hamlet*, 'When sorrows come, they come not single spies / But in battalions.' "

Lottie pointed to the grainy picture of Kayla at the bottom of page 14. "Isn't that the saddest thing you've ever seen? And she can't afford the surgery to repair the damage."

The bell over the door jingled, signaling incoming customers. "I'll see to them," Grace offered, and went up front.

"Can't you just imagine how that young woman feels every time she looks into the mirror?" Lottie asked. "It makes me want to punch that she-devil's lights out."

The bell jingled again, so Lottie went next. I put down the newspaper, reflecting on the article as I returned to my flowers. Delphi was definitely not a nice person. I hadn't thought about it before, but after seeing Delphi in action, I could understand why Libby had spent so much time at our crowded and often chaotic house.

"Grace is waiting on customers in the parlor," Lottie bustled in to say, "so I'm gonna run those three funeral arrangements over to the Happy Dreams Funeral Home."

Two minutes after Lottie left, the bell jingled again, so I went up front. But when I stepped through the curtain, no one was there. Granted, amid all the bright flowers, centerpieces, and tall green plants, people sometimes blended in. Still, I sure didn't detect anyone. I looked into the parlor, where Grace was pouring tea for three women seated at the table in front of the window.

"Did someone just come in?" I asked her.

She shook her head. Had I imagined the jingle? I started back for the workroom only to hear a rustle of leaves. I stopped and turned to scan the room, my gaze landing on two seven-foot-tall dieffenbachia plants in the back corner. Also called dumb cane, the big-leaved giants made terrific decorating accents. *Dieffenbachia amoena* had green and white variegated leaves, while the striking leaves of 'Rudolph Roehrs' were pale chartreuse with dark green edges and veins.

I saw a dead leaf lying on the ground in front of one plant and bent to pick it up. That's when I noticed a pair of brown boots behind one of the large pots. The boots came with a pair of green and tan camouflage pants. I jumped back. Someone was crouched behind the plants.

"Is the coast clear?" a voice whispered.

"What?" I asked, backing toward the curtain.

A branch parted and a green face appeared. "Is the man across the street gone?"

"Oliver?"

Moving cautiously, he stepped out from behind the plants, glancing around as though he expected to be attacked by enemy soldiers. Wearing camouflage fatigues and face paint, he held a green-gloved finger to his lips, then jerked his head toward the front door and whispered, "Outside. Sitting on the cement bench directly across the street. Is he still there?"

Keeping one eye on Oliver, I looked out the bay window at the courthouse lawn. "All I see are two elderly women on the bench."

"He was there a minute ago."

"Who was?"

"The *man*. The feds. Big gov. Big Bro—they're always watching, you know. You can't be too careful."

I didn't know what to say. I glanced out again and spotted a policeman checking parking meters along the courthouse side of the street. Was that the *man* he'd seen?

He motioned me away from the window. "I'm on a covert operation"—he glanced over his shoulders—"for bamboo."

"Bamboo—as in plants?"

"Yes, ma'am. Tools of the trade. The Japanese used bamboo shoots as instruments of torture in World War Two." He held out his hand to demonstrate, looking particularly gleeful. "You jam those suckers right under the fingernails. The pain is unbearable."

Well, *that* was creepy. "So . . . why do *you* want the plants?" Did I really want to know?

He straightened with a jerk, clicked his heels together, and saluted. "Ma'am, the commander has requisitioned them, ma'am. Will you comply?"

"If you stop talking to me like I work at the PX."

Oliver blinked several times. "You know what a PX is?"

"It's a post exchange, like a general store. I watch *M.A.S.H.* reruns."

"Cool. So do you have bamboo plants?"

"You're in luck. We got a new shipment in two days ago. They're very popular now."

"The commander always has to be on top of the latest trend, ma'am."

"Are you talking about your mother? Do you mean that Delphi sent you *here*?"

"She didn't specify where, ma'am."

That made more sense. I couldn't imagine Delphi willingly giving me her business. "Thanks, Oliver."

He placed his hand on my shoulder and said very solemnly, "You're O.O.T.T.O."

I'd never heard that one on *M.A.S.H.* Out-and-out titillating turn-on? Probably not. "What is O.O.T.T.O.?"

He glanced around, then said quietly, "One of the trusted ones. Remember that."

Time to move on. I pulled a plant from the display in the bay window. "The bamboo plants come in these decorative twelve-inch clay pots. Will that be okay?"

At his single nod, I asked, "How many do you need?"

"Thr—four."

"I'll bring out the others. Have a seat."

Oliver followed me to the workroom instead. As I

opened one of the walk-in coolers, he gazed curiously around the busy room. "A person could really hide out in here."

Inside the cooler I stepped around deep buckets of blossoms, looking for the bamboo plants. "It's amazing how quickly Libby's art shop came together," I said, making conversation.

"It's not Libby's shop," he said, standing in the cooler behind me.

"Is your mother the owner?"

He bent to examine a rose, pricked himself on a thorn, and immediately sucked the wound. "Part and parcel," he said. "Overlord and landlord. Business as usual."

I hated when people talked cryptically. It made me feel dumb. I located the other three plants all the way at the back and had him help me carry them out. "Is it nice to have your little sister back home again?"

Oliver selected a plump yellow daisy from a bucket on the floor and began to pluck the petals. "An ally is always welcome. Two forces are mightier than one. . . . Loves me, loves me not . . . Besides, Libby is way better at playing the obedient child. Takes the heat off me."

I was beginning to think that his military guise was his way of coping with Delphi. We carried the pots to the cash register, where I wrote out a statement and handed the yellow copy to him. He immediately whipped out his wallet, counted out the money, then laid the bills *and* my statement on the counter.

"This is your copy," I said, pushing the piece of paper toward him.

"Never leave evidence. Always pay in cash. You never know who'll be checking your receipts."

Obviously he didn't want Delphi to know where he'd purchased the plants. "Are you parked out front?"

"Not for a covert operation. We always use the rear."

I found boxes to hold the plants and we carried them to the back door. Oliver motioned for me to stand back. Then he opened the heavy fire door and peered cautiously outside. When he was sure the alley was safe, he carried one of the boxes to the pastel green van that said BLUME'S ART SHOP on the side. When the boxes were loaded, he saluted me. "Ma'am, thank you, ma'am. Remember"—he glanced around—"this is a *covert* operation. We must never speak of it again."

My mother stopped by Bloomers during her lunch break the next day to show us her latest artistic endeavor— a jacket made entirely of beads, but not those pretty little colored beads that were used to make bracelets and necklaces. These were giant wooden beads, like the massaging backrests cabdrivers used for long days behind the wheel. Not an attractive look for a jacket.

"What do you think?" Mom asked eagerly.

"It's quite unusual," Grace replied tactfully.

"Really nice," Lottie said, trying to sound admiring.

Mom took it off a wooden hanger and held it open. "Abigail, will you model it for us?"

I slipped my arms into the sleeves and then couldn't move. Not only was the jacket so heavy that it flattened my breasts; it was so thick that I couldn't put my arms against my sides. I rotated like a bird on a spit so they could see.

Grace tapped her chin thoughtfully. "Might be a bit awkward to wear about town."

"Kind of breezy, too," Lottie said, pinching her lips to keep from laughing.

"It's not designed to wear," Mom said, helping me out of the jacket. "I'm taking it down to Blume's. Libby invited me to include it in her 'Fashion as Art' display."

I gaped at her. My mom was taking her jacket to *Libby's* shop? I should have been relieved, but instead I felt betrayed.

"I feel so validated as an artist," Mom said happily. "To think that my work will be displayed in a real art gallery."

"How lovely, Maureen," Grace said. "We're so proud of you, aren't we, Abby?"

They both must have noticed my stricken expression, because Lottie immediately threw a meaty arm around my shoulders and gave me a shake, as though to wake me from my shock. "You bet we are."

"How did this invitation come about?" I asked as Mom placed her jacket on the hanger.

"We discussed it at dinner Friday night. Don't you remember?"

"I was at the far end of the table, Mom. All I could hear was Portia crunching her beans."

"Your father was telling Libby about my hobby. Then Libby asked if I had ever considered selling my art, so I explained that I brought them here. She asked to see some of my work, so I invited her over to see my new creations. You should have seen her face, Abigail. She was absolutely amazed. Now I'm going to be one of her featured artists. Can you believe it?"

"That's great," was all I could think to say. No way could I tell Mom anything hurtful, but I doubted Libby had been amazed. Appalled was more like it. So what was Libby really after? Did she want Mom's art to make me jealous? Or did she want my mom?

"I should get this down to Blume's." Mom started toward the door, then paused. "Will you come with me?"

No way! was on the tip of my tongue. Watching her hand Libby the jacket that should have been in my shop was the last thing I wanted to do. But I caught a vulnerability in Mom's expression that told me she was nervous. Maybe having me at her side would give her a boost of confidence. Or maybe I just wanted to be there to remind Libby whose mother she was.

I smiled. "Sure. I'll walk over with you."

The relief in my mom's eyes made my decision the right one.

Ten minutes later, I opened the *other* yellow door and watched Mom carry in her pride and joy du jour. I followed her inside, then stared around in astonishment. Libby had re-created Bloomers' interior.

She'd copied my shop cleverly. In place of my wreaths and swags, her walls were filled with art. Her curtain was ice blue, not purple, and her display furniture held clay, wood, and glass sculptures instead of flower arrangements. A small alcove on the right even held a white wrought iron table and chair set, with a small coffee bar nearby. It wouldn't be obvious to the casual observer—but I knew.

My gut feeling had been right. Libby was out for revenge. She had taken over my cousin, my haircut, my mother's art, and my seat at our family dinner, and now she'd stolen the look of my shop inside and out. Where would it end? How far would she go to get even with me?

"Mom," I said quietly, taking her arm, "let's go back to Bloomers."

"Why?"

"There are things you don't know about Libby."

"Abigail, don't be jealous. Even if I don't show my art at Bloomers anymore, I still love you. This is a big opportunity for me, honey. You understand, don't you?"

I gazed into her hopeful eyes, ready to make a stronger case, but I couldn't do it. The art meant too much to her. I glanced around for Libby, but saw only a hulking, thick-bodied woman perched on a stool behind the counter, immersed in a paperback, oblivious to our presence. She had a small head topped by short, coarse, steel gray hair; beady eyes; a long, narrow nose; and no chin to speak of. She had on a shapeless blue denim jumper over a dingy white shirt with a scarf at her neck that looked like a man's red bandanna.

When I cleared my throat, the woman looked up, obviously annoyed that her concentration had been broken. "Wotcher want, then?" she snarled with a strong cockney accent. "We're not open fer business yet."

If this woman was Libby's salesclerk, her shop was doomed.

"My name is Maureen Knight," Mom explained with her patient teacher's smile. "I'm supposed to bring this jacket over for the fashion display."

The woman's beady eyes bugged at the sight of the jacket. "Wot? That thing 'ere? Yer not serious?"

Mom looked shaken, so I said firmly, "May we see Libby Blume, please?"

"Not 'ere," the woman grunted. "'Er muvver popped

in, din't she, and they took orff. 'Er bruvver's in back if'n yer want ter talk wif summin else."

Mom glanced at me for help. "Libby left with her mother," I interpreted. "Her brother's in back if you want to talk with someone else." Wow. Watching all those mysteries on BBC America had finally paid off.

"Can I just leave the jacket here with a note for her?" Mom asked.

"No skin orff my teeth," the woman said, returning to her paperback.

If she *had* teeth. What could Libby have been thinking to hire such a coarse, unprofessional clerk? I suspected I knew the answer but hoped I was wrong. "I didn't catch your name," I said, as Mom scratched out a hasty note.

"Tilly Gladwell," the woman muttered, drawing herself up as though she were royalty, "not that it's any business o'yers." She looked up with a scowl when Mom laid the jacket on the counter in front of her. "Not 'ere! Over there." She pointed to an empty table next to the curtained doorway, then, with a sharp huff of displeasure, turned back to her book.

"She must be a temp," Mom said, trying to put a good spin on it, as we walked back toward Bloomers.

Or a very bad copy of Grace—until Libby could get the real thing.

That evening, when I went to Down the Hatch to meet Marco for dinner, Gert, the waitress, who had been there as long as the fake carp, informed me that Marco was meeting with a potential client in his office. Suspecting it was Libby, I slid into our booth, ordered a Miller Lite, and watched the evening news on the television mounted on the wall, waiting for his meeting to end.

Fifteen minutes later, Libby breezed past the table with only a brief hello, confirming my suspicions about the client. I smiled to myself. Marco had obviously refused to take her case.

At that moment, he slid onto the bench opposite me. "How's it going, Sunshine?"

"Super. So, I guess you told Libby to hit the bricks."

Marco signaled to Gert to come take our order. "No, I took her case."

CHAPTER FIVE

"**Y**ou didn't!" Stunned, I put my hands against the sides of my face. "This just keeps getting worse."

"It appears Libby has a legitimate problem, Sunshine. I'm going to look into it for her."

"She's playing you, Marco, just like she's playing my mom."

"What are you talking about?"

"Libby convinced Mom to put her art on display at Blume's Art Shop."

"Maybe Libby likes your mother's art."

"No one likes my mother's art. Why do you think we store it in our basement?"

"You should be glad your mother has an outlet for her stuff. Now you're off the hook."

"The point I'm trying to make is that everyone falls for Libby's act, including you!"

"Have a little faith in me, Abby. Libby is genuinely frightened."

"Of what? The boogeyman?"

Leaning toward me, Marco said quietly, "I'll tell you this in confidence only because I was going to ask you to work on this case with me anyway. Libby is being stalked. She's getting hate mail, e-mails, and threatening phone calls, to the point where she's afraid to go out alone. She believes the stalker may be someone from college with whom she had problems before."

"Do you know how easy it would be for her to claim someone is stalking her? Libby could mail *herself* threatening letters."

"She could, but why would she? Why do you want to believe the worst about Libby?"

"Because I know her. She looks harmless on the outside, but inside she's all screwed up."

"No, you *knew* her, Abby, when she was eleven years old. Give her a break."

I sat back and crossed my arms. "I'll give her a break when she gets a life of her own and stops copying mine."

Marco sat back, too, clearly irked. "Let's just drop the subject. Nothing I say is going to snap you out of this funk. I think you should take a pass on working on her case, too. There's no way you can be objective."

"Those were the next words out of my mouth," I replied testily.

"You want to order?" he grumbled, nodding toward our waitress standing patiently at the end of the booth.

"I need comfort food, Gert," I told her.

"One grilled cheese and tomato sandwich with sweet pickles on the side," she said, marking it on her pad.

After Marco had given her his order, I said to him,

"You know what I'd like you to do? Walk down to Libby's shop tomorrow. See for yourself how she made it look like Bloomers."

"Okay, so Libby admires you and tries to emulate you. It's awkward, but it's not a crime."

"You still don't get it. She's not just emulating me, Marco. She's hijacking my life. Look at all the things she's done to be like me, even changing her name to sound like mine. I thought you of all people would understand how frustrating this is for me."

"You realize this is about the past, don't you? You can't stand it that Libby admires you because you still see her as that little pest you had to babysit."

"She *was* a pest, and I didn't even tell you the half of it. Because of her showing up everywhere I went, my friends stopped asking me to hang out with them. Libby was at my house so much that my mom started buying her Christmas and birthday presents, and my brothers called her their *other* little sister. She didn't just read my diary, Marco. She made entries in it—as me! But the absolute worst thing she did was to tell a guy whom I secretly liked that I had a major crush on him. She told him I had written his name all over the inside of my locker and then she opened it up and showed him the signs *she* had hung there! I was mortified."

"And you've never forgiven her, have you?"

I opened my mouth to deny it, then closed it again. Could Marco be right? Was Libby's behavior driving me crazy because I had never forgiven her? Was I blowing this thing all out of proportion because of grudges I still carried? I sat back, my mind reeling as my thoughts spun backward to those open wounds of my youth.

Marco reached across the table and took my hands. "Let go of the past, Sunshine."

Let go. Sure. As if it could be that easy. I gazed at Marco's handsome face and knew he was only trying to help. "Maybe you're right."

"I'll do whatever I can to make it better." He rubbed his thumbs in the middle of my palms. "You know those foot massages you like so much?"

I sighed dreamily. Was there anything better than a thorough foot massage, especially when delivered by a hot hunk with more on his mind than feet?

Marco lifted one of my palms to his lips and nibbled it, sending tingles of ecstasy up my arm and straight to my core, which was rapidly turning molten. "And how about a bottle of that Italian wine we discovered at that great little restaurant on Rush Street to go with your massage?"

I took it back. A foot massage, a hunk, *and* a glass of Brunella—now, *that* was the best.

"And maybe top it all off with dark chocolate truffles from your favorite candy shop?" He raised an eyebrow to entice me. "My mother went home. My place is all mine again."

"Now, *that* sounds like a plan," I said, fanning my face. If he didn't stop kissing my palm soon, I was going to dissolve into a puddle of euphoria.

"Would you two get a room?" Gert drawled, waiting to set our plates on the table.

I gave Marco a little smile as we drew apart. "We were just discussing that."

When Gert left, I leaned forward to say in a sultry voice, "What time shall we launch your, um, Abby initiative? I can meet you at your place when you get off work this evening."

"You're on, Sunshine." Marco gave me a hot glance as he picked up his burger, but he stopped centimeters from his mouth. "Damn. I'll have to take a rain check. I promised Libby I'd start on her case tonight."

Not tonight! My molten core cooled as a wave of disappointment washed over me. A protest was on my lips, but I managed to stifle it. If Marco wanted me to let go of the past, then that's what I'd do. Although I still suspected Libby was playing him, I'd go out of my way to demonstrate that I was a benevolent person, not a begrudging crank. And if my prediction about Libby proved to be true, he'd just have to learn it the hard way.

"I'll hang on to that plan until you're free," I said cheerfully.

He squeezed my hands. "That's my Sunshine."

Between running the bar and working on his PI cases, Marco was tied up for the rest of the week, so I made it a practice to drop by the bar after I closed the shop, so we could at least have a beer together. Without fail, however, Libby would show up soon afterward to discuss the latest developments in her case, which made it nearly impossible to block out my animosity for her. Still, I tried, even when other shop owners kept stopping me to say how much Libby and I looked like sisters, and what a great kid she was, and wasn't I glad she had returned to town? In each case I managed to smile and nod—and quickly move on.

To demonstrate even further to Marco that I was willing to let bygones be bygones, I made up a big floral arrangement for Libby's grand-opening celebration on Friday and walked it down there myself just before closing time on Thursday. Oliver had just flipped the sign in the door to CLOSED, but when he saw me through the glass pane, he let me in, saluting as I passed.

I stared around at the balloons and streamers hanging from the ceiling, and the big, colorful splash of roses, orchids, spider mums, gerbera daisies, and more that were artfully positioned in designer vases all around the shop. Obviously, Delphi had gone somewhere else for her flowers. At least I could claim one arrangement, even if I had brought it down myself.

"The place looks great," I told him. I glanced around and saw three of my potted bamboo plants on display in an Oriental art exhibit. "What happened to the fourth bamboo plant, Oliver?"

"It wasn't requisitioned, ma'am."

Hearing Delphi's angry voice and some unpleasant cockney screeching coming from the back room, I said, "Should I come back later?"

He took a seat on a stool behind the counter. "You'll miss the show, ma'am."

I set the flower arrangement on the counter just as Delphi cried, "You're a thief! A crude, lying, sticky-fingered thief! Don't you dare deny that you took money from the cash drawer, you wart-covered cockney toad. Give it back."

"'Oo d'yer think you are, talkin' ter me that way!" Tilly fired back.

"The woman who's going to have you deported, that's who!" Delphi shouted.

Tilly burst through the curtain and headed straight for

the counter with Delphi in hot pursuit and Libby trailing after, looking anxious and unhappy.

Oh. *That* show.

"Out o'me way, you barmy swine," Tilly bellowed, nearly shoving Oliver off the stool as she reached beneath the counter for her purse. She swung to face her accuser. "Just try an' 'ave me deported," she sneered. "You'll be sorry you ever crossed Tilly Gladwell, you will."

"Oliver," Delphi commanded, "call the police!"

I glanced over at him and found him entranced in the whole spectacle as though it were live theater. I tapped on the counter. "You'd better call 911."

As Oliver reached for the phone, Tilly headed for the door muttering swearwords.

"Don't you walk out of here!" Delphi shouted, her pixie face red with rage. But Tilly charged straight out the door with Delphi fast on her heels yelling threats.

"Mummy, don't!" Libby cried, racing behind. "You might get hurt!"

Through the window I watched as Delphi caught up with Tilly and tried to wrestle the purse away, while Libby stood off to the side wringing her hands. Being larger, Tilly gave Delphi a shove that sent her sprawling, then quickly loped up the block and around the corner, moving surprisingly fast for a woman her size.

Hearing the wail of a police siren, I decided a quick exit was in order. I couldn't afford to be caught in the middle of another fracas.

"Ma'am?" Oliver called as I darted for the door. "You didn't leave a bill for the flowers."

"They're a gift," I called back. "Happy grand opening."

Too late. A squad car pulled up and two officers got out—one of them Reilly.

At once Delphi marched up to them and began to rattle off her complaints, while Libby stood mutely at her side. As the other officer took off in pursuit of the would-be thief, Reilly pulled out his notepad and pencil, listening to Delphi as his gaze quietly took in the scene. I edged away from Blume's, hoping my brown corduroy jacket and khakis would blend in with the brick front, but he spotted me anyway. Damn my red hair.

Not again! Reilly's look said when he saw me. I gave him a little wave and headed in the opposite direction.

"Abby!" he barked. "Stick around."

Yikes. "I'll wait on the bench across the street," I called, and darted away before he could protest. Once the other officer returned—without Tilly—and took over interviewing Delphi and Libby, Reilly came across, sat down beside me, and stretched out his long legs.

"Please believe me, Reilly, I wasn't involved. All I did was carry over an arrangement for their grand opening."

"I'm not accusing you of anything. I just wanted to get your take on the situation."

"Now you're talking." I gave him my explanation, which he dutifully recorded. When he was done, I said, "Now I'd like your take on something, Sarge." I pointed across the street. "Does anything seem odd about Blume's Art Shop?"

"Odd how?"

"I don't know . . . maybe that Blume's Art Shop looks just like Bloomers, down to the sign and yellow door? And then there's Libby, who has turned herself into a blond copy of me. If she ever dyes her hair red, it'll be hard to tell us apart."

Reilly squinted his eyes at Libby. "You're right. That's quite a resemblance."

"I'm glad you agree, Reilly. I think Libby is copying me on purpose because I wouldn't let her work at Bloomers. Everyone else thinks I'm making a big deal out of nothing—imitation is the sincerest form of flattery, blah, blah—but they don't know her like I do. So is there anything I can do to make her stop copying me and my store?"

"Has she stolen your credit card, driver's license, or taken out a mortgage in your name?"

"Well, no, but—"

"There's no law against what she's done, Abby."

I crossed my arms and scowled at the ground.

"What does Marco think?"

"He thinks I'm harboring grudges against Libby from the past," I grumbled, "because I used to babysit her and she was a monster."

"Are you harboring a grudge?"

I sighed. "Maybe."

"Take the advice of a wise old divorced man, Abby. Move on."

Blume's grand-opening celebration day came without one mention in the newspaper of Tilly's theft. I went to the ribbon-cutting ceremony at nine o'clock because I'd told Libby I would, and because I was still trying to demonstrate that I could forgive and forget. My mom was there, beaming proudly beside her beaded jacket, and Jillian was there, too, dressed in a designer outfit, posing for the photographer from the *New Chapel News*.

Standing beside the photographer was crime reporter Connor MacKay, who'd covered a murder investigation that I'd entangled myself in a few months back. Connor had enchanting green eyes and a wide smile that could coax the spots off a Dalmatian, but after he tried to trick me out of confidential information so he could score a big story, I'd made it a point to steer clear of him. However, this time I was trapped.

"Well, if it isn't Libby—er—Abby Knight," Connor said with a wink, sauntering my way.

"Not funny, MacKay."

"Sorry. I'm having a hard time telling you two apart. What do you think of Blume's Art Shop? Kind of reminds me of another shop on the square."

"So you see it, too?"

"Hard to miss that bright yellow door. How do you feel about that?"

I was so ready to tell him. Then I reminded myself that I wasn't there to smear Libby's name. I was there to show what a good person I was. So I forced a smile and said, "Can there ever be enough yellow doors in town?"

He held up his pen and reporter's notebook. "Can I quote you on that?"

Did I want to be named in an article about Libby? "Let me put it this way, Connor: What kind of flowers would you like at your funeral?"

The weekend passed too quietly. Although Marco managed to squeeze in our nightly phone conversations, he was too busy to see me, so I buried myself in my work. Meanwhile, Libby and her art shop were garnering lots of attention, the store was always crowded, and everyone liked her. And although Libby's presence on the square was grating, and my gut was still telling me that there was more behind her behavior than simple admiration, I didn't say a word. Thank goodness I had Nikki to talk to. She might have been the only person who believed me.

Then, five days ago, just before we opened for business, I spotted Libby across the square getting out of a yellow Corvette convertible with a black ragtop.

"She has a car like mine!" I ranted to Lottie and Grace, who were standing at the big bay window with me. "Do you still think I'm overreacting?"

"I must say, that is an extraordinary coincidence," Grace conceded.

"I've been trying to put the past behind me and give Libby the benefit of the doubt, but *that*"—I jabbed my index finger toward the shiny Corvette—"makes my blood boil."

"I wonder where it's gonna end," Lottie said.

A sudden chill ran through my body. "I don't know, and that's what really disturbs me."

I phoned Marco to tell him about Libby's new car, but got his voice mail. I left him a message asking him to call, but I didn't hear from him. Finally, at eleven o'clock that morning I hurried down to his bar—and there was Libby having a cup of coffee with him at *our* booth. She turned around to see who came in, then gave me a smug little smile, as if to say, *He's next.*

Fury rose up inside me like an ugly, uncontrollable

beast. I didn't trust myself to confront her. Instead, I marched straight past the booth and into the middle of Marco's office, where I stood with my back to the door, my arms crossed, and my foot tapping angrily against the carpet.

Marco followed, shutting the door behind us. He came up behind me and put his hands on my shoulders. "Are you all right?"

"Why is Libby here?" I demanded, turning to face him.

"Take it easy, Sunshine. She wanted me to see a letter she got this morning."

"It came this morning? How convenient. She showed up here every evening last week, totally monopolizing your attention, and now she's added mornings to her list."

"Aren't you exaggerating a little?"

"Libby is playing you, Marco, and you've fallen for it hook, line, and sinker."

He sighed. "Don't start that again."

"Did she tell you she bought a car like mine?"

"It's twenty years newer, and her mother bought it for her as a surprise."

He knew! And he hadn't even bothered to warn me. "So what if it's newer? It's still a yellow Corvette convertible. And I'm not buying the surprise-gift bit."

"Why? You know Delphi has the money to do it."

"Why would Delphi buy an older Corvette with no air bags, no CD player, and none of the modern conveniences when Libby already has a Mercedes SL convertible?"

He crossed his arms and leaned against the door. "I suppose I'm going to hear why."

"Because Libby asked for it. That Vette moves her one step closer to taking over my identity. And you know what that leaves for her to take over? My hair color—and *you.*"

"For God's sake, Abby—"

"Bow out of her case, Marco. Refer her to another PI. You don't need the work."

"I've already accepted a retainer."

"Give it back."

"It's not the money. I gave my word, and you know I don't go back on my word."

"Even if she's lying to you?"

Marco's expressive mouth took a downward turn. "I asked you to trust me on that."

"I wish I could, but she's got you buffaloed just like everyone else."

His frown turned to an irritated scowl. "No one is buffaloing me."

"Please, Marco, make up something. Tell her that you forgot that you made a prior commitment . . . or that your mother took ill. Seriously, Libby is deranged. Who knows where this will end? Maybe she'll try to do away with me."

"Okay, now you're being irrational."

"I'm not irrational and my instincts aren't wrong. You've got to send her to someone else."

"I need to be able to call my own shots, Abby, and I need you to trust me."

"Trust works both ways."

He pressed his lips together and said nothing, which meant he wasn't going to budge on the matter. What was wrong with him? Why wouldn't he believe me? "Give her back her file, Marco, or I'll—" I searched for a way to make him understand how strongly I felt.

"You're giving me an ultimatum?"

Was I? "I wish I didn't have to."

"Then don't."

Frustrated, I flapped my hands against my sides. "Then give Libby back her file."

"We're going in circles. I'm not going to give Libby back her file, and you're not going to be happy unless I do, so let's just call it a draw, okay?" He turned to walk over to his desk, as though the matter were settled.

"Do you expect me to just sit on the sidelines and watch her manipulate you?"

Marco sat in his chair and regarded me steadily. "I believe you're the one doing the manipulating, Abby."

My mouth dropped open and my cheeks blazed with heat. "Is that what you think? That I'm trying to manipulate you? Fine. Then maybe I should leave."

"Abby, stop. Don't say another word until you cool down and think about what you're saying."

"I know what I'm saying," I retorted in the heat of the moment. "Maybe *you* should think about what you're doing."

His jaw muscle twitched. "Maybe you should take your own advice, since you can't seem to give up your need for control—or this obsessive idea that Libby is out for revenge."

First I was irrational, then manipulative, and now an obsessive control freak? Fuming, I spun around and stalked to the door. "It seems we're at a stalemate, Marco. I don't know what else to do to convince you how serious I am about this except to walk out."

"Walk out . . . on us?"

"I guess so."

It was a dramatic moment worthy of a good soap opera. Unfortunately, it didn't have the effect I'd hoped for. Instead of trying to stop me, Marco said nothing, just continued to regard me, as though he didn't really believe I meant to do it. Which I truly didn't want to do. The problem was that now I'd drawn a line in the sand. How could I back down? *Way to go,* my conscience chided. *How does it feel to jam yourself between a rock and a hard place?*

Hard.

I waited a moment longer, my hand on the doorknob, giving him time to relent. Finally I said, "Good-bye, Marco."

I opened the door and stepped into the hallway, still hoping he'd stop me. He didn't.

CHAPTER SIX

Present

"That's about it, Dave," I said, reaching for a tissue from the box on his desk to wipe my eyes. "I've been holed up at Bloomers ever since, working late, trying to keep my mind off Marco and Libby. I haven't heard from Marco since that day, but I *have* seen Libby. She's sporting red hair now, just like mine. Customers say they can't tell us apart."

Dave sat back, tapping his pen on the legal pad. "Intriguing."

"I knew Libby had a plan in mind when she took over my identity, but she comes off so innocent that no one would believe me." I glanced at my watch. "It's been half an hour. Think you can find out now who her victim was?"

Dave picked up the phone. "Considering that you were wrongfully arrested, I'm sure the prosecutor will bend over backward to be of assistance to us."

Dave placed the call to the DA, Melvin Darnell, and

was put through immediately. "Mel, I'm here with my client, Abby Knight. We need some answers as to what happened this morning. Can you help?" He listened a moment, gave me a thumbs-up, then began to jot notes on his yellow pad. After a few more minutes, he said, "Thanks, Mel," and hung up.

"Okay, the good news first," he said. "You don't need a lawyer."

I sighed in relief. I was in the clear—at least for the present. "Victim?"

"Libby's mother, Delphi Blume."

"No way!" I sat back as the icy shock rolled over me. Delphi was dead? By *Libby's* hand? "How was she— how did it happen?"

"A blow to the head is what it appears at first glance. The body was discovered in the alley behind Franklin Street. A witness out walking his dog early this morning noticed a yellow Corvette idling at the other end of the alley. The car sped away as he approached, so he got only a glimpse of the driver's red hair. His dog found the body. It had been wrapped in a blanket and left between two big garbage bins behind your shop."

I was so stunned I couldn't speak. Behind *my* shop! A redhead driving a *yellow* Corvette. Who else could it have been but Libby? Leaving the body behind Bloomers must have been the last step in her plan. She probably had an airtight alibi all worked out.

My heart began to race. What was *my* alibi? Nikki could sleep through a tornado. I could easily have slipped out and returned without her ever knowing. "The police didn't even question me, Dave, so how were you able to get me released?"

"The rookie trooper didn't have a clue as to who you were. Once everyone calmed down, they realized that you had no reason to commit murder, nor were you likely to have done so. And you were fortunate that your dad sent Sergeant Reilly to intercede in your behalf."

"My dad sent him?" Then my parents had heard the news, too. No wonder there were so many messages from them.

"After Reilly explained your concerns about Libby's odd behavior," Dave continued, "the police were willing to concede their mistake."

"I just can't believe it. Libby—a murderer?"

"It would appear so, especially since she's missing. That's why the APB went out—with a description matching yours."

"Something must have gone wrong with her plan. Maybe someone alerted her that I'd been released and she realized she was in trouble. But still, why would she kill her mother? That woman gave her everything she wanted. Libby adored Delphi."

"They could have had an argument, Abby. If Libby was off balance to start with, maybe she snapped. Crimes of passion happen all the time, you know."

I rubbed my forehead, trying to make sense of everything. Libby had gone to such great lengths to look like me. . . . Was that simply so she could get even with me? Or was her plan to get even with me *and* get rid of her mother—and let me take the blame? But if that were true, why had she felt the need to worm her way back into my family? Why had she coaxed my mom into exhibiting her work at Blume's Art Shop? Why had she schemed to take Marco away from me?

"I'm so confused, Dave."

"You'll drive yourself crazy trying to figure it out. Leave it to the detectives. If you want more information later on, I'll do what I can to help."

Martha buzzed in to tell Dave the prosecutor was on the line. I started to get up, but Dave motioned for me to sit. Then he put the receiver to his ear. "How's it going, Mel?" He listened a moment, then sat forward, reaching for his pen to take more notes. "I'll be right there." He hung up and looked at me. "They have Libby. The police spotted her in her Corvette pulling into the alley behind her shop about nine this morning. She's been in custody for a while, but the DA wasn't told until just now. The cops were probably hoping to get a confession from her first."

I watched Dave put his legal pad in his briefcase "Why does Mel want you there?"

"Libby asked for me."

Now she was even stealing my lawyer? "You're not going to represent her, are you?"

"There's no reason I shouldn't."

"You heard my side of the story. Isn't that a conflict of interest?"

"Think back to your law school days, Abby. There's no case against you, hence no conflict." He stood up and walked with me to the door. "Want to come with me?"

"Seriously? You'll let me get involved?"

"I think Libby already made sure you were."

At the police station we had to go through two security checks, then were taken to a conference room where Chief Prosecuting Attorney Melvin Darnell was waiting with a slew of paperwork for Dave. He appeared to be surprised—and embarrassed—to see me.

Well over six feet tall, Darnell had a wholesome, country-farmer appearance, with thinning blond hair, a ruddy complexion, and a slow smile. As usual, he wore a light-colored suit, white shirt, and robin's-egg blue tie, believing that a prosecutor should never wear black, as it might give a jury a negative impression.

With him was a classy-looking blond woman wearing a black suit over a melon top with a colorful silk scarf around her neck. She had a natural look—little makeup and a smooth, golden complexion. Her thick hair was gathered in back in a loose bun held by black and gold chopsticks, and she wore a flat black leather shoulder bag across her body, resting on the opposite hip, as though to protect herself from pickpockets—or to conceal a gun.

"This is Lisa Wells," Darnell said, "the newest member of our detective bureau. She's going to head up this case."

"I've known Lisa for a few years," Dave said with a smile, shaking her hand. "Lisa, this is my assistant Abby Knight."

As I shook her hand, Darnell narrowed his eyes at me. "Assistant, huh?"

"Abby used to clerk for me, so I asked her to take notes for me today." Dave opened and closed his right hand. "Sometimes my arthritis acts up. You don't have any objections, do you?"

Darnell seemed to suddenly remember my run-in with the state trooper. "No objections."

"Good," Dave said, tossing me a quick wink. "And

that brings me to my next question. Are you charging Libby Blume or not?"

"All indications are that Miss Blume is guilty," Darnell said, "but we're still gathering evidence, so as of now no formal charges have been filed."

"You'll give me a heads-up if and when that happens, I trust?" Dave asked.

At Darnell's nod, Dave said, "So is my client free to leave?"

"Unless she wants to cooperate with us," Lisa said with a bright smile.

Dave returned her smile. "I think you both know that my standard operating procedure is never to allow my client to speak to the police."

"It was worth a try," Lisa said.

"Go get your client," Darnell grumbled.

The conference room was a small, windowless box with dingy white walls and a black-and-white asphalt floor that was stained and cracked from wear. In the room were a standard government-issue steel desk, gray metal folding chairs around a long veneer-topped table, and an old coffeepot on a hot plate sitting on a stand in the corner.

Peering through the small glass door pane, I could see Libby hunched over the table at the far end, her head nestled in her arms, her red hair spilling over them. I glanced down at my own outfit—brown boots, khakis, and a green sweater—then at hers: brown boots, khakis, and a brown sweater. My identical twin could have been sitting in that room.

Hearing the door open, Libby raised her tearstained

face. I stayed out of sight until Dave had introduced himself; then I slipped quietly through the doorway. The instant Libby saw me, she ran toward me, arms outstretched like those of a child needing a hug. Though I was still fuming inside, there was nothing I could do but let her hug me.

"Abby," she sobbed, her head on my shoulder, "Mummy is d-dead!"

She said it as though Delphi had been my mom, too. It made me want to shake her until her teeth rattled. Instead, I found myself comforting her. "I know, Libby. I'm so sorry."

She lifted her head, her cheeks wet with tears, her red-rimmed eyes searching mine as though she was desperate for answers. "Someone m-murdered her, Abby, and the police arrested me! Why? Why would they arrest *me*? I loved Mummy. Now she's dead and they think I killed her!"

Her sobs turned to a deep keening as she held on to me with a grip that no one could have pried loose. Her grief certainly seemed genuine, but Libby had fooled me before.

"Who could have done it, Abby? Who?"

"I don't know, Libby." But I had a few suspicions.

She was sobbing so hard I could barely understand her. "Wh-what am I going to do without her? I c-can't go on. How will I go on?"

"You'll manage, Libby. You have Oliver."

"Oliver?" she cried. "He's no help. He's hopeless. Mummy had to take care of him. Now he'll be my responsibility."

"Abby," Dave said, "why don't we head back to my office? We can talk there."

"Come on," I said to Libby, treating her as though she were eleven years old again. "Let's go with Dave so he can help you get this sorted out."

"We have to find out who did this, Abby," Libby said. "We have to."

"Yes, we do," I said, and meant it.

I put my arm around Libby and she wrapped her arm around my waist, leaning heavily against me as I helped her out of the room. She was trembling all over and looked so pale I thought she might faint. I couldn't imagine the state I'd be in if my mother had been killed.

Back at the law office, Martha seated us in Dave's conference room and brought in coffee. I opted for water and asked for a yellow pad so I could take notes. I knew Dave didn't need my help, but I was too keyed up to sit idly by. Besides, I might catch something he missed.

Libby sat at the head of the long, oval table, and Dave sat at her left, so I took a seat opposite him, where I could see them both. I especially wanted to be able to watch Libby's face.

"Ready to answer some questions?" Dave asked her.

Libby reached over and squeezed my hand, as though she needed my strength.

"Everything you tell me is in total confidence," Dave said. "I can't relate our conversation to anyone under any circumstances, and neither can Abby, so you must be totally honest with me no matter what you did or didn't do. In return, I'll do everything in my power to help you."

"Okay," she said meekly.

Dave began by asking for personal information, such as date of birth, members of the family, and education, before he got down to the important part—Libby's alibi.

"Can you account for your whereabouts at five o'clock this morning?"

"I was sleeping."

"In your own home?" Dave asked. At her nod he said, "Can someone verify that?"

"I live by myself"—Libby's eyes welled with tears—"in a condo Mummy bought me."

"That's not going to cut it in a courtroom, Libby," Dave said. "This is a question that could be asked in front of a jury, so you'll have to do better than that. We need to find someone who can put you at home at the time of the murder, because a redhead in a yellow Corvette was seen leaving the site where your mother's body was found."

Libby's face lost all color. "It wasn't me," she said with quivering chin. "I didn't get up until nearly seven o'clock this morning. And when I left the building, my car was parked where it always is. There has to be a mistake. It must have been another redhead in a yellow . . ."

With a gasp, she turned an accusing gaze on me.

CHAPTER SEVEN

"**D**on't even think about making me a suspect," I warned Libby. "I was already arrested for that, thank you very much."

"Honestly?" Libby's eyes widened. "They put you in jail? I'm so sorry."

I'll bet you're sorry—that I'm not still locked up.

"Libby, what time did you leave your apartment this morning?" Dave asked.

"I had an appointment to meet with Sally Mitchum—a customer—at eight, to deliver some art, so I left about twenty-five minutes before eight to pick up the paintings at the shop."

"I'll need the customer's address and phone number to verify that," Dave said.

Libby gave him the info from her BlackBerry, which I also wrote down.

"Did anybody see you leave the condo or the parking

lot?" Dave asked. "Did you wave to anyone on your way to your client's house?"

She thought a moment. "Not that I remember."

"Did you go straight back to town after you met with your customer?"

"Yes."

"Does anyone else have access to your car or the keys to your car?"

"Not at five o'clock in the morning. My keys were with me all night, in my purse."

Dave jotted some notes on his yellow pad. "Is there a duplicate set?"

"Mummy kept a set when she bought the car"—Libby reached for a tissue from the box on the table, holding it beneath her eyes to stanch her tears—"in case I got locked out."

"How about your brother?" Dave asked. "Didn't you tell me earlier that he lived with your mom? Wouldn't he have access?"

"Oliver lives in the apartment over her garage and comes and goes from her house whenever he likes, but he wouldn't hurt Mummy. She supports him."

"When you went to your car this morning," Dave continued, "was it parked *exactly* where you left it last night?"

"I think so. It was in my parking space." She paused, her forehead wrinkling, then looked up in dismay. "My car seat! I had to move my seat up because it was farther back than usual."

I'd been watching Libby's expression closely, and this sudden recollection of the car seat seemed to genuinely astonish her—which gave me my first doubt about her guilt.

"How tall is Oliver?" Dave asked.

"Five foot ten, but you don't think—" She shook her head. "No. That's impossible."

Was Libby having doubts about her brother or giving us a performance?

"How tall are you?" Dave asked her.

Libby glanced at me with a tearful smile. "Five foot two, just like Abby."

"Do you ever leave your keys lying around your art shop?" Dave asked.

"I usually drop them on my desk next to my purse."

"Is this desk in a private office?"

"No, we've partitioned off an area in our storage room."

"Would you list your employees for me?" Dave asked.

"It's just Oliver and me and Mum—" She caught herself, then instantly burst into tears, holding her hands over her face. "Oh, God, what am I going to do? How can she be gone?" She wept so hard she had to gasp for breath, and I found myself comforting her again as my own eyes welled up. I vowed to call my mother as soon as I left Dave's office.

"Have some coffee," I urged, my voice thick and raspy. "It'll make you feel better."

"Would you like to take a break?" Dave asked her gently.

Libby shook her head, quieting after a moment. She blew her nose, then took a deep breath and said in a wavering voice, "I'm sorry. I still can't believe . . . it doesn't seem real, like I'll wake up in the morning and this will be just a horrible nightmare."

"I understand," Dave said.

"Does Oliver know yet?" Libby asked, reaching for her cup with trembling hands.

"I don't know," Dave said. "I haven't heard any news about your brother."

"He must be wondering where we are," she said, almost to herself. "I can't think why he hasn't tried to call me. Do you mind if I check my cell phone?"

"Go ahead," Dave said.

She took out a bright pink phone and flipped it open, pressing buttons with her thumbs. "He didn't call. Maybe he's at the shop." She tried there, with no luck. "Where could he be?"

"Did you have just the two employees?" Dave asked. "Your brother and your mother?"

"Yes. Oliver is my deliveryman and Mummy is my"—she paused as she caught her mistake—"*was* my bookkeeper."

"Don't forget Tilly," I said, remembering the Grace wannabe.

"Tilly," Libby said with disdain. "She was our clerk until Mummy fired her after Tilly stole money from the cash register."

"What's Tilly's full name, and where can I find her?" Dave asked.

"It's Tilly Gladwell. I've got her address back at the shop. . . ." Libby's eyes widened. "What if she killed Mummy for firing her? Tilly did threaten her."

"We'll have to talk to her and see what she says," was all Dave would say. "Now, you said your mother was your bookkeeper. Was that in addition to running her talent agency?"

"She doesn't own the talent agency anymore. She's just a consultant."

Dave paused to write it down. "Okay, Libby, this might be painful, but I have to ask if you've had any arguments with your mom witnessed by anyone, or overheard by anyone, that you can remember?"

"No," she said forcefully, swiping the tears that spilled down her cheeks. "We were very close. Everyone will tell you that we got along famously."

"Did your mom have any enemies that you know of? Anyone she fought with? Anyone who might have had a grudge against her, or was angry with her? In other words, can you think of any reason why another human being would want her dead?"

"Everyone loved her except for Tilly and one of Mummy's clients—I think her name was Kayla—who claimed Mummy forced her to have plastic surgery that didn't turn out the way she wanted. It was a lie, of course."

I made a note to tell Dave the truth about the lawsuit later.

"Do you know who her lawyer was?" Dave asked Libby.

"No."

"Was the suit filed here in New Chapel?"

"I think it was Chicago."

"In federal court?"

"I don't know. I was away at school." Libby began to rub her forehead. "But I should know. I mean, it affected Mummy's life. I'm sure she told me." She was so agitated that she pounded her fist against her forehead, then burst into tears. "I'm a terrible daughter!"

I reached for Libby's hand and squeezed it reassuringly. "You weren't a terrible daughter." Why had I said that? I didn't know what kind of daughter she was.

"I can get that information from the clerk's office," Dave assured her. "Now, Libby, I have another painful question, so are you okay with continuing?"

She gave my hand a quick squeeze back, then nodded.

"When was the last time you saw your mother?" he asked.

Her chin started to tremble. "Yesterday, at her house for dinner. We always have dinner together unless she has a late meeting." Libby let go of my hand to hold the tissue to her eyes.

"You and your mom?"

"And Oliver, usually, but he went out last night. He plays war games with his stupid friends. Mummy says if he weren't such a loser, he'd be dating."

Dave looked back at his notes. "You said Oliver is your half brother, right?"

"We have the same mother, but he has a different father, also a loser, by the way. Mummy had Oliver change his name to Blume so he wouldn't be tainted."

Wow. Delphi sure controlled her children's lives.

Dave asked her, "Did your mom seem worried or distracted yesterday, or did she indicate that she was frightened or in trouble?"

"No. We discussed plans for a new event at the shop. She was in a good mood."

Dave jotted more notes, then glanced at me. "Abby, anything you want to ask?"

He had no idea! But since he probably wouldn't appreciate me going into a tongue-lashing on the whole identity-theft issue, I kept it short. "Just two. Any progress to report on your stalker case?"

Libby's gaze shifted away from me. "I don't think so."

Gaze shifting. Hmm. Wasn't that a sign of deception?

"Just one more thing," I said. "Why did you get a yellow Corvette like mine?"

Libby glanced at me in surprise. "You're not angry, are you? Honestly, Abby, it was because I absolutely fell in love with yours, and I knew no amount of money would make you give your car up, so Mummy found another one for me through a dealer in Chicago. She couldn't locate any 1960 models, but"—Libby's chin quivered—"she tried."

I glared at her. She brazenly admitted to coveting my car, then had the audacity to seem surprised that I was upset. I had to sit on my hands so I didn't wrap them around her throat.

"Are you done, Abby?" Dave asked.

I was too furious to speak, so I pressed my lips together and gave him a quick nod.

"Then I have one more question for you, Libby." Dave sat forward, his gaze focused on Libby's face to catch the tiniest nuance of expression. "I need to know if you've ever been convicted of a crime, either a felony or a misdemeanor, in this state or any other state, or had any other legal problems."

There was a momentary hesitation before she answered. "No."

"You're sure?"

Another hesitation. "Positive."

A big red flag went up in my mind. Hesitations usually meant uncertainty. Why had Libby hesitated? Was there something in her past that she didn't want us to know about? I underlined the note I made on it.

Dave glanced at his own notes. "Then what we haven't covered is the financial side. You haven't been charged, but just in case you are, I'd like to do a preliminary investigation to make sure our bases are covered. That means I'll need a substantial retainer."

"Mummy opened an account for me at the New Chapel Savings Bank, so all you need to do is contact Rita and she'll issue you a check."

Dave wrote it down, then capped his pen and sat back. "Okay, Libby, you can go home or go back to work—just stay close to town. If the prosecutor does decide to charge you, he'll contact me first and I'll call you immediately. Do you have any questions or comments?"

She thought a moment, then shook her head.

"Then that does it for the time being," Dave said as we all stood up. "The minute I have any news I'll contact you."

"Thank you, Dave," Libby said, shaking his hand. "I know you'll take good care of me."

She walked to the door, then paused to look back. "I do have one question. You mentioned a preliminary investigation. Does that mean you'll be hiring an investigator?"

"That's my usual practice," Dave said.

Libby smiled at me, and I thought, *Oh no. She's going to ask me to do it.*

She looked at Dave and said with a straight face, "Then I want Marco Salvare."

CHAPTER EIGHT

"**M**arco's a good PI, Abby," Dave assured me after Libby had left the office. "I would have hired him anyway."

"But can't you see she's still at it? She knew that would make me angry."

"Dave," Martha said, poking her head in the doorway, "you have court in ten minutes."

He gave Martha a nod, then began to pack up his briefcase. "While I'm at the courthouse, I'll check on that lawsuit filed against Delphi Blume."

"Good, because Libby didn't have the whole story. I was told there was a judgment against Delphi, so she filed bankruptcy to keep from paying up, which meant that her client"—I glanced over my notes to find the girl's name—"Kayla never collected a dime."

"Good to know. I'll get the particulars today." He stood up, ready to leave.

"I have a question for you. While I was in the lockup, I

found out that there are at least a dozen women who've been waiting a long time for a hearing. They don't have bail money and can't afford a lawyer, so they're stuck. Why is that happening? Why aren't there more hearings?"

"Sad to say, Abby, it's all about money. There just aren't enough dollars available to hire enough judges, prosecutors, and public defenders to monitor all these cases. You're talking about adding two to three hundred thousand dollars to an already tight budget."

"But there has to be some way to help people in that situation."

"There is. Allocate more money. Unfortunately, the county's budget has all sorts of interests tugging at it. The same goes for the state. There's usually federal money lying around, but it takes an interested bureaucrat to work through the red tape to get it."

"What if I could find an interested bureaucrat who could get at the money?"

"Then a courtroom could be set up in the jail, staffed with a judge, prosecutor, and public defender. They could meet every other day to review the inmates' files and move them through the system quickly."

"So all I need to do is find someone who will take it up as a cause."

At Dave's skeptical glance I said, "Don't worry. I've got enough on my plate at the moment, but I do intend to pursue it as soon as I get this matter with Libby cleared up."

He put an arm around my shoulders and walked me into the hallway. "You don't need to clear anything up, Abby. Marco is a smart man. He'll find out if Libby is the murderer. Now, go back to Bloomers and forget about it."

Forget? With Libby on the loose and a murderer roaming free—both of whom might be one and the same? Not a chance.

As soon as I left Dave's office, I called my dad to assure him I was fine and thank him for sending Reilly to the jail for me. Then I called my mom's cell phone to leave her a message, since she'd be in class with her kindergarten kids. "Hey, Mom. I just wanted to let you know I'm fine and heading back to Bloomers now. Talk to you later. Bye . . . oh, and, Mom, I love you."

The instant I hung up, my phone rang. The caller ID was unfamiliar, so I answered with a tentative, "Hello?"

It was a reporter wanting to know how I felt about Libby murdering her mother, then trying to pin the crime on me. I was about to tell him where to stuff his question, because clearly he had already decided that Libby was guilty, but then I had a better idea. I told him I'd give him a comment if he would write a piece about a problem at the jail. But after I explained the situation, he said he'd get his comments elsewhere, thanks.

It was nearly one o'clock, so I detoured to the deli to pick up lunch, only to spot Connor MacKay standing in line for a sandwich. Quickly, I turned to duck out before he caught sight of me, but then I remembered my promise to my cell mates. So I waited until Connor had paid for his food and was about to walk past me; then I let my purse slide off my shoulder onto the floor.

"Oops," I said, and when we both stooped to retrieve it, I pretended to be surprised to see him. "Connor! Who knew you were such a gentleman?"

"Well, if it isn't New Chapel's notorious redhead," he

said loud enough to draw every eye in the place. "Bust out of jail, Libby? Oh, wait. You're Abby."

"You're a riot act, MacKay. Too bad you're not a real reporter, because I have a story that would make headlines."

"I'm all ears, sweetheart."

So was everyone else in the deli. I leaned closer to say, "How about somewhere more private?"

"Rosie's Diner is around the corner. Want to join me?"

"I thought you'd never ask."

Back at my apartment that evening, I fed Nikki's white cat, Simon, and made myself an omelet with tomatoes, mushrooms, basil, and feta cheese—my new favorite supper. Then, wrapped in a cuddly robe, I curled up on the sofa in front of the TV with a happily purring Simon in my lap. Yet even in that tranquil setting I felt distracted and restless. I tried to make myself believe it was the shock and exhaustion from my grueling morning, but I knew it was more than that. More even than losing Marco.

Two images kept replaying in my mind. The first was Libby's face when she told me her mother was dead. I knew that if I'd just lost my mother, my expression would have mimed exactly what I saw in Libby's. Could anyone fake that soul-shattering grief?

The second was when it hit Libby that her mother was truly gone from her life. Either she was an actress worthy of an Oscar or a daughter devastated by a heart-wrenching loss. I wanted to believe she was the killer only to satisfy my need to understand why she'd stolen my identity, yet because of those two images, a sliver of doubt kept creeping back in.

What if Libby hadn't killed Delphi? It seemed a remote possibility, yet what if someone else had taken advantage of there being two women in town with red hair and yellow Corvettes, either of whom could be made to look guilty? What if I'd done such a good job of portraying myself as the victim of her identity scam that I'd doomed Libby to a conviction of murder and given the true killer a way out?

I wrestled with those questions until midnight, when Nikki got home from her evening hospital shift in X-ray.

As soon as she saw me, she dropped her purse and ran across the room to give me a hug.

"I've been trying to reach you all afternoon. The news is all over the hospital. Are you okay?"

"I'm fine. Sorry if I worried you. I had to shut off my phone because of all the calls I was getting. Everyone wants the inside scoop on the murder."

"Is it true Libby killed her mom and dumped her body behind Bloomers?" Nikki asked, obviously wanting the scoop, too. "Wait! Don't answer that yet. We need ice cream first." She ran to the kitchen and returned with two spoons and a container of Lighten Up. She handed me a spoon, scooted my legs off the sofa so she could sit beside me, then said, "Tell me everything."

Because she was my best friend, I did just that, for over half an hour, managing to polish off about a fourth of the container at the same time.

"I am truly sorry," Nikki said, "for not taking you seriously before."

I stopped licking ice cream off the spoon. "You didn't take me seriously?"

"Promise you won't hate me, but I thought you were

overreacting. Now it's obvious that Libby was planning to pin this murder on you all along."

"That's what I thought at first, but now I'm not so sure."

"Are you kidding me? Why else would she go to those lengths to look like you?"

"I know, Nik, but Libby adored her mother. Why would she murder her?"

"Maybe she only pretended to adore her. From what you told me about Delphi, I could see some causes for resentment there. I mean, the woman pretty much ran Libby's life."

"But Libby didn't seem to mind."

"You can't seriously believe she's innocent, not after the hell she put you through. Come on, Abby, she caused you and Marco to split up."

"Did she? Or did I drive him away because I'm a control freak?"

"You've always been a control freak. It never bothered Marco before."

"Maybe he didn't say anything before. Maybe Libby merely brought it to a head."

"Or maybe Marco decided to let it seem like you broke up in order to fool Libby so he could find out what she was really up to."

"I wish I could believe that, Nik, but you didn't hear his voice or see his expression when I threatened to walk out. And at that point, I had such a head of steam going that there was no way I could back down. I knew I shouldn't give him an ultimatum—my dad always says to never use a threat that you aren't prepared to carry out—but the words just slipped out."

"But you *were* prepared to walk out, weren't you?"

"I really didn't believe it would come to that. I couldn't imagine Marco not trusting my instincts—or not giving Libby her money back. Boy, was I wrong. It really hurts, Nikki, to think that after I've helped solve five murder cases, he wouldn't have a little faith in me."

"Truthfully, Abby, I'd be more pissed off than hurt. And now Marco will be investigating another case for Libby. How will that ever work?"

"I'm pissed, too, Nik, and I'm not sure how it will work, although technically Marco will be investigating for Dave. Will it be possible for Marco to conduct an impartial investigation? And if Libby is indicted for murder, will she be able to get a fair trial?"

"I see what you mean, especially now that everyone in town is convinced she's evil."

"That's the crux of my dilemma, Nik, because I'm the one who convinced them."

"You know what I think?" Nikki stretched out her legs, leaned her head against the back of the sofa, and ran her fingers through her short, spiky blond hair, clearly beat after a long shift at the hospital. "I think we should get some rest and figure out what to do about it tomorrow."

Lying in the darkness of my bedroom, I tried to take Nikki's advice, but my conscience wasn't in a mood to cooperate.

Admit it. You know what you have to do if you want to see that justice is served, and you can stop pretending to sleep, because you're not fooling me. So do you want to get some rest tonight or do you want me to keep nagging?

Anything to stop that nagging. But if I was to see that justice was served, I'd have to investigate, and to do that, I had to come up with a plan, a place to start my investigation. I remembered the notes I'd made at Libby's interview and padded softly to the kitchen for my purse, nearly tripping over Simon, who assumed I'd awakened to feed him. I spooned out a dollop of cat food, then sat at the kitchen table with my sheet of yellow paper. Some of my notes were things Libby had said, and some were my own recollections:

1. Delphi bought Libby a condo.
2. Libby left her condo at 7:35 a.m., met with client Sally Mitchum around 8 a.m., returned to town, was picked up in her yellow Corvette behind her shop.
3. Car parked in Libby's space as usual, but seat pushed back farther than normal. Tall person.
4. Oliver—5'10", Tilly at least 5'9".
5. Delphi had a set of Libby's car keys. Others who had access to keys at work: Oliver, Tilly.
6. Delphi supported Oliver, who lived above her garage and had access to her house.
7. Delphi fired Tilly and threatened deportation. Tilly vowed to get even with Delphi.
8. Delphi did Libby's bookkeeping.
9. Kayla sued Delphi for plastic surgery botch-up. Settlement a no-go. Delphi filed bankruptcy. Kayla's height? Access to car keys? Probably not.
10. Last time Libby saw Delphi—Sunday for dinner. Oliver playing war games.

11. Oliver is L.'s half brother. Delphi made him change name to Blume.

12. Delphi in a good mood Sunday evening, didn't appear worried or nervous.

13. Delphi found yellow Corvette that Libby wanted.

14. Libby claims to have no criminal record. Really.

As I read over the list, it was apparent how much influence Delphi had over Libby's and Oliver's lives. Too much control could cause a lot of resentment, which could be a motive for murder. But how much resentment would it take to push someone too far? Tilly and Kayla also had strong motives, but of the two, only Tilly had access to Libby's car keys. However, at such an early stage I couldn't rule anyone out.

My first step, I decided, was to use my lunch hour to pay a visit to Libby's customer Sally Mitchum, to see what she could tell me about Libby's behavior yesterday morning. From there I'd stop at the hardware store and the lock-and-key shop to ask if anyone had copied a Corvette key. I yawned, my eyelids growing heavier by the second.

"Are you happy now?" I asked my conscience, after I'd tucked myself back in bed.

I was asleep as soon as I hit the pillow.

First thing I did the next morning was to grab the newspaper from outside the door. The banner headline read, FORMER MODEL MURDERED, and beneath it were two photos—one a recent shot of Delphi coming out of the courthouse, and the other of a younger Delphi at the height of her modeling career. The front-page article was mainly about her career, with only sketchy information on the crime. The real story was on the inside, accompanied by a photo of Delphi standing with her arms around Oliver and Libby, taken at the grand opening of Blume's Art Shop.

According to the article, Libby was being considered a person of interest, which, as anyone who watches television knows, means that she was the main suspect. The article mentioned that several other persons were being questioned, but didn't list any names. The focal point was that a daughter was being questioned in her famous mother's death. Thank heaven my arrest wasn't mentioned.

At least Connor MacKay stayed true to his word and wrote a great exposé on the plight of the women in jail, which made me hope that the people with the power to fix the problem had been embarrassed into doing so.

My cell phone rang just as I was heading out to work. I checked the caller ID and saw that it was Bloomers. "Sweetie," Lottie said, "we have a predicament. I've got a good client on the other line who wants to know if we can do a floral centerpiece for her party tonight."

"That doesn't sound like a predicament, Lottie."

"Except that she wants the flowers to be made out of fruit and veggies. Now, you know I'm strictly a traditional gal, so if you want to try it, I'll tell her so, otherwise—"

"I'll do it." No way was I going to turn down business, especially for a good client.

"Think you'll have it ready before closing time?"

"Even better, tell her I'll deliver it around noon. I've got to run an errand then anyway. I'll stop at the market and pick up the supplies now."

Food made to look like flowers. Hmm. Well, I always loved a challenge. I dug through the kitchen junk drawer for Nikki's flower-shaped cookie cutter and melon baller, threw them in a paper bag, and flew out the door, making up a grocery list as I headed for the market.

When I arrived at Bloomers an hour later, I had two bagsful of fixings. With Lottie's help, I cut poblano peppers into the shape of dark green leaves, then rimmed a glass bowl with them. Using the cookie cutter, Lottie cut pineapple slices into daisylike flowers that I then topped with blueberries to make the centers. Pale green honeydew melon slices shaped with a serrated blade became the daisy's leaves. Small strawberries strung on raffia became bleeding heart vine, and grapes became the centers of orange-peel flower petals. I misted the fruit with a light lemon-juice spray to keep it from turning brown, then wrapped it in clear cellophane and tucked it into the cooler. A multiuse centerpiece—colorful *and* edible.

Grace came in to admire it. Then Lottie got out the camera to take a picture of it. "Great work, sweetie. I could never have come up with that."

There was another reason why I loved being a florist. None of my law professors had ever had such praise for my work. "Is that the best you can do?" and "What were you thinking?" were the usual remarks.

"So," Lottie said as I began to arrange a bouquet of chocolate cosmos, dahlias, and cockscomb, "have you and Marco decided to investigate Delphi's murder?"

"Why?" I asked cautiously, knowing neither of my assistants liked me to get involved in criminal matters. Plus they didn't know about my breakup with Marco, and I wanted to leave it that way.

Grace said, "We're a bit apprehensive about how easily Libby deceived us, and we're afraid she might be clever enough to outwit the police, too, and turn the spotlight back on you."

"So if you do decide to look into it," Lottie said, "we'd be glad to help."

They were encouraging me to get involved? That was a first. "Thanks. I appreciate the offer. And since you asked, would one of you go to the Recorder's Office and find out whose name is on the title for Libby's condo?"

"We're on it," Lottie said.

I wrapped the bouquet in floral paper, slipped on my heavy corduroy jacket, picked up the fruit-flower arrangement, and headed out to make my deliveries. Maybe I wouldn't miss Marco's help at all.

Stowing the fruit arrangement in the foam carrier in Lottie's station wagon, I made the delivery to a delighted client, then headed out to Sally Mitchum's house in a newly developed subdivision on the outskirts of town. After a fifteen-minute ride, I located her sprawling brick two-story house, and with the bouquet in hand, I rang the bell.

A slender, white-haired woman in her sixties came to the door. She had on a navy running suit, white sneakers, and a sweatband around her forehead, as though she'd just come back from a run. "Libby," she exclaimed in surprise. "Good heaven, I just read about—oh! I beg your pardon. You're not Libby Blume."

"It's a common mistake. I'm Abby Knight. I own Bloomers Flower Shop."

"Of course. I've been to your shop. You really do look like Libby, you know. I'm Sally Mitchum, by the way. Are those flowers for me?"

I handed her the bouquet. "They're a gift from Bloomers—well, from me."

"They're beautiful," Sally said, peeling back the paper. "What did I do to deserve them?"

"I'm hoping that you'll answer a few questions about your appointment with Libby yesterday morning."

"I've already spoken with a detective. That should be enough."

"Except that I want to make sure Libby gets fair treatment, because right now it's looking a little dicey for her. The cops seem to be focusing on Libby as their prime suspect when I know there are other persons of interest out there."

Sally studied me with shrewd eyes. "Are you saying she's innocent, then?"

Yikes. I'd have to sidestep that question. "My only concern is that the cops investigate all persons of interest."

"I see. Are you related to Libby?"

"No."

"Amazing resemblance. Is she a friend?"

I shook my head, so Sally said, "Then why do you care?"

"Because I believe every person is entitled to equal treatment under the law."

Sally raised an eyebrow. I didn't think she was buying it. "Then do you do this for everyone, or just for people who look like you?"

She had me there. "Whether Libby looks like me or not has nothing to do with . . . well, it does have something to do with my investigation, but . . . see, I used to babysit her and . . ." How could I sum up my reasons when they were so entangled with my emotions? "Look, I just want to make sure Libby gets a fair shake. So can I ask you a few questions? Please?"

"I have to say, Abby, you've certainly got me intrigued." She pointed to two wicker chairs on her front porch. "Have a seat. I'll be right back."

I perched on the edge of a bright tropical-print cushion and waited. In a few moments Sally returned, wearing a warm fleece jacket over her running suit and carrying two orange mugs filled with steaming hot cocoa. She handed me a mug, then turned her chair to face mine. "Now tell me your story. Tell me why you hate injustice."

I blinked at her in surprise. "I don't have a story."

She leaned forward to look me in the eye. "I think you do. A lot of people hate injustice, but not everyone does something about it. So why do you?"

I shrugged. "My dad was a cop. I guess it runs in the family."

"Then why didn't you become a cop?"

"Me? They couldn't pay me enough to put my life on the line every day. Actually, they don't pay enough for *anyone* to do it. My dad was shot while chasing down a drug dealer and now he's paralyzed. He'll be in a wheelchair the rest of his life. And here's the irony. The dealer who went to prison is already out." I could feel angry tears welling up, so I changed topics.

"Anyway, I feel responsible for Libby's predicament

because I raised a stink about how she made herself over to look like me. I prejudiced people's opinions against her and now they assume her purpose was to pin the murder on me. So I need to make sure she isn't falsely accused because of what I've said."

"That's very admirable." Sally patted my hand. "See? You did have a story. Now drink your cocoa and I'll tell you *my* story."

So I did, and learned that Sally was a psychologist whose daughter got hooked on heroin at the age of sixteen. The girl was arrested and put into lockup, where she died from a drug overdose. Because of that, Sally had become a victims' rights advocate.

Nikki firmly believes there are no such things as coincidences, and I was beginning to think she was right. So I told Sally my other story, the one about the women who'd been held much too long in lockup—including the sixteen-year-old girl who should never have been put there in the first place—and how I'd managed to get Connor MacKay to do a piece for the newspaper on their situation.

"I saw the article," Sally said, her keen gaze on me, "and I admire your courage, Abby. I was particularly moved by the plight of that young girl—Maria, I think her name was. We women need to help one another, you know? So I'm going to help you. You see that house across the road? The one with the big iron gates at the front? A member of the House of Representatives lives there. I've campaigned heavily for him in the past and he owes me a few favors, so I'll walk over there this evening and see what he can do about this injustice."

"That would be terrific, Mrs. Mitchum. Thank you! Will you let me know what he says?"

"You bet I will. Now, I believe you had some questions about Libby?"

"Yes," I said eagerly, digging in my purse for my notepad, "like what time she showed up yesterday morning and how she appeared—calm, nervous, whatever."

"Libby arrived around ten minutes after eight o'clock, stylishly dressed, her hair clean and shiny—just like yours, actually. She seemed flustered, but said she'd been held up by a slow freight train on the way and hated being late for an appointment, which could have accounted for her upset. She brought over several art prints so I could try them out here at home. She left around eight forty-five so she'd be back in time to open her shop."

I made a note of it, wondering why Libby felt she had to open the shop when she believed her mother and/or Oliver would be there.

Sally checked her watch. "We're going to have to wrap this up so I can get to my office. I have clients to see."

"Sure. I just need to verify that Libby was driving a yellow Corvette."

"No, Libby came in a van with *Blume's Art Shop* written on the side."

CHAPTER NINE

Libby wasn't driving the Corvette? But that meant that she hadn't been coming from Sally's house, as she'd claimed, when the police picked her up in her Vette. Why had she lied?

I knew Sally needed to go, so I thanked her for being so helpful, and she reiterated her promise to call me after she'd talked to the congressman.

As I drove up the country road pondering the new information, the railroad-crossing signals ahead started flashing and then the gates went down. I was betting it was the same crossing where Libby had gotten stuck. I counted the engines as they chugged past—three of them, which meant I was in for a long wait. No sense letting the time go to waste. I pulled out my phone and checked in with Grace to see what she'd learned at the Recorder's Office.

"The title to the condominium is in Delphi's name," Grace said. "She paid for it outright. There's no mortgage."

"Did Delphi quitclaim the deed to Libby?"

"No, it's all hers, and Blume's Art Shop is leased in Delphi's name, as well."

"So Libby lives in a condo owned by her mother and works in a shop leased by her mother, and Oliver lives over his mother's garage. Delphi was either very generous or wanted to control her children's lives. Either way, I don't think Libby or Oliver would have wanted to pull that financial plug."

"Unless perhaps they wished to inherit her money and run their own lives. It's something to think about, isn't it?" Grace asked.

"I'm sure the cops have already thought about it." I glanced out the window to check on the train and saw a long line of boxcars still to come, so I turned my thoughts to another puzzle: Who drove Libby's Corvette to get rid of the body?

"I'm going to swing by Ace Hardware and Gandy's Lock and Key on my way back," I told Grace. "I want to see if anyone came in to have a duplicate Corvette key made."

"Take your time, dear," Grace said. "This is important."

When the gates went up, I started across the tracks only to see a green Prius crossing from the opposite direction. My heart quickened when I spotted Marco at the wheel, but he gave me only a nod as we passed. I nodded back. That was it, a passing nod, as though we were mere acquaintances. It felt like someone had a hand around my heart and was squeezing tight.

At the hardware store I went to the key department in the back and rang the buzzer. A moment later a pleasant-looking older man appeared. "Can I help you?"

"I was wondering if you've copied any Corvette keys lately. It would have been for an older model, say, 1980?"

"You're the second one to ask me that question today. I'll tell you what I told him. No one asked me to make a copy of a Corvette key. But I don't work every day, so you'll have to check back with Fred after three o'clock today. He works this counter when I'm not here."

I gave him my business card. "Would you tell Fred to be expecting my call?"

I stopped at Gandy's next, a tiny, triangle-shaped shop tucked into a corner lot on Concord Avenue, where I found the locksmith, Mr. Gandy, about to head out on a call. "I already talked to a detective *and* a private investigator," he said, climbing into his van. "If you want the information, check with one of them."

"Would you tell me if the PI's last name was Salvare?"

"That's him."

Damn. Marco had beaten me to the punch. Now I'd have to see if Dave Hammond would tell me what information Gandy had given Marco, since I wasn't about to call Marco myself. I had another question for Dave anyway, so as soon as I got back to Bloomers, I called him, catching him between appointments.

"Hey, Dave, I have some news for you. I went out to see the customer Libby saw yesterday morning—Sally Mitchum—and she mentioned that Libby was driving the Blume's Art Shop van, not the Corvette, which means Libby *wasn't* on her way back from Sally's house when she was picked up by the cops. What do you make of that?"

"Nothing, until I talk to Libby."

That was a typical lawyer answer.

"Why were you visiting Sally Mitchum, Abby? You're not conducting the investigation. You wouldn't be investigating on your own, would you?"

Oops. Time for some artful dodging. "Sally's helping me with the jail situation, Dave. She has a neighbor who's a congressman, and she's going to ask him to get some federal money for the county courts to help move people through the system quicker. Isn't that great?"

"Sure is. I hope it works."

Damn. I could forget about asking Dave for more information on the case.

I stepped into Bloomers to find the Ladies' Poetry Society meeting under way. The elderly poetesses gathered weekly in the parlor to share their original poems while munching on Grace's buttery scones and downing pots of tea. I scurried past just as one of the members began to read.

" 'Ode to a Varicose Vein.' 'Oh, purple vein, how I hate thee. / Inching up my calf, to my knee. / I will sigh when you reach my thigh. / But I'll take a pass when you reach my—' "

I stuck my fingers in my ears and dashed past the doorway. There were some subjects that just didn't lend themselves to poetry. In the workroom, I plunged into the orders on the spindle, trying to erase the image in my mind of Marco's quick nod at the railroad crossing. I still couldn't believe we'd broken up. I wanted to cry when I thought about that painful scene in his office. I hadn't asked for much, just for him to give Libby back her file. Stubborn male!

The more I thought about it, the angrier I got. By the time Dave Hammond called at three o'clock, I was really fuming.

"Abby, Marco phoned me earlier. He went out to interview Sally Mitchum, but she told him she'd done enough talking and referred him to you for any further information."

It was a good thing Dave couldn't see me, because I was grinning from ear to ear. Score one for the florist.

"I thought you said you went to see Sally about the jail problem, Abby."

"Can I help it if other subjects come up in the course of normal conversation?"

"Such as what vehicle Libby drove to her appointment? Is there anything more?"

I could tell Dave wasn't happy with me. "There might be."

He sighed, clearly frustrated. "You don't need to get involved. Marco is on the job."

"But therein lies the problem, Dave. Since Libby had hired Marco to work on another case for her, someone has to make sure he gives Libby fair and unbiased treatment on the murder investigation. Besides, you were the one who said Libby made sure I was involved."

"Look, Abby, if anyone understands your feelings about Libby and Marco, it's me, but you're wrong about Marco. He's a pro. He can deal with it."

It was useless to try to change Dave's mind, so I decided to use a different tactic. "Okay, fine. The truth is, I'm just being nosy. You know how I love to poke around in things, and you also know there's no use in telling me not to poke, right?"

He sighed again, this time in resignation. "Right."

"So how about we make a deal? I'll share all my information with you if you'll do the same for me."

"Do I have a choice?"

That didn't even merit an answer. "Do you have your pen handy?"

After I gave Dave the information Grace had gleaned at the Recorder's Office, I said, "So what information has PI Salvare turned up?"

"Nothing yet."

That meant he'd struck out at Gandy's. Ha. I was one step ahead of Marco. Now if I could get to Fred at Ace first . . . I glanced at the clock. Yikes. It was past three. I needed to call right away. "I'll let you know the moment I learn anything new," I said, and hung up.

Just as I opened the phone book to look up the number, I heard screams coming from the shop, followed by some heavy thuds and a flurry of excited chatter. Dropping the phone book, I dashed through the curtain to see what was happening.

In a word, chaos. On the floor lay half a dozen senior citizens, their wrinkled arms and stockinged legs flailing. The other poetesses watched their fallen compatriots from the sidelines, hiding giggles, while Lottie and Grace did their best to give aid. In the midst of it all stood Mom, looking horrified.

Then I saw the reason for the chaos: giant wooden beads all over the floor.

I knelt to help one of the ladies who was lying on her back, laughing hysterically.

"Abby, you should have seen us," she wheezed, wiping tears from her eyes. "We came out of the parlor chattering away, not looking where we were going, just as those danged beads went shooting all over the floor." She started laughing again, which made her cough. "I haven't laughed this hard in years."

"Do you need to go to the hospital?" I asked, thinking of the potential lawsuits I faced.

"Oh, heavens, no. I got a bump on my rump is all, and believe me, it's well padded. Give me a hand and help me up."

Grace and I each took an arm and helped the woman to her feet. As she and the others left Bloomers, chuckling, and rubbing sore backsides and elbows, I said a quick prayer that none of them had been seriously injured. My mom, I noticed, was quietly packing her beads into a box.

"I'm so sorry," Mom said to me after the poetesses left. "I wanted to bring you my newest piece of art, a lovely beaded lampshade, because"—she burst into tears—"I wanted to apologize for not believing you about Libby, and for being such a traitor! What was I thinking, taking her my jacket?" Gulping back tears, she said, "Then the plastic threads came apart and my lampshade broke, sending beads everywhere. Oh, those poor, unsuspecting ladies!" She handed me the box and wept into her hands.

"Mom, you're not a traitor," I said, putting an arm around her. "It was a chance for you to showcase your art in the best environment for it. I understood that."

"We mustn't cry over spilt milk, Maureen," Grace said, "or spilt beads in this case."

"Sweetie," Lottie said to her, "don't fret. The ladies weren't injured."

"Abigail," Mom said, sniffling, "do you forgive me?"

"There's nothing to forgive, Mom. It's okay."

"We didn't believe Abby, either," Lottie said.

"To think Libby killed her *mother*," Mom said, her big brown eyes red-rimmed.

"Mom, let's not condemn Libby until we have all the facts, okay?"

"Would you like some tea, Maureen?" Grace asked. "It'll soothe you."

"Thank you, Grace, but I'm going home to gather every bead in my house and take them to the Goodwill store. And I promise you my next hobby won't have anything to do with beads!"

"Do you know how to knit?" Lottie asked. "Because I belong to this great knitting club. We meet every Wednesday evening at KnitWits, just around the corner, and we have a ball."

"I'd like to try it," Mom said, dabbing her tears with a tissue.

I patted Lottie on the back. Good idea. Knitting was a harmless hobby—as long as Mom didn't jab anyone with her knitting needle.

I glanced at my watch. Yikes. It was three thirty and I needed to call Fred. "I have to get back to work," I said, giving my mother a hug.

She put her hands on either side of my face and stared me straight in the eye. "I really am sorry for not believing you, Abigail. I love you. I hope you know that."

"I love you, too. Mom." Wow. Mom didn't say that very often. Maybe something positive had come from Libby's return to New Chapel after all.

I left Lottie giving my mom the particulars on her

knitting club and hurried to use the phone at my desk in the workroom. I called Ace and asked for Fred, and after what felt like hours, he finally picked up.

"Hi, I'm Abby Knight, and I'm investigating the Delphi Blume murder. I was wondering if you could tell me whether you'd copied a Corvette key in the past week."

"Well, isn't that a coinkydink?" Fred said. "I was just handed your phone message."

"What phone message?"

"The one in my hand that says an investigator called about a key. Isn't that you?"

Oh, no! Marco must have phoned Fred, too. "Well, I *did* call earlier." No need to mention that my call was in person. "So . . . about that Corvette key?"

"The thing is, I'd have to know who ordered the copy. That's the way our system works."

"Oh. Well, then, how about Tilly Gladwell? She's a large, stout woman with short gray hair and a heavy cockney accent."

"Now that you mention it, I do remember a woman like that. I could barely make out what she was saying. Let me see. . . . Did she have a key copied, or was she here for something else?" There was dead air for a few minutes. Then Fred said, "I don't see her name in the system, so it wasn't a key."

"How about a thirty-year-old man about five feet ten inches tall, long, narrow face, short brown hair, thin build, possibly wearing military-style clothing? Goes by the name of—"

"Oliver Blume? He's in here all the time, buying things."

"Did he have a key made?"

"Not while I was here. Last time he was in, he bought a gray utility blanket."

The kind that Delphi's body had been wrapped in? I wrote myself a quick note to ask Dave about the blanket. "Do you have a copy of the receipt?"

"You'd have to check with Sheila in the office about that, but I can tell you right now, unless he paid by check or credit card, his name wouldn't be on any receipt."

I thanked him for his help and hung up the phone just as Grace came through the curtain with a cup of tea for me.

"I have some news for you, dear. I asked a friend of mine who works at the British embassy in Chicago if she would inquire into Tilly Gladwell's background. I thought it might help to rule her in or out as a suspect. But as it turns out, Tilly is in London."

"She flew back to England?"

"No, dear. She never left. The clerk who worked for Libby is not Tilly Gladwell."

CHAPTER TEN

Tilly was an impostor?

"The real Matilda Gladwell," Grace explained, "is a lady of high standing in London society. Two months ago, one of her housemaids, a woman who went by the name of Cora Fraime, stole Matilda's passport and a large sum of cash and fled the country. Sadly, that was when Matilda discovered that Cora had quite a criminal background. *Fraime* was just one of the aliases she's used over the years. She was also Cora Fink, Cora Bell, and Corabelle Finklestein."

"Did you find out if Cora's criminal background included murder?"

"Not yet, dear. I'm still waiting for that information."

"Okay, Grace, let's suppose Cora is the killer. She's a large woman, so she would have had to push Libby's car seat back, right? That's how Libby claims she found the seat that morning. So that's a plus in the suspect column. But Cora doesn't have red hair."

"A wig would easily solve that problem," Grace said. "If Cora has used aliases before, then she might have used disguises, as well."

"True. So let's say Cora gets a copy of Libby's car key, borrows her Corvette, puts on a red wig, and drives to Delphi's house. How does she get inside? Ring the doorbell?"

"Why not? Or perhaps her criminal talents include breaking and entering."

"Or, if Delphi left her purse in Blume's back room, Cora could have snatched her house key and had a copy made when she had one made of Libby's car key."

Grace frowned in thought. "Then everything would hinge on Cora having the opportunity to take the necessary keys without their owners realizing they were missing, then get to a store to have copies made, and return the originals to their owners' key rings. It seems too cumbersome and much too risky. If Cora is indeed a criminal, then it's quite possible she knows how to hotwire an auto and pick a door lock."

"That's very good, Grace."

"Of course it is, dear. Now let me see what I can find out about wigs that have been purchased here in town in the past two weeks."

Grace left just as Lottie breezed through to gather arrangements we'd made for a funeral. "I convinced your mom to come to my knitting club tomorrow night," she announced proudly. "Isn't that great? She can't do any harm with yarn. Now we can all breathe easier."

Where my mom's art was concerned, was that even possible?

I hummed contentedly as I gathered supplies for another arrangement. No matter what my problems were, when I immersed myself in flowers, everything else receded. Twenty minutes later, I stepped back to look at the finished product and declared it a success.

As the client had requested, I'd fashioned a real romantic beauty using lots of pink and red roses in graduated tones that blended spectacularly ('Chapeau de Napoleon', 'Duc de Guiche', and 'Celsiana'). Then I backed them with sprigs of lady's mantle (*Alchemilla mollis*), lamb's ears (*Stachys*), and the delicate greenery of euphorbia, all set in an old-fashioned cream-colored ceramic pitcher with red roses painted on the sides. I wrapped my creation in clear cellophane, tied with a pink ribbon at the top, tagged it, and placed it in one of the coolers.

"Abby," Grace said, coming into the workroom, "I checked with salons all over the county and none report the sale of a long-haired red wig anytime within the last three weeks."

"Great," I said with a sigh. "If that wig was ordered through a catalog or over the Internet, we'll never track it down."

"Never say never," Grace admonished. "If the wig was ordered, then someone had to deliver it."

"Someone like UPS or FedEx! You're a marvel, Grace."

"Merely the Watson to your Holmes, love." She paused as the bell over the door jingled. "I'll see to that and track down the delivery later."

"Thanks, Grace." Before I started another order, I turned off my creative juices long enough to phone Dave to see what he could tell me about the blanket found with Delphi's body.

"Abby, I was just about to call you," he said.

"Really? What's up?"

"Marco's frustration level."

I wondered if he could hear the smile in my voice. "PI Salvare is frustrated?"

"He seems to think you're trying to thwart his investigation."

"What? No way! Tell him he's being—irrational." That was one of the labels he'd given me, and it still smarted.

"Hold it. When did I become your go-between?" Dave asked.

"I didn't ask you to be the go-between. It must have been PI Salvare."

"*PI Salvare?* That's what you're calling him now?"

"You don't want to hear my other choices." *Weasel* came to mind.

"Abby," Dave said, switching to his gruff voice, "I'm talking to you as your lawyer and your friend. If this problem between you and Marco is going to hamper my ability to protect Libby in any way, shape, or form, then this is going to be our last conversation on this case."

Yeesh. I couldn't let that happen.

Lottie came back from making her delivery just then, and I didn't want to talk in front of her about Marco and me, so I said, "Not a problem, Dave. I'll stop by your office at five to discuss it. And maybe you can find out what kind of blanket Delphi's body was wrapped in."

"I'll do my best. See you at five."

By the time I'd locked Bloomers' front door, cut across the courthouse lawn, and made it up the creaky stairs to Dave's office, it was a few minutes after five o'clock.

"I'm here," I said breathlessly, brushing my wind-tossed hair away from my face as I dashed in the room. Then I stopped dead in my tracks.

Marco was sprawled in one of the two chairs facing Dave's desk, his long legs stretched out in front of him, his hands behind his head. I glanced at Dave with a furious scowl. He'd set this up. He should have warned me so I could've prepared myself.

At once Marco rose, giving me a solemn nod even as those dark eyes raked over me, making my heart beat as wildly as it had the first time we met. He was wearing his familiar black leather jacket over a sienna T-shirt with blue jeans and black boots. Although his gaze was as impudent as ever, his eyes appeared tired. A late night with Libby, perhaps?

"I didn't know we were having a conference," I said, giving Dave a pointed look.

"I thought we needed a meeting of the minds," Dave replied. "Have a seat."

Feeling not only miffed but also as nervous as if I were on a blind date, I forced myself to act cool as I casually removed the green knit scarf at my throat, slipped off my navy peacoat, and sat down. Marco waited until I was in the chair; then he sat, too. But if he thought his gentlemanly ways still impressed me . . . he was right, damn it.

"Now, then," Dave said, "as long as you're both going to be investigating this case—"

"Hold it," Marco said. "Abby doesn't need to investigate. I thought you called her in here to explain that."

"Excuse me?" I said. "I wasn't *called in.* This isn't the principal's office. I happen to be conducting my own private investigation."

"For what purpose?" Marco asked.

"Because I don't think you can be unbiased."

"You're questioning my professionalism?"

"Actually, yes."

"Hey!" Dave said as Marco and I began to argue. "Both of you sit quietly and listen to me. First of all, Marco, you know that when Abby sets a course of action, there's no deterring her. Right?"

Marco grunted what sounded like, "Yeah," then glanced at me, frowning.

I almost stuck my tongue out at him.

"And, Abby," Dave said, "you can't thwart this investigation. If people refuse to answer questions because you've already talked to them, that's interfering with my ability to protect my client, and I won't have it."

Oops. I was glad I'd kept my tongue in check. If only I could've said the same about that fiery blush on my face.

"So here's the way it has to be," Dave said. "You're either going to work together or—"

"No!" we both said, and began to talk over each other until Dave put his fingers between his teeth and whistled so loud that Martha came running.

Dave waved her away, then pointed at us. "I don't care what's going on in your personal lives—you work that out for yourselves—but either you both cooperate on this investigation or I'll hire another PI, and, Abby, you can forget about asking me for any further information." He paused to let his words sink in, then said, "Am I making myself perfectly clear?"

Marco had a white-knuckled grip on the arms of his chair, and I thought for sure he was about to tell Dave to hire someone else for the case. But then his fingers relaxed, he leaned back, and he gave a nod of agreement. Why had he conceded so readily? He didn't really need the work. Was he staying in it for Libby?

Dave glanced at me, waiting for my answer. What could I say? That working with Marco was impossible, given our lack of trust in each other? That I couldn't look into his eyes and not think of the relationship we'd been building that now seemed lost? That I couldn't hear his voice and not remember all the romantic things he'd ever said to me? Was there any way to keep my feelings out of it?

Would a professional investigator let a private matter stand in her way? that little voice of reason asked. But I already knew the answer. Even though I wasn't a PI, I could at least conduct myself in a professional manner. I glanced at the chiseled hunk on my right who was staring straight ahead, his smooth skin blurred by a five-o'clock shadow, his fingers tapping the arms of his chair. Fine. If Marco could do it, so could I.

"I'll cooperate," I said to Dave. I'd just have to tuck my feelings about Marco in a big box, lock them up tight, and throw away the key . . . maybe into Lake Michigan.

"Okay, then," Dave said. "Let's see what we've got so far." He opened the file on his desk and reviewed the papers inside. "Abby, you asked about the blanket found on the body. According to the police report, it was a gray utility blanket. Does that mean anything to you?"

"Sure does. Oliver bought one matching that description at Ace Hardware last week. And if he paid by credit card or check, there should be a receipt that proves it."

"That certainly throws more suspicion on him," Dave said.

Marco opened his own file, pulled out a piece of paper, and slid it across the desk to Dave. "Here's a copy of Delphi's irrevocable trust. Upon her death, each child is to inherit half of her estate. So it's possible that Oliver wanted to get his hands on his inheritance early."

"But why kill the golden goose?" I argued. "Oliver's mother bought him everything he wanted. You'd think he'd want to let her continue to make money so he could preserve his inheritance while continuing to mooch off her. And why would he have thrown the blame on his sister when she was his ally?"

"His intent might have been to make *you* look guilty, Abby," Dave pointed out.

"But he'd have to realize that it would also incriminate his sister," I said.

"I think I'll pay Oliver a visit," Marco said. "Maybe I can get some answers."

"Good luck with that," I murmured, reaching into my purse for my notes.

Marco fixed me with the penetrating gaze that always made my knees go soft. "Why?"

"I doubt that Oliver will talk to you. You're *the man.*"

"He'll talk to me. We're not strangers. I've already met him at the bar. I'll just use my ranger background to get him to talk, since he likes the military so much."

Marco must have forgotten that Libby had been with Oliver at the time. Oliver alone was a whole different ball game. But I merely gave a *whatever* shrug.

"Do you have the autopsy report yet?" I asked Dave.

"No," he answered, glancing through the file. "And all

the coroner's statement says is that the death was not accidental and would be preliminarily classified as a homicide. Let's see what else is on the police report. . . . Time of death was between four and five in the morning."

"Still dark out then," Marco noted. "Easier to dump the body."

"That reminds me," I said to Dave. "Did you ask Libby about driving the van to Sally's house rather than her Corvette?"

"Libby told me that when the cops found her, she had just parked the van in the alley behind her shop so Oliver could use it later. She had left her Corvette in the alley earlier that morning and was in the process of moving it to a parking garage. The cops asked where she'd been, and she stated she had been to see her client Sally Mitchum. She didn't specify which vehicle she'd used because she didn't realize the importance of it at the time."

It sounded logical enough.

"Here's some new information on Delphi," Dave said. "Her body was discovered wearing a pair of pink silk pajamas, a pink silk robe, and matching slippers."

"Then we know she wasn't killed in her bed," I said. "If she took time to put on a robe and slippers, she must have gotten up for some reason—maybe to answer the door."

"Libby and Oliver have house keys," Marco said. "It wouldn't have been for them."

"Maybe it was Tilly Gladwell, the clerk Delphi fired," I said, eager to wow them with Grace's discovery. "Tilly had a motive, obviously, and the opportunity to have a copy of Libby's car key made. Not only that"—*drumroll, please*—"but according to Grace's source at the British embassy, Tilly is an impostor. Her real name is Cora. The real Tilly Gladwell is a wealthy Londoner."

Dave raised both eyebrows, clearly impressed, but Marco didn't say a word. So I told them about Cora's criminal background, along with Grace's belief that Cora knew how to hot-wire cars and pick locks and might have purchased a wig to commit the crime.

"Grace learned that no red wigs were sold by any salons in the county in the past three weeks," I said, "but that doesn't rule out catalog or Internet sales, so Grace is going to try to track down all deliveries made to our suspects to see if any of them came from a wig supply house."

"Good luck with that," Marco muttered, then gave me a look that said, *Take that!* His gaze lingered a moment longer than necessary, a little hotter than I would have expected, too, given the state of our relationship. For a split second, even the corner of his mouth quirked, that sexy little upward curve that always drove me wild. Was he flirting with me? By the hot flush on my cheeks, my body thought so.

But then his provocative little grin was gone—or maybe it had never been there, just wishful thinking on my part.

"If this Cora broke into Delphi's home," Dave posed, "wouldn't she have attacked Delphi in her bed?

"Maybe Delphi heard a suspicious noise and got up to investigate," Marco said.

"If Delphi is like most women," I reasoned, "she'd call the cops first. And don't forget, Delphi is a former model. She wouldn't risk bodily harm. Now, if she thought it was Oliver or Libby coming in, she'd put on her robe and slippers and go see what they were up to. Maybe Delphi surprised Cora."

"Until we find out where the initial crime scene was," Marco said to Dave, "we're wasting our time speculating. For all we know, Delphi might have been killed in the Corvette."

"She was in her pj's," I said, "and probably without makeup. She wouldn't have left her house that way unless there was a weapon pointed at her."

"There was no mention of any weapon in any of the reports I have," Dave said, "so that's an unlikely scenario. I'll call the prosecutor first thing in the morning and see if he knows where the initial crime scene was, and I'll let Detective Wells know about Tilly being an impostor. Anything else we need to discuss tonight?"

I reviewed my list and said to Dave, "What about Kayla Olin? She seems to have a strong motive—a damaged face and ruined modeling career."

"I requested a copy of the court docket from her lawsuit and a copy of the bankruptcy filing," Dave said. "They should be ready tomorrow afternoon."

"I did a preliminary workup on Kayla," Marco said. He pulled out an eight-by-ten glossy photo and placed it on Dave's desk. "I got this off of the talent agency's Web site. That was Kayla at the age of sixteen, before her surgery."

"She was beautiful," I said. "She didn't need any work done."

"According to what I found, Kayla is five feet nine," Marco said, "tall enough to need to push Libby's car seat back. And her dark hair could have been dyed red. I went to the address I have for Kayla—her mother's house—but her mother wouldn't let me see her. She was very anxious to keep me away from her daughter. I'm still trying to find out where Kayla works so I can talk to her there." Marco closed his file. "That's all I have."

"For our next meeting," Dave said, "I'll see if Detective Wells knows where Cora is. Marco?"

"Besides tracking down Kayla, I'm going to interview Oliver," Marco said.

"I'll follow up on the wig search," I said.

"If Marco has any trouble with Oliver," Dave asked, "will you assist, Abby?"

I didn't glance at Marco, but I guessed he was bristling at the thought of needing my assistance. "No problem. Oliver and I are simpatico."

Dave pushed away from his desk. "Let's plan to meet again tomorrow at five o'clock."

I slipped on my peacoat, grabbed my purse and scarf, and walked out of the office. "Good night, Martha," I called, tossing the end of my scarf over my shoulder and swinging my hips a bit more than was necessary as I sashayed out the door. I knew Marco was right behind me, but I pretended I didn't.

As I headed down the long flight of stairs that let out onto the sidewalk below, the door at the bottom suddenly burst open and there, outlined by the glow of the streetlamp, stood Libby. With her features in shadow, it could have been me standing there.

"Oh, Marco, thank God I found you!" she cried, wringing her hands. She pushed past me to run up the stairs to him. "Someone just tried to kill me."

CHAPTER ELEVEN

Leave it to Libby to steal the scene every time. But after that shocking declaration, there was no way I could depart without knowing more. I turned back to see Libby cradled in Marco's arms, both of them sitting on the carpeted steps. Libby was wearing a black peacoat and a white silk scarf shot through with silver threads, silver boots, and a silver and gold plaid purse, as usual looking like me, only ten times more chic.

"It was awful," Libby cried, shuddering against him. "I closed up at five and drove home, stopping at my mailbox to pick up the mail. But when I pulled down the little door"—she buried her head against his leather jacket—"a snake tried to bite me."

"What kind of snake?" I asked.

She turned to glance at me, only then realizing I had stuck around. "A hideous, scaly brown snake."

"How long was it?" I asked.

"I didn't stop to measure it!" she cried. "Besides, it was coiled up."

"Was it thin?" I persisted. "Maybe it was a garden snake that crawled in for a nap."

"It was fat, okay? Besides, the door was shut. Someone put it there on purpose."

"Abby," Marco said quietly, giving me a glance that said, *Don't press her. She's upset.*

Poor baby. Unfortunately, I wasn't finished with Libby because I had a hunch she had made up the snake, just as she had her stalker. She seemed to like the role of victim.

"Did it bite you?" I asked, ignoring Marco's lowered eyebrows.

"No, I drew my hand back before it could strike." She gazed into Marco's eyes and in a whiny voice said, "I was peering inside, ready to reach for the envelopes, when it lifted its head and started to hiss at me. Honestly, Marco, it could have bitten me in the face." She put her hands over her eyes and began to wail, "Someone wants me dead, too."

She was so melodramatic I almost laughed, but my conscience reminded me that I was still judging her by past behavior. Maybe a snake really had been in her mailbox. Until I could prove otherwise, I had to give her the benefit of the doubt. *Hmm.* Maybe I should have a look.

"Come on," Marco said to Libby, "let's go up to Dave's office and get you some water. Then you can let Dave know what happened."

As Marco ushered Libby up to Dave's office, I left the building and headed toward the parking lot to get my car.

Halfway down the block I heard Marco call, "Abby, wait up."

I stopped and turned. What a sight he was, striding up the sidewalk in his leather jacket and tight jeans. He was so masculine he took my breath away. "Did you want something?" I asked, trying to sound bored.

"Yeah, I want you to stay away from Libby's mailbox."

"I don't know what you're talking about. I'm going home."

"Right. Home via Libby's street. You're not fooling me. I could tell by your questions that you weren't buying her story."

"Marco, I truly don't know what to believe about Libby's story."

He studied me, as though trying to determine if I was being straight with him. I gazed back, hoping to look convincing while not noticing how the glow from the streetlamps lit up the gold flecks in his chocolate brown eyes, which always made me go all soft and gooey inside. *Be a pro,* my conscience chided. But it was too late. I *had* noticed his eyes.

Apparently, I also hadn't convinced him of anything. "Look, I know you're going over there," Marco said, "so you might as well ride with me."

Sit beside him in the very same car in which we used to make out? I took a step backward. "I don't think so."

"If there *is* a snake in her mailbox, do you want to be the one to find it? Besides, if we carpool, you'll save gas."

That was certainly a selling point, considering that my Corvette, with gas prices so ridiculously high, was burning up half of my pitiful income every month. Still, riding in his car was bound to bring back many bittersweet memories. "Thanks, but I'll pass."

Marco arched one eyebrow. "We're supposed to cooperate, remember?"

He was challenging me, knowing full well that I had never been able to turn down a challenge. The question, though, was why.

"My car's around the corner," he said, his mouth quirking devilishly.

As we headed south through town, crossing the highway to an area where new condos and town houses had seemingly sprung up overnight, I sat stiffly in Marco's passenger seat, determined not to let his proximity get to me. It was a losing battle, however, as soon as I caught a whiff of his spicy-musky aftershave lotion I loved so much. From the corner of my eye I could also see his right hand on the steering wheel, the hand that had often held mine. I stared out the side window, wishing I hadn't agreed to ride with him.

Marco knew right where to go, turning down one curving street and up another. How many times had he been here? He wound deeper into the new development until he reached a cul-de-sac of brick and cedar two-story town houses, where the mailboxes stood on posts at the bottom of long, curving driveways.

He pulled up near a large black metal mailbox whose door was slightly ajar. Then he reached across me to open the glove compartment, removing black gloves, a flashlight, and his tiny digital camera, sending the seductive aroma of his aftershave past me yet again. We got out of his car and cautiously approached the mailbox. Marco glanced around, saw a thick twig lying near a bush close by, and picked it up.

"Stand back," he said, then used the twig to free the latch, causing the door to swing down. When nothing slithered out, Marco shone the flashlight around the interior, using the twig to push the envelopes aside so he could see all the way to the back. Wearing heavy gloves, he carefully removed the envelopes, handed them to me, then scanned the inside again.

While his attention was diverted, I quickly shuffled through the stack of envelopes, trying not to think of how many laws I might be breaking. The first two were from utility companies; the third was addressed to Libby in a bold script, the strong, diagonal letters topped with sharp points and long tails. To me it seemed like angry writing.

There was no return address on the envelope, just a hastily scribbled *R. Shah.* The date stamp said PITTS-BURGH, PA. *Hmm.* Hadn't Libby attended school in the Pittsburgh area?

"Nothing inside the box," Marco reported, switching off the flashlight. "The door wasn't shut tight. The snake must have escaped."

Or maybe the reptile had never been there in the first place.

As we walked back to the car, Marco took the envelopes from me and glanced through them, pausing at the one with the angry writing. Was it the handwriting that had caught his attention, I wondered, or was it the name R. Shah? Could it be a letter from Libby's stalker? Would a stalker put his name on the envelope? I didn't think so.

Marco merely tucked them in his inside jacket pocket and got into the car.

"I meant to ask earlier," I said, trying to sound casually interested, as we pulled away, "have you had any luck tracking down Libby's stalker?"

"I'm about to wrap up that case."

Was there really a stalker? I wanted to ask, but I knew he wouldn't tell me anything. I was so used to being able to discuss ideas with him that it was hard not to get angry all over again. The problem was, I wasn't sure whom to be most angry with—Libby, Marco, or myself.

Maybe I could tie my question in with the murder investigation. "Is it possible Libby's stalker murdered Delphi?"

"I don't think they're related," Marco said. He looked like he was about to say more, but he stopped himself. Damn those confidentiality clauses.

"Could the snake be connected to the murder case?" I asked. "Maybe a warning of some sort?"

"It could be, which is why I'm going to inform the cops and let them look into it. Or it could be nothing more than a prank."

"If the snake was a warning, wouldn't you think the perp would have left a note?"

"Not necessarily. The snake could have been put there to shake Libby up, remind her that the killer is still out there."

By his answer I knew Marco didn't think the letter from R. Shah had anything to do with the snake. So why had the envelope made him pause? The only explanation I could come up with was that it tied in with the stalker case.

Marco turned on the radio, and the song "Sexy Back" was playing. He glanced at me. "Remember that song? Wasn't that Ross Urban's ring tone?"

He was referring to a suspect in the last murder case we'd worked on together. "Ross and Jess, the Urban legends," I said, and couldn't help but laugh at the memory. "That was a morticians' convention I'll never forget."

"It isn't every day that you get locked in a coffin," Marco said.

"Not just any coffin," I said. Then he chimed in with me, "A *phone booth* coffin."

We laughed together, and our gazes met, making my heart constrict in agony. We'd worked hard to break that case, and I'd nearly gotten myself killed doing so. But as always, my hero had been there for me. How painful that memory was now. Marco turned his attention back to the road and I turned to stare out my window. We rode back the rest of the way in silence.

"Thanks for the ride," I said when he dropped me off at the parking lot near Bloomers.

He waited until I was safely inside my car, then took off. I watched his taillights disappear in my rearview mirror, missing his good-night kisses more than ever.

Be a pro, that annoying little voice in my head whispered. Well, fine. I'd just turn off my heart, then. Grumbling to myself, I pulled out my notes and a pen and wrote at the bottom of the paper, *R. Shah, Pittsburgh, PA.*

"Okay, R. Shah," I said aloud. "You and I need to talk."

I got into work half an hour early on Wednesday so I could do an Internet search on the mysterious R. Shah, only to find two dozen orders for funeral arrangements waiting, and the deceased was none other than Delphi Blume, which meant her body had been released by the coroner's office. The autopsy report, then, must be done. Maybe Dave would have a copy by the time we met that afternoon.

I did a quick white pages search for all the R. Shahs in the Pittsburgh area and found three listed. I called the first number and struck out. The man who answered had no idea who Libby Blume was. He was also hard of hearing, and kept saying, "Who?" I had a strong hunch he wasn't the person I was looking for.

At the second number I got a machine recording that said, "Roshni and Sam here. Leave your name and number."

Was Roshni R. Shah? I left a message asking her to call me if she knew Elizabeth/Libby Blume. I tried the third R. Shah and reached a woman who had no idea who Libby was and hadn't attended college with anyone by the name of Blume. But if I wanted a free mobile phone, she had a deal for me.

Next I did a Google search on Roshni Shah and discovered she had a MySpace page that said she went to college at the University of Pittsburgh, which was also where Libby had gone to school. Coincidence? I thought not.

With the arrival of Lottie and Grace, I put the case on hold to work on the funeral orders, since Delphi's viewing was scheduled for six o'clock that evening at the Happy Dreams Funeral Home. The funeral service was set for the next day.

When I took a break midmorning, I checked my messages and saw one from Sally Mitchum. I called the number and reached her on her cell phone.

"Abby, I talked to my neighbor the congressman about the problem at the jail," Sally told me. "He promised to look into it, so I'll check back with him in a few days to see if he's as good as his word. He did say that with the financial problems the state was having, the federal government was our only hope to rectify the situation, but that it would take time to work through all the various levels to get to the proper funding."

"That's a start, Sally. I really appreciate your help."

"I don't know if it will come to anything, but I always keep my promises. And by the way, I've made it my personal crusade to see that young Maria is treated justly."

Feeling hopeful that something would be done at last, I hung up with a smile. Then Grace came in to tell me that she'd had no luck tracing the wig with either the post office or FedEx. "They're mum on the subject. Privacy laws and all that."

But she had persuaded our friendly UPS deliveryman to disclose that he'd delivered over thirty packages to Blume's Art Shop in the past three weeks, but none to Libby's home address, and only one to Delphi's address, which could have been for either Delphi or Oliver. Unfortunately, the guy couldn't help us any more than that.

"There has to be some way to find out if Tilly or Oliver bought a wig," I said.

"I'll put on my thinking cap," Grace said, and went to attend to some customers.

As Lottie and I worked on the stack of orders that afternoon, I found myself constantly checking the time, wishing it were five o'clock. The reason for my eagerness was Marco, of course, which was infuriating because I couldn't get him off my mind.

Still, at ten minutes before closing time, I put away my tools and supplies and slipped into the tiny bathroom in back to check my hair and douse my lips with peach-flavored lip gloss. And just before I walked into Dave's office, I paused to put on my best imitation of a model's bored yet sophisticated expression. Then, after a deep breath, I glided in, right shoulder first, then left, butt tucked under, chin angled daringly, one hand on my hip.

"Hi, Dave," I said in a sultry voice, giving him a cool smile. I turned to give Marco an elegant nod—only to find his chair empty.

CHAPTER TWELVE

Dave was watching me with some amusement. "If you're looking for Marco, he had to run home to make a wardrobe change. He'll be here soon. If you want to wait in the conference room, you can make that entrance again when he gets here."

With a furious blush, I flopped into the chair. "I'll pass."

"When are you two going to kiss and make up?"

"What makes you think I want to make up with him?"

From outside the office I heard Marco's sexy, deep voice: "Afternoon, Martha."

I quickly crossed one leg over the other and tossed my hair back.

"Well," Dave said, "*that*, for one thing."

As always happened when I saw Marco, I felt a surge in body heat that I knew was turning my cheeks pink. He sauntered in like James Bond, wearing a tailored black suit, ivory shirt, and silk tie, looking hotter than ever. I wanted to devour him like a chocolate bar.

Before I made a fool of myself, I rummaged through my purse to find a pen and my notes, mumbling a quick, "Hi," to his, "Afternoon."

"Are you going to the funeral home for the viewing?" Dave asked Marco.

"Yep. How about you?"

"I'm going to stop by after supper," Dave said.

They both paused, obviously waiting for me to announce my plans, which until that moment had been up in the air. I hadn't decided if I wanted to show my face at Delphi's funeral or not, considering that most of the town would probably mistake me for Libby. "Um, I have to go home to change clothes first."

"Why?" Marco asked. "You look great."

I glanced down at my outfit with a blush. "In this old thing?" Well, okay, it was new, a skirt and sweater I'd gotten on the last-ditch sales rack at H&M. "Thanks."

"It looks good on you," Marco said. "Really good." He wasn't looking at my outfit, though. He was gazing into my eyes, a hopeful glimmer in his brown ones, as though he were extending an olive branch, seeing if I would accept it. But I couldn't. Maybe it was just my foolish pride, but it still rubbed me the wrong way that he wouldn't trust my gut feelings, not even a little. So I looked down at my hands in my lap and said nothing.

"Let's move on," Dave said. "We have a lot to cover. Marco, your report?"

"I wasn't able to track down Kayla or Oliver," Marco said. "Kayla seems to be holed up in her mother's house. I haven't been able to catch her coming or going. Oliver wouldn't answer his apartment door, and Blume's Art Shop is closed until next Monday. I haven't seen the van around, either. I asked Libby if she knew where he was, but she hadn't seen him since yesterday evening. He seems to be keeping himself scarce, too."

"Try Harrigan Park," I said. "Guys play war games there all the time."

"Did that," Marco said. "He wasn't there. I even talked to the guys he hangs out with, but they hadn't seen him in a few days."

"Oliver is very fearful of being followed," I said. "Maybe he thinks you're tailing him. Maybe he'll come out of hiding only for a face he trusts."

"If you can find him and get him to talk to you," Marco said, "be my guest."

"I'd rather you went with Abby," Dave said to Marco, "just to be on the safe side."

There was a long moment of silence, during which I stared at my notes. "That's okay," I said finally. "I don't need help."

"No, Dave is right," Marco said. "If you can track Oliver down, let me know when you plan to talk to him and I'll be there."

I'll be there. His words were like tiny darts straight into my heart. Was it just a month ago that he'd said to me, *I'll always be there for you, Sunshine*? Now there were ifs attached.

"I meant to ask this earlier," Dave said to Marco. "Did Libby receive any written threats or phone calls after the snake incident?"

"Nothing," Marco said.

Dave made a note, then said, "Abby, your report?"

"Lots of packages were delivered to Blume's Art Shop and to Delphi's home, but none of the carriers would reveal information about them, so I'm at a dead end on the wig hunt. Maybe I should just drop that thread. The red wig idea was pure speculation anyway. And, as you both realize, we can't turn a blind eye to the possibility of Libby being guilty." I resisted the urge to glance at Marco for his reaction, but I guessed he wasn't smiling.

"Just a reminder," Dave said. "I'm not trying to prove Libby's guilt or innocence. I only want to direct the guilt *away* from her. And don't sell yourself short on your wig theory, because when I called Detective Wells this morning, she said they'd just finished processing several strands of red hair that they'd found on the blanket wrapped around Delphi's body. And guess what? The strands were synthetic."

"Wow," I said. "Grace guessed right. Then whoever carried Delphi's body to the car must have been wearing the wig."

"Did Detective Wells finally admit to the likelihood of the killer being someone other than Libby?" Marco asked.

"Not in so many words," Dave said. "That doesn't necessarily mean she'll act on it unless she sees other evidence pointing toward another suspect and away from Libby, so we'd better come up with that evidence soon."

"I'm puzzled by the wig strands found on the blanket around Delphi's body," Marco said. "Aren't the strands sewn in? Wouldn't it take some force to pull them loose?"

Both men looked to me for answers. "Sorry," I said, "I've never owned a wig—well, unless you want to count that Bride of Frankenstein fright wig I wore for a costume party once. . . . That's it! I should have thought of that before. The wig must have come from a costume shop, not a wig shop, because a cheap wig would shed all over the place. I'll call around to the costume shops in the area and see if I can find out who bought a red wig recently."

"Do the cops know yet where the initial crime scene was?" Marco asked.

"Delphi's kitchen," Dave replied, "where it appears that Delphi was struck with a wine bottle. They found an unopened bottle on the floor amidst dirt and debris from a broken potted plant, but they're still processing the evidence, so there's no fingerprint analysis yet."

"How about the autopsy report?" I asked him.

"It came in just a while ago," he said, shuffling through the expanding stack of paperwork. "In a nutshell it says death came as a result of blunt-force trauma to the right temporal area, consistent with blows from a smooth, spherical object, causing internal hemorrhaging of the brain. No other bruising on the body was found, but the fingernails were broken and the fingertips were covered in blood. That was consistent with the detective's report that said Delphi was found facedown with hands outstretched as though she'd been trying to pull herself forward. However, the blow that eventually killed her was most likely delivered while she was standing."

"It sounds like Delphi was trying to get away from her attacker," I said.

"If someone grabbed the wine bottle and whacked her in the head," Marco said, "it sounds like a crime of passion, done in the heat of anger."

"No way," I said. "Buying a wig, having a key made—that murder was planned."

"Not necessarily," Marco said. "The wig might have been used to trick Delphi into opening the door, making her think it was Libby without her house key. The killer might have gone there with other intentions, but when Delphi didn't cooperate, the killer turned violent."

"Detective Wells needs to talk to Cora," I said. "She's big and rough and has a criminal record."

"They haven't located her yet," Dave said. "Detective Wells was pretty darned embarrassed when I told her about Cora being an impostor."

"The detective should have done her homework," I said.

"Next suspect, Kayla Olin," Dave said, placing a paper on the desk so we could see it. "This is a copy of the docket sheet that shows the chronology of Kayla's case against Delphi and her agency. The lawsuit was filed over three years ago, and the plaintiffs were Kayla Olin, and Karen and Robert Olin—probably the girl's parents."

Dave picked up the report to scan it. "Depositions were taken, settlement conferences were held, mediations were attempted, and hearings were continued—looks like Delphi's lawyers dragged it out as long as they could. Let's see. . . . Okay, here we go. The jury's verdict against the defendant was entered in the amount of one and a half million dollars."

"Wow!" I said. "That was a *huge* award."

"Delphi filed a praecipe for appeal thirty days later," Dave noted. "Six months after that, the original judgment was affirmed and entered of record, which means that Delphi's appeal failed." He put the docket sheet aside and picked up another. "This is Delphi's bankruptcy filing in which the judgment was wiped out. It's date-stamped October fourteenth of this year."

"Three weeks before the murder," Marco pointed out. "Timely."

"I hear what you're saying," Dave said, "but it wasn't

like Kayla hadn't known what was coming. Her attorney would have warned her what the bankruptcy would do to her judgment."

"It's one thing to be told what could happen," Marco argued, "and quite another to have it become reality. Kayla could have held out hope that the judge would exempt her claim, and when that hope was taken away, she decided to get even with the woman who destroyed her life."

"Kayla's not even twenty years old," I argued. "That's a pretty drastic step for a young woman to take. Besides, she must have sued the surgeon and got some money."

"You're right," Dave said. "The doctor's insurance company settled with her, but it's under seal, so there's no way to know what that amount was. However, those policies usually have a hundred-thousand-dollar limit."

"A hundred grand isn't bad, but it's a far cry from one and a half million," Marco said. "And I can't help but wonder why her mother is being so protective of her that she won't even let her daughter speak to me."

Dave checked his watch. "Let's meet again tomorrow at five. Do you have your game plans now?"

"I'll keep trying to get in touch with Kayla," Marco said, "and I'll see if I can track down Cora."

"I'll follow up on the wig and try to make contact with Oliver," I said.

"Remember," Dave said, "if you do set up a meeting, take Marco along."

"You didn't tell Marco he had to take me along when he went to Kayla's house."

"That's because I haven't almost been killed going after murderers," Marco said. The corner of his mouth twitched as he stood up, as though he was teasing me. "So, maybe I'll see you at the funeral home later?"

I gave him a coy smile. "Maybe."

Considering how often I'd been to the huge old Victorian house that housed the Happy Dreams Funeral Home, I shouldn't have felt ill at ease. Then again, it wasn't every day that I saw my clone standing in front of a coffin greeting well-wishers. Libby was wearing a smartly tailored black knit dress with a black patent belt and heels and gold jewelry, her red hair fashioned into a loose chignon at the nape of her neck, and a lace handkerchief in her hand, looking every bit the bereaved daughter. I had opted for a gray sweater dress with a black belt, and a black patent headband in my hair. Even so, I was still offered condolences.

A line of people stretched around the perimeter of Parlor A and through the hallway to the front door. I was betting most had come out of curiosity. They'd been reading about Delphi for years and wanted to catch a last glimpse of the once-famed model.

To my surprise, Oliver was nowhere to be seen. I glanced around to see whom else I knew and caught sight of Marco standing a few yards from Libby. He appeared to be scanning the room, too, and when our gazes met, he gave me a nod of acknowledgment. I brightened at once, then dimmed. It was so hard to get used to him not being my boyfriend.

When my turn in line finally came, Libby wrapped her arms around me as though we were long-lost sisters, and there we stood, locked in an embrace, rocking back and forth, as she wept and keened, her red head pressed to mine. "You'd think they were twins," someone whispered behind me, only to be hushed.

"Mummy's really gone, Abby," Libby wailed. "She's really gone."

Taking my hand, she led me to the coffin, where she fussed over her mother's hair. "They did it all wrong. Mummy would be so upset. I'd better call Mrs. Dove in here and have her fix it." She swung around, seeming not to notice the curious faces staring at her.

"Mrs. Dove?" she called loudly. "Mrs. Dove, Mummy needs you."

"Your mom's hair is fine, Libby," I whispered in her ear, turning her toward the coffin. "Get a grip. Where's Oliver? Why isn't he here with you?"

Libby glanced over her shoulder as though she hadn't realized her brother was gone. "I don't know. He *was* here." She spotted Marco and motioned him over. The crowd watched with growing interest as we formed a huddle at one end of the coffin.

"Do you know where Oliver went?" Libby asked.

"I haven't seen him since I told him I wanted to talk to him later," Marco said. "He probably slipped out when the people started pouring in about fifteen minutes ago."

"I'll look for him," I said, and turned, only to have Libby grab my wrist and pull me back.

"Why do you both want to talk to Oliver?" she asked.

"We just need to clear up a few things," Marco assured her.

"What things? Is Oliver in trouble?"

"Calm down. There're just some things I want to ask him," Marco told her.

"What *things*?" Libby demanded like a petulant child.

"Libby, you hired me to do an investigation," Marco said firmly. "Are you going to let me do what I need to do?"

As though her father had scolded her, Libby instantly became docile. "Yes."

"Good. Now go back to the line of people waiting to talk to you."

Libby gave him a teary-eyed glance. "Will you stay with me until Oliver comes back?"

Oh, ick. How could Marco put up with her? "I'll see if I can find Oliver," I said, and walked away in disgust.

I stepped out of the parlor and glanced around. The hallway ran up the middle of the old mansion from the front door, through the grand foyer, between the two funeral parlors, then, farther back, between the lounge area (once a morning parlor) and a kitchen, to the back door. Hmm. Where would Oliver be? Maybe Max and Delilah had seen him.

As I started toward the kitchen, I heard, *"Psst."*

I turned and glanced down the hallway, but no one was in sight.

"Psst. Over here."

The whisper came from Parlor B, so I stepped to the doorway for a look inside. Because the room wasn't in use, wooden shutters had been drawn beneath the heavy burgundy brocade drapery, blocking out all light, making it hard to identify the shapes inside.

"Is the coast clear?" the whisperer asked.

"Oliver, is that you?"

"Sh-h-h! Is the *coast* clear?"

Yep, it was Oliver. "Why are you hiding? You should be standing beside Libby."

A hand shot out, grabbed my arm, and yanked me into the room, pulling me behind the door. Another hand covered my mouth. "I'm being followed, ma'am," Oliver whispered in my ear. "Don't blow my cover."

CHAPTER THIRTEEN

Oliver had a *cover*? As a grieving son—or lunatic?

"Do you understand?" he asked. He didn't sound threatening, just frightened.

I nodded. I could have elbowed him hard in the abdomen and gotten away, but my instincts were telling me I wasn't in danger, and I needed to talk to him anyway, so I decided to play it out, see who was following him and why.

When he removed his hand from my mouth, I whispered, "You're not being followed, Oliver. Marco Salvare just wanted to talk to you. You know who he is—the owner of Down the Hatch. He's the private investigator your sister hired."

"I know who Salvare is," Oliver said. "This is someone else. You've got to find out who he is, ma'am. It's vital to the mission."

"You want *me* to find out?" I took a step back and bumped my head on the door. "How am I supposed to do that?" I asked in a low voice, rubbing my head.

"Libby showed me her scrapbook. You solve cases. This should be a piece of cake. A cakewalk. A walk in the park."

"You don't need me, Oliver. Just confront the guy. Ask him what he wants."

"Can't do that, ma'am. He might be with the feds. They hate us paramilitary men."

"Have you actually seen this person?"

"Not face-to-face, ma'am, but he's out there. He drives a black car that cruises by my place at midnight every night, on the dot, spot-on. One time I came home and my door was ajar. I know he bugged my apartment."

"Did you check for bugs?"

Oliver glanced around. "Those government agents are sneaky, ma'am. They know where to place bugs so they can't be found. Right now he's in that crowd across the hall. I felt his eyes on me, watching, waiting, waiting and baiting."

"Why would you have a tail? Have you done something wrong? Broken any laws?" *Committed murder?*

Oliver leaned closer. "They find reasons to put people like me away, ma'am."

"People like you?"

"You know what I mean."

Lunatics? "So, basically, you want me to follow the person who's following you."

"I don't care how you do it, ma'am. I'll pay you a thousand dollars to learn his identity."

Wow. That would pay for the repair of one of my coolers and leave some cash to spare. Still, I had to proceed with caution. If Oliver wasn't the killer, neither was he the sanest person I'd ever met. "If I find out who your tail is, what are you going to do about it?"

He thought for a moment, then said cryptically, "First I have to know who I'm dealing with, ma'am. Know thine enemy. Enemy mine."

I'd have to set up a surveillance to see if Oliver had a tail, then trace the guy's license plate. Then I could decide if I wanted to turn over the information to him. Oliver was right. It would be a piece of cake—and hopefully my bargaining tool, as well.

"Tell you what, Oliver. I'll take your case if you'll answer some questions first."

He hesitated. "What kind of questions, ma'am?"

"About your mother's death."

I could see the hollows where his eyes were, and knew he was staring at me, debating whether to cooperate. "Are you working with Salvare, ma'am?"

"No, I'm an independent operator."

"Would you explain that, ma'am?"

"Come on, Oliver. You saw Libby's scrapbook. I like to solve cases. How about if we discuss this somewhere else, say the coffee parlor at Bloomers tomorrow morning, at nine?" Where I'd have lots of witnesses if he tried anything.

"Will there be people around?"

"Just me, my two assistants, and maybe a few customers."

"I'll take a pass, ma'am."

"Would you feel better if I made it at eight o'clock? We don't open until nine, so it would be just me and my two assistants, who'd be busy getting ready for the day."

"Here's the deal. You call me when you get the information. Then I'll meet you. Meet and greet. Remember, this is strictly between you and me. Not a word to *anyone* about your undercover assignment. Agreed?"

Suddenly, there was a commotion in the hallway just outside the parlor. At once Oliver flattened himself against the wall and began to inch away from the door. "He's looking for me, ma'am. You have to help me."

"Don't panic," I told him. "I'll go see what's happening."

I hurried to the doorway just as two men hustled a tall, slender woman out of the parlor across the hall. I recognized the men as Max Dove's employees, but the woman was unfamiliar. She was wearing a black cape and a black hat with an attached scarf that wrapped around the lower half of her face and tied at the throat. Was that who Oliver believed was following him?

"Let go of me!" the woman cried, and began to pull back and kick as they forced her to the front door. "I only came to pay my respects."

In her struggles, her scarf came untied and her hat fell back, revealing her face. Judging by the misshapen nose and mangled lips, I was betting she was Kayla Olin.

I stepped out of the parlor just as Libby came dashing out from the opposite side, with Marco right behind. "Tell the police to handcuff her!" she called to the men. "She's crazy."

"Was that Kayla Olin?" I asked Marco.

"Kayla the killer Olin!" Libby said spitefully.

"Take it easy," Marco said as a crowd gathered in the doorway behind them. "You don't have any proof of that."

"I saw that crazed look in her eyes," Libby cried. "Do you think she came here to pay her respects to the woman she sued? More like coming back to inspect her handiwork—and killing me while she was at it. I'll bet she's the one who left the snake in my mailbox, too."

Oh, brother. Libby the victim again. I headed toward the front door to try to catch Kayla.

"Make sure she's arrested, Abby," Libby called. "It's about time Mummy's killer is brought to justice!"

"Wait up, Abby," Marco said, starting after me.

"Marco!" Libby whined. "You can't leave me now. I need you."

I marched back to her, pointed toward the darkened parlor, and said through gritted teeth, "Your brother is in there. *He* should be standing beside you, not Marco."

"Marco," Libby whimpered, hanging on to his sleeve, totally ignoring me, "don't leave."

I left them to work it out and hurried outside, where Max's assistants were holding on to a subdued Kayla as two cops got out of a squad car and came toward them. One of the cops was a female that I didn't know. The other was Sergeant Reilly.

"We'll take it from here," Reilly said to the men, pretending not to see me. He removed his handcuffs from the leather holder on his belt while his partner instructed Kayla to stand against the squad car with her hands on the roof so she could pat her down.

"Why are you arresting her?" I asked Reilly, who had no choice but to notice me now.

He moved me off to the side. "Why is it that every time I show up at a scene, you're there? Do you wander around town looking for trouble? Do you keep a police scanner strapped to your ankle?"

"All that girl did was come to the viewing. That's no reason to handcuff her."

Reilly dipped his head and said quietly, "No, but

walking out of Starke-Porter while she was on a suicide watch *is* a reason."

My mouth dropped open so far, a bowling ball could have fit inside. Starke-Porter was a mental-health-care facility located across the street from the county hospital. "A suicide watch? How long has she been there?"

"Several weeks, until she slipped out three days ago."

The day before Delphi was murdered. "Do you know anything else about her case, like why she tried to kill herself?"

"Nope. You know everything I know."

"Sarge," his partner called, "you want to take this?"

Reilly's partner was holding something that glinted silver in the streetlight. While Reilly grabbed an evidence bag from the squad car, I stepped up for a closer look. It was a scalpel.

"Found it in a pocket inside her cape," the other cop said quietly as she deposited the knife into the bag. She handcuffed Kayla, removed her hat, and tucked her in the backseat. Kayla went without a whimper, her head bowed.

Maybe Libby had been right after all. Maybe Kayla *had* come to kill her.

"Fill me in," Marco said, striding up to us.

I pretended to peer behind him. "Where'd you leave your ball and chain?"

He gave me a scowl. "Libby persuaded Oliver to stand beside her."

I had a hunch it was Marco who did the persuading. "Reilly, would you show him what you showed me?" I asked quietly.

Reilly opened the bag and Marco peered inside. His eyebrows rose in surprise.

"Kayla Olin walked out of Starke-Porter three days ago," I told Marco, "while she was on a suicide watch. And it was the day before Delphi's murder."

Marco glanced at Reilly. "Does Detective Wells know that?"

"If she didn't, she'll know soon enough," Reilly said, starting toward the car. "We've got to get this woman back to Starke-Porter. I'll catch you later."

As the squad car pulled away, Marco turned toward me, a glimmer of satisfaction in his dark eyes. "What do you think about Kayla being a strong suspect now?"

"The timing of her escape could be a coincidence," I said.

"Pretty hefty coincidence, especially considering that bankruptcy ruling three weeks ago."

"How would Kayla get a copy of Libby's car key? Or know where Libby lives? Libby hasn't been in town long enough to make it into the phone book."

"Kayla could have followed her home," Marco reasoned. "You have to admit it looks pretty suspicious when she shows up here with a scalpel."

"Did she threaten Libby with it?"

"No, she bypassed the line and walked directly to the coffin. Something about her behavior struck me as odd, so I tried to engage her in conversation. Then she backed away as though she were afraid of me, and that's when Libby saw her and started to panic. I alerted Max's assistants, and they called the cops."

"How did Libby recognize Kayla? Half of her face was hidden."

"I'd say by her eyes. You wouldn't forget those eyes."

"Why? Were they crossed?"

Marco frowned, not appreciating my attempt at humor. "They were striking."

"If Libby recognized Kayla, that means she knew her previously, which is inconsistent with what she said at her interview. She led us to believe she was unfamiliar with Kayla and didn't even know much about the lawsuit because she was away at college during that time."

"Why would Libby lie about knowing her?"

Maybe because that's what liars do, I was about to say. But I held my tongue. "Skip it. Are you going to try to see Kayla?"

"I'll have to contact her doctor at Starke-Porter to see if Kayla is up to it." He paused as visitors came out of the funeral home. "I guess we should get back inside." He strode toward the door, then glanced back when he noticed I wasn't behind him. "Aren't you coming?"

"My work here is done. But don't let me stop you from rejoining the party."

He frowned in thought as he reached for the door handle, but he didn't go inside. Instead, he turned around and came back, falling into step beside me as I started toward the parking lot. "I'm done, too," he said. "Libby doesn't need a babysitter."

Yes! "I don't know about you, but I'm beat," I said. "I'm going home to enjoy a leisurely bubble bath, a glass of chilled wine, and a big chunk of rich, dark chocolate." I sighed dreamily, then cast him a quick glance to see if my daydream had had any effect on him.

Oh, yeah. Marco was gazing at me as if I were a hot fudge sundae. Perhaps he was even picturing me in that bubble bath. *Gaze on, hungry man, because you aren't getting so much as a nibble until you apologize for believing Libby and not me.* "So what are your plans?"

"I"—he paused, then sighed wearily—"have to get back to the bar."

I was halfway home when I remembered that I was supposed to find out who was tailing Oliver. So much for the leisurely bubble bath. I turned around and went back to Happy Dreams, where I drove around looking for any sort of big black sedan in the area. When that produced no results, I parked around the corner from the funeral home, a good distance away from the streetlight so no one would spot my yellow Corvette, and walked back to the parking lot to do a visual search. I found an older-model black Cadillac, but an elderly couple came out of Happy Dreams and drove away in it. The Blume's van was still there, I noticed, but not Libby's car. I wondered if the police were still holding it as evidence.

For the next hour I stood in the shadows of a recessed doorway kitty-cornered from the funeral home, shivering with cold, because I hadn't brought my warm coat and I couldn't risk being spotted in my car. Had I known I was going to be doing surveillance, I would have borrowed Nikki's little beater car. At least I had on dark clothing.

When the last of the visitors had gone and the parking lot had emptied out, Libby and Oliver came out and drove away in the van. I waited to see if anyone pulled out behind them. Then I dashed to my car and followed at a safe distance as Libby took Oliver to his apartment over Delphi's garage.

The Blumes' stately redbrick home sat on a large

corner lot in a historic part of town, built at the end of the horse-and-buggy era, when coach houses were still a necessity. Delphi had converted hers into a three-car garage with an apartment above. Both the home and the coach house had black shutters and gray slate mansard roofs. A ten-foot-tall black wrought iron fence enclosed the property, with gates both front and rear.

I had to park on the side street to avoid being seen— a yellow car could be a real handicap when working a case—but I was still able to watch Oliver enter the fenced-in yard through the rear gate and climb the wrought iron stairs to his apartment. The house and most of the grounds had been sealed off with yellow crime-scene tape, but the cops had left a path open for him.

I saw a light come on in his window; then I waited another half hour to see if a black sedan happened by, but finally had to leave when my eyes kept shutting. Stakeouts weren't really my thing, especially when I hadn't planned for them. I'd have to do better if I wanted to earn that thousand bucks.

On Thursday morning I arrived at Bloomers well before eight o'clock, hoping that Oliver would decide to show up after all. But the next hour came and went, and then it was nine and customers started to come in, most heading for the parlor for their morning coffee. Because of his mother's scheduled funeral service, not to mention his desire for privacy, I knew there was slim chance of him stopping by later.

"Sweetie, last night your mom took to knitting like a duck to water," Lottie gushed as we snipped flowers at our big table in the workroom. "You'd think she was born to those needles. The gals loved her, too. I think she's found herself a new hobby."

"That's great, Lottie. Now she can knit in the evenings and keep my dad company in front of the television instead of throwing clay in her studio. And there won't be any art to sell, either, so everyone wins."

"Abby, love," Grace said, coming back to the workroom, "you have a phone call from Oliver Blume. He said it's urgent."

I dashed over to my desk to pick up the receiver. "Oliver?"

"Where were you last night, ma'am? You were supposed to keep watch."

"I did. I sat outside the funeral home until you left. Then I parked near your apartment for another half hour, and not one suspicious car passed by. I really wasn't prepared to stay longer. That's something I have to plan for."

"He came by. By and by."

"What time?"

"Midnight. Night after night at midnight. I saw him from my window. Flash, flash, flash."

"Did he take photographs?"

"Yes, ma'am. Night after night."

"Did you see his camera?"

"Didn't have to, ma'am. It's what he does every night."

"But how do you know?"

"Why else would he slow down?"

How about for the stop sign on the corner? I sighed inwardly. So what did I have? A dark sedan that drove by at midnight every night, and a guy whom Oliver had never seen who took photos of him with a camera he'd also never seen. Either Oliver was smoking something potent or he was paranoid. Maybe both.

"I'll be there before midnight tonight, Oliver. If someone is shadowing you, I'll find him."

There was a click and the line went dead. I hung up and rubbed my temples. What had I gotten myself into? I was starting to wonder if a thousand dollars would be enough.

Nine orders had come in overnight, so Lottie and I dug in, happy as larks doing what we loved best. For me, that did not include thinking *or* talking about Oliver or Libby. Sensing my mood, Lottie occupied herself by humming along with a Willie Nelson song on the radio as she covered a foam cross with 'Milva' roses in a lovely peachy gold color. I simply immersed myself in the delightful aromas and textures of the flowers.

Thirty minutes later I had created a contemporary funeral spray of pink roses, white lilies, purple hydrangeas, and an Oriental lily called 'Tiara' that I particularly liked because it was pollen free and had gorgeous pink and purple flowers. I was so blithely in the moment that I even joined Lottie as she belted out a chorus with Willie. Midway through the morning, however, Grace appeared to snap me out of my reverie.

"I'm sorry to interrupt, dear, but Dave Hammond is on the line."

With a regretful sigh, I put down an uncut stem of French tulips for the next arrangement to answer the phone at my desk. "What's up, Dave? And don't say Marco's frustration level. We're cooperating."

"Maybe you two are, but Kayla Olin isn't. Marco talked to her doctor first thing this morning and got permission to interview Kayla, but when he got to Starke-Porter, Kayla refused to see him. Do you want to try?"

So the Salvare charm had failed to work, had it? "I'll go over during my lunch hour. Will you let the doctor know I'm coming?"

"I'll take care of it."

I hung up and there stood Grace and Lottie, waiting eagerly for me to update them on the case. So, feeling in lighter spirits, I filled the women in on the latest developments, including the information Dave had gathered, my visit to the funeral home, Kayla's surprising appearance there, and my new job as Oliver's private eye.

"Are you sure working for Oliver is a good idea?" Lottie asked, frowning in concern. "He seems to have a few bats in his belfry, if you know what I mean."

She meant wacko, and I couldn't disagree. "I won't put myself in danger. Besides, I'm not convinced anyone is actually following Oliver, but I'll humor him and see what turns up."

"Let me see if I understand this," Grace said. "Libby hired Marco to find her stalker, and now Oliver has done the same with you? Don't you find that a bit odd?"

"Everything about Libby and Oliver is odd," I said. "And that reminds me, I never got a return phone call from Roshni Shah. Maybe she didn't get my message."

"Is she the young woman who wrote the letter to Libby?" Grace asked.

"Yep, the one with the angry writing. She might have no connection to what's going on here, but I think it's worth pursuing."

"Would you like me to follow up on the wig by calling costume shops in the area?"

"That would be a big help. Thanks, Grace. Oh, and would you do one more favor? See if any of the pet shops in town have sold a big brown scaly snake recently, and if so, to whom."

I finished the arrangement, stowed it in the cooler, then sat at my desk to make the call. This time, a young woman picked up the phone. "Roshni Shah?" I said.

"Yes. Who's this?"

After I explained who I was and my purpose for phoning her, she said angrily, "What is it with you people? I'm trying to cut Betsy out of my life, and you keep pulling me back in."

"Okay, wait. You lost me. Is *Betsy* Elizabeth Blume?"

"Yes. She was my roommate at U. Pitt. last year. We shared an apartment off campus. And what a nightmare that was."

Boy, could I empathize. Once a pest, always a pest, no matter what anyone said. "Has someone else contacted you?"

"A detective from New Chapel—Lisa Wells I think her name was. And a private investigator, too, with an Italian-sounding name."

"Marco Salvare? Did you talk to him?"

"No way. I wouldn't even talk to the detective until I got confirmation from the police that she was for real. I don't trust Betsy and I don't want anything more to do with her. So I'm sorry, but please don't bother me anymore."

"Roshni, wait. Don't hang up. I understand where you're coming from. I used to babysit Lib—er, Betsy, and I'd like to cut her out of my life, too."

"So let's both cut her out starting now. Good-bye."

"Please hear me out first, and if you still don't want to talk, I'll respect your decision."

I heard her sigh. Then she said reluctantly, "Fine. I'll give you five minutes."

Five minutes to describe the hell my life had become with Libby in it. Ready, set, go.

"Okay, first of all, Betsy is calling herself Libby now. Notice how it sounds like *Abby*? Now let me tell you what she's done since she came back from school, starting with when she decided she was going to intern at my flower shop." I continued with the story, squeezing in as much as I could in my allotted time, reaching the point of my false arrest.

"I know I'm out of time," I said, "so I'll just end it by saying that now I'm trying to find Delphi Blume's killer, whether it's Betsy or not, because I feel like I prejudiced the whole town against her and that's not acceptable to me. Everyone deserves justice, even pests. That's why I was hoping to get some information on Betsy's behavior while she was at school. So could I just ask you a couple questions, and if you don't want to answer them, that's fine? If you want to check me out online, I'll give you my Web site address."

I gave her the URL, then waited while she checked. Clearly, Roshni wasn't taking any chances. "Can we make this short?" she asked, coming back on the line. "I really have to be somewhere."

"Absolutely."

"Go ahead, then."

"Would you explain why you want to cut Betsy out of your life?"

"I'll make it real simple. Betsy Blume is a stalker."

CHAPTER FOURTEEN

*L*ibby was a stalker? Wow. Was it a coincidence that she was now claiming to be the one being stalked—or was she cleverly turning the tables? "Did Lib—er, Betsy stalk you while you were roommates?" I asked Roshni.

"She didn't stalk *me*. She stalked her art professor's husband, Nolan Grant. He had to get a restraining order to stop her."

Libby had lied to Dave! She'd totally denied having any legal problems.

"Can you believe that Betsy is *still* hounding me to send her news and pics of Mr. Grant?" Roshni asked. "I mean, okay, so she's wild about the guy. He isn't interested. Grow up! I told her point-blank that I didn't have time for her ridiculous fantasy life and I wasn't about to get into trouble by helping her live it out, but she doesn't get it."

"What was her fantasy life?"

"That she was going to marry Nolan Grant, adopt the

Grants' twins, and teach art at the college, as if Professor Grant was simply going to disappear. It was like Betsy thought she could just take over the poor woman's life. Is that insane or what?"

Insane—and familiar. "Would you tell me how it started?"

Roshni heaved a sigh, as though she didn't even like to think about it. "During our senior year, Professor Grant would hire Betsy occasionally to babysit her twins, until she found out that Betsy had developed a big crush on her husband and had even tried to seduce him. Needless to say, Betsy wasn't hired again, but that didn't stop her. She dyed her hair dark brown and had it styled just like Professor Grant's. Then she started dressing like her, and even bought a brand-new Mercedes because Professor Grant drives one—an *old* one, but still."

Even more familiar.

"Things got really feisty after that. Betsy started following Mr. Grant everywhere, showing up wherever he went—she even brought a picnic basket to his office so they could have lunch together—as though she really was his wife. He warned her to stay away, and so did the professor, but they finally had to get a restraining order. Betsy almost didn't graduate because of her conduct, but her mom flew in at the last minute to talk to the dean, then whisked Betsy away immediately after graduation.

"I thought Betsy had finally given up on her fantasy, but she'd barely been home a day when she started calling me, asking me to give Mr. Grant messages from her, and wanting me to take photos of him with my cell phone and send them to her. I told her no way, but she wouldn't drop it. I finally stopped taking her phone calls and wrote her a letter telling her if she didn't leave me alone, I'd file a restraining order, too."

"I can understand why you don't want anything more to do with Betsy," I told her. "By the way, just out of curiosity, what is the professor's first name?"

"Well, it's Patricia, but everyone calls her Patsy."

Patsy and Betsy. Abby and Libby. Creepy. "When you first met Betsy, what was she calling herself?"

"Elizabeth."

"Did she change it to Betsy after she started working for Professor Grant?"

"That would be about right."

"How many letters have you sent to Betsy since she's been home?"

"Just one."

"Have you called or e-mailed her?"

"I e-mailed her several times to tell her to stop bugging me, but no phone calls. I don't ever want to hear her voice again."

"Has she tried to phone you?"

"Not for about a week."

"Did Betsy ever mention that she was being stalked?"

Roshni laughed. "Is that what she's claiming now? Trust me, once people at school got to know her, they kept their distance. She was bossy, snobbish, and very immature."

"Did she have any boyfriends?"

"She dated, but like I said, once her personality came out, the guys shied away."

"Thanks, Roshni. You've been very helpful."

"Do me a favor, Abby. Next time you see Betsy, tell her I moved to Australia and left no forwarding address."

I hung up and made notes about the call. So Elizabeth "Betsy" "Libby" Blume had taken over someone else's identity, too. Very interesting. I wondered if Marco had uncovered that tidbit yet. If he had, then he'd probably figured out that Libby had made up the stalker story. Perhaps that was why he said he was about to wrap up the case. In any event, I'd have to let Dave know about the restraining order.

I thought back to the day Libby showed up at Bloomers, fully expecting me to welcome her with open arms. After what I'd just heard, I was betting that Delphi had promised Libby a job with me as an incentive to stay in New Chapel, where Delphi could keep an eye on her. When I wouldn't take Libby on as my intern, Delphi had probably panicked, fearing Libby would head back to Pittsburgh, and then when Delphi couldn't bully me into changing my mind, she must have dangled the art-shop idea in front of Libby, like a carrot to a horse.

I was also betting that Libby had been more than glad to accept that offer. What a great way to get even with me for rejecting her. Set up a shop as close to mine as possible, then proceed to take over other elements of my life, including my boyfriend. It was almost a duplicate of what she'd done to Professor Grant.

Yet, as infuriating and odd as Libby's behavior was, I still didn't see a connection to Delphi's murder. Delphi had come to Libby's rescue at least twice, which would tend to make most people grateful, not murderous. Then again, Libby wasn't like most people. But she certainly was a puzzle. How could one very bright, *exceptionally* attractive young woman manage to annoy so many?

I checked my watch. Yikes. I had only an hour left

before I had to see Kayla. I still had a stack of funeral orders to do and two assistants hovering at the table behind me, waiting to hear the newest revelation about Libby. I turned with a smile. "Okay, ladies, I'll give you the scoop while we work."

Kayla Olin was slumped in a small upholstered chair in a semiprivate room of the mental-health facility staring forlornly out the window. The room was painted in soft, soothing pastel colors and smelled strongly of laundry detergent and disinfectant. Luckily, she didn't have a roommate, which gave us some privacy.

"Kayla?" I called softly from the doorway. "Hi, I'm Abby Knight."

When she didn't respond, her doctor, a kind, older woman, said, "Kayla, this is the young lady I mentioned earlier who wanted to come by. You said you'd talk to her."

Kayla turned, staring at me with empty eyes. She had beautiful, long, silky auburn hair and big violet eyes framed by thick black lashes. But there her beauty ended. Her long, thin nose had such a sharp point at the tip that she could have burst balloons with it. Her lips were huge and lumpy, as though someone had tried to stuff them with tapioca, and her chin jutted forward unnaturally. She was truly a tragic sight.

"Come in," she said in a lifeless voice, turning back toward the window. She was wearing a blue print shirt and jeans with soft slippers on her feet.

I glanced at the doctor, who gave me an approving nod. Before she brought me to Kayla's room, I'd spoken with the doctor, asking for her professional opinion as to whether she thought Kayla was angry enough at Delphi to murder her. The doctor wouldn't give me a definite answer, but indicated that she didn't think Kayla was a danger to anyone but herself. Kayla had been admitted to the hospital's psych ward after attempting to commit suicide by overdosing on pills, which she'd done after learning that Delphi's bankruptcy was final. Kayla had been moved to Starke-Porter a week later, but because of her depression, had continued to be on a suicide watch.

The doctor pointed to another chair next to the empty bed. "You can use that. Kayla doesn't have a roommate right now."

I scooted the chair closer to Kayla, trying to find something chatty to say to break the ice, but everything I came up with sounded lame. I finally decided to simply explain why I was there. "So, Kayla, let me start by telling you a little bit about myself—"

"Just tell me what you want from me," she said in a weary, defeated voice.

Okay, so I'd cut to the chase. "I know what happened to you, Kayla, with your plastic surgery and all, and I think you got a raw deal."

"You know what Delphi did to me?"

"Yep. The surgery, the trial, the judgment, and the bankruptcy." I decided not to mention her suicide attempt.

Her deformed lips twisted into a scornful smile. "So are you writing an article about how I got screwed by the famous belly babe who promised to make me a huge modeling success?"

"I'm not a reporter, just a florist who's interested in your case. If you don't mind, I'd like to ask you some questions about it."

"Go away." She turned back to the window.

I couldn't blame her for refusing to talk to me. What did I have to offer? If I were sitting in her chair, what would I want to hear?

"Look, I may be just a florist, but I'm really good at solving problems. Maybe I can help you solve yours."

She glanced at me in disbelief. "My *problem*? Are you referring to my face?"

"Well, that depends. . . . Would it offend you?"

She scoffed. "Like anything could offend me more than looking in the mirror."

"Would you consider having more plastic surgery?"

"Do you really think any health-insurance company would cover the cost? Believe me, I tried, but they consider it elective surgery, a *cosmetic* procedure. I'm lucky that my mom has decent health insurance or I wouldn't be here to get help for my depression."

"Would you at least talk to a plastic surgeon?"

"What good will that do?"

I crossed my fingers behind my back. I was going out on a very big limb to get Kayla to talk to me, and I hoped it worked. "My brothers are doctors, and they have doctor friends that they trade favors with. You know how lawyers do pro bono work? Well, what if I ask my brothers to see if one of their friends, someone who's a plastic surgeon, would do surgery pro bono for you?"

Her lifeless gaze suddenly sharpened. "Seriously?"

"Seriously. My brothers are good guys. If they can help you, they will." Especially if I reminded them of some big favors I'd done for them. Then it would be payback time.

Tears filled her violet eyes as she said angrily, "Don't tell me this if you don't mean it, because I don't want to get my hopes up for nothing. I mean, look at this disaster of a nose. I don't think there's any way it can ever look normal."

"Just wait and see what the surgeon says, okay? And if he believes he can help you, then I'd like you to answer some questions for me. Is that a deal?"

She nodded, wiping tears off her face.

"Super. I'm going to page my brothers right now and get the ball rolling. I'll let you know as soon as I hear back. How does that sound?"

She nodded again, sniffling, then suddenly lurched toward me and gave me a hug, sobbing on my shoulder. I patted her back, relieved to notice that I wasn't getting any bad vibes from her, which I would if she was the killer. Or maybe I just didn't want her to be.

I left Kayla and went to the lobby to call the hospital across the street, hoping one of my brothers was doing rounds. When neither one answered his page, I called Jordan's cell phone.

"Hey, Sis. What's up?"

"Jordan, I have a huge favor to ask. But first, remember last year when you forgot to send Kathy an anniversary gift, and I rushed over there with a big, beautiful bouquet of her favorite, deep pink 'Duc de Guiche' roses and said they were from you?"

"What do you need?" he asked with a sigh.

I explained Kayla's problem and crossed my fingers. "Do you know anyone who'd be willing to help her?"

"It's not a question of knowing someone, but whether Kayla is a candidate for further surgery, and even more important, whether the surgeon will do it for free."

"Can't you find someone who owes *you* a favor?"

"Well . . . how about if I promise him an anniversary bouquet, too?"

Like I needed to be giving away free flowers. "Fine." My phone beeped, signaling a text message coming in. "Wait, Jordan. Mom is texting me." When had she learned that?

I switched screens and saw her message: *Knttng mat'l arrvng Fri. Din@ hm.*

I switched back to Jordan. "Looks like we're having dinner at Mom's house this week instead of the country club."

"Why?"

"I'm not sure. Her message just said that her knitting material was arriving. Go figure."

"What did she order, a boatload of sheep?"

"Yeah, right."

"I think we should be scared, Abby."

"Come on, Jordan. She took up knitting. What's there to be scared about?" Wait. Had I actually asked that question?

When I returned with a sandwich from the deli, Lottie was taking an order from a customer in the shop, and Grace was serving coffee and scones to two groups of chattering ladies. I greeted the customers, poured myself a cup of coffee, and went to the workroom to eat. On my desk was a note in Grace's beautiful script. *There is but one costume shop and it's in the next county. I spoke with a gent there who will look into the purchases of red wigs and get back to me. Yours, Grace.*

In the middle of eating my sandwich, my cell phone rang, so I dug it out of my purse and saw Jordan's name on the screen. "Hey, Sis," he said. "I found a surgeon who's agreed to take a look at Kayla. When he finishes his rounds at the hospital later today, he'll head across the street and have a look."

"Cool! You're a godsend, Jordan. Thank you so much!"

"You bet. I'll see you at Mom's on Friday. Say your prayers."

I hung up smiling. Now, hopefully, I could get some answers from Kayla, and also get her the help she needed. With the clock ticking on the case, I'd have to pay her another visit this evening before visiting hours were over. I'd been looking forward to some downtime for myself, but that would have to wait until after I'd questioned her. Then I could go home, run that bubble bath and—oh, wait. I still had Oliver's case to work on.

I turned to glance at the older of our big walk-in coolers, which was even now groaning and thunking as though it were on its last leg. "I hope you appreciate what I'm doing for you."

"Whom are you talking to?" Lottie asked, coming through the curtain.

"The cooler."

Lottie rolled her eyes. "Sorry I asked."

Fifteen minutes before closing time, I got a phone call from Dave Hammond to cancel our meeting. "I have to see a client at the jail," Dave said. "He was just picked up on a warrant. And afterward I promised my wife I'd take her out to dinner for her birthday."

I was disappointed, mainly because I wouldn't get to see Marco. "Tell her 'Happy birthday' from me. Any news from the prosecutor's office?"

"They finished processing Libby's yellow Corvette, but didn't turn up anything incriminating. Libby's prints were all over the car, but that's to be expected. They found strands of Delphi's hair in the trunk and on the utility blanket, but they didn't find anything that pointed to any other suspect. How about you?"

"I talked to Libby's former college roommate today and found out that there's a restraining order out against Libby."

"For what?"

"Apparently she had her sights set on a professor's husband and stalked the guy until he was forced to file the order to get her to leave him alone."

"Well, that's discouraging news. Okay. I'll make it a point to talk to her about it. I hope the prosecutor doesn't find out."

"I think he will, Dave. Detective Wells spoke with the roommate, too."

"Damn."

"On the good-news front, I'm going to see Kayla Olin this evening. She promised to answer questions for me."

"Good work, Abby. I've got to get over to the jail now, so let's plan to meet tomorrow at five. I'll phone Marco to let him know."

At seven thirty, a staff member at Starke-Porter accompanied me to Kayla's room, per their rules. "Kayla's not with a doctor, is she?" I asked.

The woman peeked inside, then shook her head. Kayla was lounging against a pillow in her bed, watching TV.

"Hi, Kayla," I called from the doorway.

"Abby, come in," she said eagerly, waving me in as she sat up. She had a big smile on her face, revealing beautiful teeth behind her misshapen lips. "Guess what? The plastic surgeon thinks he can repair my face! Isn't that awesome? He's a reconstructive specialist—he fixes people who've been in bad accidents. And my doctor came by afterward and said I can go home tomorrow if I want to. Oh, Abby, I can't believe this is happening."

Thank you, Jordan. "That's great, Kayla. Have you told your mom?"

"Yes, they let me call her right after the doctor left. Mom was so happy she cried. If the surgery works, I can go back to school and get my degree so I can earn decent money and help out with all the bills. It's been really hard on us since my dad died. I can't thank you enough."

I smiled at her, wanting to rejoice in her good fortune, but a little voice inside urged caution. If the evidence came back strongly pointing to Kayla, there was a good chance that she wouldn't see any of her dreams come true. Maybe I'd been unfair to dangle hope in front of her when it might be snatched away.

Then again, I could turn around and walk out without asking her anything. Don't ask, don't tell, or, as Grace always said, ignorance was bliss. I'd simply report back that after questioning Kayla, I'd crossed her off the suspect list—and pray like hell that she was innocent.

Yep, that sounded like a good plan. "Listen, Kayla—"

"I know. You have questions for me." She took a deep breath. "Go ahead. I'm ready."

CHAPTER FIFTEEN

"**W**hy don't I come back another time?" I told Kayla. *Like in a dozen years or so.*

"Please stay. I'll answer whatever you'd like. I owe you that much, at least."

I searched her damaged face and hopeful eyes. I'd always heeded my gut feelings before, with good success, and right now they were telling me that Kayla didn't kill Delphi. So I decided to go for it. I pulled my notebook and a pen from my purse and readied them.

"I need to ask you about your relationship with Delphi. I know it's a painful subject, but I want to make sure you don't become the top suspect on the detective's list."

Kayla's eyes widened in alarm. "I didn't kill Delphi."

"But you have to understand that in the detective's eye you had a motive and an opportunity. You did check yourself out of here the day before she died."

Kayla groaned, dropping her head back against the

pillow. "I wanted to go home. I missed my mom. And listening to the sounds that go on here all night was making me feel worse."

"I totally understand. Why don't we go over your background information? How old were you when you signed up with Delphi's agency?"

"Sixteen. I did catalog modeling for about two years. Then Delphi began to hint that I could really go places if I had facial work done. My parents refused to let me go under the knife, so Delphi stopped getting me modeling assignments. She told me no one wanted me, that my face wasn't good enough. I kept pleading with my mom to let me have the surgery—after all, Delphi was providing it for a very reasonable cost by a surgeon she knew—until finally Mom convinced Dad to let me go ahead with it."

Kayla's eyes welled up. "It was horrible. I was in so much pain. I knew before the bandages were removed that something had gone terribly wrong. And Delphi never once came to see me and wouldn't even return my phone calls, as though the doctor had warned her that he'd botched it. Then my dad died suddenly—he was only forty-two—and I know it was because of what I was going through. And I couldn't have corrective surgery because I had to use the money I got in the doctor's settlement to help my mom keep our house and pay off my dad's medical and funeral expenses, because his insurance company denied most of our claims."

Kayla wiped tears from her face and said bitterly, "Delphi Blume was poisonous. She micromanaged every one of her clients' lives and ruined mine in the process. I hope she's rotting in hell for what she did to me and my family."

"I understand why you went into a depression, Kayla. No one should have to go through what you did. But feeling as you do about Delphi, why did you go to the funeral home last night?"

Kayla reached for a tissue to blow her nose, then gazed at me through bleak, red-rimmed eyes. "I shouldn't have gone. I'm really sorry now. It wasn't fair to her family."

"But why did you go? Did you intend to hurt Delphi's daughter?"

Kayla glanced at me in horror. "No! Why would I do that?"

"Why did you have the scalpel?"

"I took it when I left here because I was planning to kill myself, but then I went to the restaurant where my mom works as night manager and stood outside, watching her through the window. She looked so tired and sad that I just couldn't put more sadness in her life. I went home and hid in the backyard that night. She found me there when she got off her late shift, and I begged her not to send me back to the hospital. She wasn't happy about it—I think she was afraid I'd try something while she was working—but she let me stay."

"Was that Sunday night?"

Kayla paused to think back. "Yes."

"What time did your mother find you in the backyard?"

"It was sometime after one o'clock in the morning."

"Can she verify that you were at home at five thirty a.m. on Monday morning?"

Kayla nodded vigorously. "Mom made me sleep in her room so she could watch me, and she doesn't leave for her day job until nine thirty."

"Good. That establishes your alibi. What happened next?"

"For the next two days I rested and read paperbacks. Mom wouldn't let me watch the news or read the newspaper because she said they were too disturbing. Then on Wednesday, while she was at work, Mom's cousin called to tell us she was thinking about going to Delphi's viewing that evening to see the famous former model in person, and I just flipped out."

"So you showed up at the funeral home intending to do what? Kill yourself in public?"

"I'm ashamed to admit it, Abby, but I wanted to disfigure Delphi so she'd see what it felt like to have people stare at you like you're a freak show. I know it sounds crazy—it *was*. Then I heard her daughter cry out and suddenly I realized how insane it was to even think that Delphi would know if I did anything to her, not to mention how it would upset her family."

"Did you have any contact with Delphi after her bankruptcy filing? Is there anyone who might have seen you talking to her?"

"I haven't had any contact with her since the civil trial."

"Do you know Delphi's daughter?"

"Elizabeth? Yes, I know her, but we weren't friends. I always thought she was a little jealous of me, to tell you the truth."

"Why?"

"When I first signed with the modeling agency, Delphi made a big fuss over me, and I don't think Elizabeth liked it. She never said anything to me directly, but sometimes she'd be at the agency when I stopped by to pick up a check and she was never friendly. One time . . . well, never mind."

"No, finish, please."

Kayla blushed. "It's really petty, but I think Elizabeth tried to sabotage my work. One time I was supposed to do a shoot at the dunes early in the morning. Then I got a message that the time had changed. When I got there, the photographers had packed up and gone home, thinking I wasn't coming. Delphi was furious with me, and swore she never left that message. And once there was a mysterious electrical fire in the old jail building where I was supposed to do a shoot, where, just by coincidence, Elizabeth happened to be. I told Delphi about my suspicions, and suddenly Elizabeth stopped showing up. Not long after that, Delphi started pushing me to have surgery, so I really didn't see much of Elizabeth after that."

"Do you think Delphi pushed you into surgery because you complained about Elizabeth?"

Kayla shrugged. "I doubt it, but with Delphi, who knows? At the time I thought I just wasn't attractive enough."

"Do you hold any grudges against Elizabeth?"

"She's certainly not one of my favorite people, but a grudge? No. I think she was jealous of me because I had her mom's attention. Honestly, after what I went through, she ought to be glad she didn't have Delphi's attention."

"Do you know where Elizabeth is currently living?"

"No. Should I?"

"I wouldn't think so. Do you own a red wig?"

Kayla gave me a puzzled look. "No."

"Great. Okay, one more question. How do you feel about snakes?"

"*Ew.* They terrify me. I can't even look at one without breaking out into a cold sweat."

"That's it," I said, putting away my notebook. "You did a great job. Will you call me after your surgery and let me know how you're doing?"

She brightened. "Sure."

I held out my hand and she shook it. "Thanks for answering my questions, Kayla. I hope everything works out for you and your mom now."

"You'll never know how much this means to me, Abby."

A nurse peered into the room. "I'm sorry, but visiting hours are over."

"Good timing," I said. "I was just leaving."

As I walked through the facility's spacious lobby, Marco got up from a chair and came toward me. As always, my heart beat faster at the sight of him. Would that ever stop?

"Did you see Kayla?" he asked.

"Just left there, as a matter of fact."

"Did she talk to you?"

"Yep." For some reason I didn't feel like being forthcoming.

"What did she have to say?"

"What did you want to know?"

Marco gazed deep into my eyes, making me blush uncomfortably. He knew I was playing coy. He pointed to a quiet corner, where steel-framed orange vinyl chairs were grouped for conversation. "Want to sit?"

I checked the time on my watch. "I have to be somewhere in a little bit, but okay, I have a few minutes."

Actually, I had all evening, since I wasn't planning to rendezvous at Oliver's apartment until close to midnight, but I didn't want Marco to know that. Better to let him think I had places to go, people to see, maybe even a hot date.

I sat down and Marco turned a chair to face me, straddling the seat. He always looked so masculine when he did that, like a cowboy on a horse. "Did Kayla talk about Delphi?" he asked.

"Yes, and after hearing her story, I'm convinced that Kayla isn't the murderer."

"Will you tell me what she said?"

With his husky voice and earnest expression, how could I refuse? So I related the conversation I had with Kayla about Delphi's murder.

When I finished, Marco said, "You're right. She should be off the suspect list. And by the way, that was great work, Su—" He stopped himself before he said *Sunshine*, changing it to, "So, how did you get her to cooperate?"

I didn't know which hurt worse, not hearing him call me by my pet name, or him not wanting to say it. "I channeled into her pain," I answered wryly. I rose and put my purse strap over my shoulder. "Speaking of pain, where's Libby tonight?"

"I wouldn't know. Where are you parked?"

"In the hospital parking garage."

"I'd better see you to your car. It's late."

We both knew the parking garage was perfectly safe; still, I didn't turn him down. It was nice to know he still cared.

"I hear you're working a case for Oliver," Marco said

as we strolled along the sidewalk. "What is it with those two and stalkers?"

"Oliver hasn't actually seen his stalker or had any communication from him, but he swears the guy follows him around and drives by every night at midnight taking photographs. And did I mention that Oliver has never seen the camera, either? I'm hoping to find out tonight whether he's telling the truth."

"You're not taking the Corvette, are you?" Marco asked as we reached my car.

"I'll use Nikki's car. She gets off at eleven tonight, so it won't be a problem."

"Remember, stay out of sight, wear black clothes and a knit cap over your hair—"

"I know the drill, but thanks." I opened the door and was about to get inside when Marco said, "Abby," and put his hand on my shoulder.

Surprised, I turned and found him inches away, gazing into my eyes as though he wanted to say something else. My blood began to heat and my pulse to race. "Yes?"

I saw a quick flicker of something—regret? sadness? —in his brown eyes; then he withdrew his hand and stepped back. "Don't forget to lock your car doors."

At 11:25 that evening I pulled up to the curb two houses away from Delphi's corner lot and positioned myself so I had a view of Oliver's apartment as well as the cross street. My cell phone and black plastic flashlight were on the seat beside me and my dad's old police-issue blackjack was within reach, just in case I needed to protect myself. Legally, I probably shouldn't have had the heavy lead baton, as they had long since been out-lawed in New Chapel, but my dad had insisted. It was ei-ther that or take him along with me.

To stay hidden as well as warm, I had donned a black turtleneck and thick sweater under my navy peacoat, with black sweatpants, thick black socks, and black boots. I had a black knit scarf around my neck, warm black gloves, and a black knit cap. All my hair was tucked carefully under-neath. Marco would have been proud.

As I killed the engine, my cell phone began to vibrate. I checked the screen and saw an unfamiliar number. I pressed Talk and heard loud music. "Yes?" I answered over the noise.

"What time will you deploy?" came a raspy whisper.

"Oliver, would you turn down the music, please?"

"It's a cover in case someone is listening. I can hear you okay—just don't use any names."

"I'm outside right now in an older-model white Corolla." I glanced up at the window over the garage and saw a yellow glow along the sides of a window shade. Then the window went dark.

"Recognition confirmed."

"How did you get my cell phone number, Oliver?"

"That's privileged information, ma'am. Over and out." He hung up.

I opened my water bottle and took a sip just as a pair of headlights shone in my rearview mirror. Quickly, I ducked down and waited until the vehicle passed, then peered over the dashboard and saw a silver SUV park in front of a house up the street. A young woman got out and went up to the house, using a key to let herself inside.

Two more vehicles passed during the next half hour,

neither of them a black sedan. I checked my watch, pressing a button to light up the face, and saw that it was two minutes after midnight. I yawned; then suddenly more headlights flashed in my mirror, coming up slowly behind me. I scrunched down as far as I could and waited. As the vehicle passed, I carefully lifted my head. It was a black Buick sedan!

I snapped two photographs of the car's bumper with my cell phone, then watched as the Buick paused in front of Delphi's garage. I could see movement inside the car, then a tiny flash of light. Had the guy taken a picture? Of what? There was nothing to see.

As the sedan drove away, I started the engine and followed at a safe distance, hoping the driver wouldn't notice me. The sedan made a turn at the next corner, continued to the end of the block, turned the corner, went to the end of the block, and turned again. One more turn brought us back to Oliver's apartment, only this time the sedan didn't slow down.

I kept as far behind the car as I dared as the driver turned the corner and started up the next block again, repeating that sequence until we were once again at Oliver's apartment. Damn, he was leading me in circles. He must have spotted me.

With nothing to lose, I gave the Toyota some gas and caught up with the sedan, hoping to catch a glimpse of the person inside, or at least get a closer look at his license plate. But the Buick sped off with a squeal of tires, taking corners on two wheels, prompting me to go way too fast to keep up. He finally turned onto a country road and pushed the pedal to the floor, kicking up a cloud of dust. I tried to follow, but when he nearly spun off the road at a curve, I backed off. There was no sense putting my life in jeopardy. I'd blown it.

My cell phone vibrated. "Yes?" I snapped, feeling out of sorts.

"Status report," Oliver said.

"I followed the black sedan, but he outmaneuvered me. I took a couple photos of the car, but I couldn't see who was inside."

He hung up. I hated when he did that.

I turned back toward town and pressed a button to call Oliver. "Stop hanging up on me. Have you noticed the black Buick following you around town at any other time of the day?"

"During the day he follows on foot, ma'am."

"Have you actually seen him?"

"Just glimpses, like the day I came down to your flower shop."

"Then let's set up a time when I can observe you while you take a stroll around the square. What are you doing at noon tomorrow? Will you be at the art shop?"

"Yes, ma'am. The shop won't be open until Monday, but Libby wants me to be there in the morning to help her with some crates."

"Okay, here's what I want you to do. At noon, walk out the front door and take the long way around the square to my flower shop. Come inside and one of my assistants will give you some flowers to take back with you, as though you'd ordered them. Then walk back around the square to the art shop. Take your time. Do some window-shopping. Talk to people, anything to stall so I can scan everyone on the square. Got it?"

"Understood, ma'am. We're a nation at war." The

phone went dead—again. A moment later my cell phone vibrated.

"Would you stop hanging up on me?" I snapped.

"I didn't know I had," Marco replied, his voice instantly soothing my jangled nerves.

"Sorry. I thought you were Oliver."

"How did the stakeout go?"

"Well, it was a good news–bad news situation. The good news is that Oliver wasn't kidding about being followed. A black Buick sedan did drive by his place around midnight just like he said. I took photos of the car but haven't had an opportunity to see if I caught the license plate number. The bad news is that I tried to follow the car, but the driver managed to elude me. At least I know that Oliver really does have a stalker."

"Do you? Think about it. If he could make the cops believe he was being stalked by his mother's killer, it would make him look like a victim, too, instead of a suspect, wouldn't it?"

"I suppose."

"Maybe Oliver hired someone to follow him, then hired you because you're inexperienced and, in his mind anyway, easier to fool. With your eyewitness account to back up his stalker story, his job of convincing the cops would be that much easier, wouldn't it?"

I hated to admit that I might have been duped, but Marco had a valid argument. Oliver had actually told me very little about his stalker. And why would the guy take pictures of Oliver's apartment or show up the same time every night? It didn't add up.

"Remember what I taught you," Marco said. "Never assume anything."

"I'll remember."

"What's your next move?"

"I've arranged for Oliver to take a stroll around the square tomorrow so I can watch for his so-called stalker. If the guy shows up, I should be able to get a clear view of him or of the license plate. Hopefully that will put an end to the mystery."

"Sounds like a plan. If you get the plate number, I'll have my friend at the DMV run it."

"Thanks. So . . . why did you call?" I was hoping Marco would say that he just *had* to know I was okay. That he couldn't have slept until he knew I was safely back home.

"To tell you that Cora is in custody. She was caught trying to sneak across the Canadian border."

CHAPTER SIXTEEN

The news about Cora wasn't what I'd been hoping to hear Marco say, but it *was* worthy of a call. As I turned into the parking lot of my apartment building, I said, "How did you hear?"

"Reilly called, so I thought I'd pass it along. I figured you'd want to know."

Marco hadn't been checking on my well-being after all. I tried to muster some enthusiasm to hide my disappointment, but it was tough. "I hope the prosecutor will take a serious look at Cora now."

"I'm sure he will. The sheriff is bringing her back from Michigan tonight. I'm guessing Reilly will be able to get more information about her interview in the morning."

"Well, thanks for letting me know. Are you still at the bar?"

"Yep."

There was an awkward silence while I tried—and

failed—to think of a witty ending to our conversation. "Well, I'm home now, so—good night."

"Night, Abby," came his husky reply, bringing back memories of our good-night kisses.

As I pulled the Toyota into Nikki's parking space, I heard a vehicle speed past the apartment building. I turned to look and caught just a glimpse of a dark green compact car. Was that Marco's Prius? Was he checking up on me after all?

Probably not. He said he was still at the bar. Still, why would he call me so late on a weeknight? He could have let me know about Cora first thing in the morning. Could it be that Marco *had* called to see if I was okay and just used Cora as an excuse? Did I dare hope?

Dream on, Abby, my little inner voice said. *Remember Marco's advice: Never assume anything.*

I parked Nikki's Corolla, then turned on the interior light to view my cell phone photos. The first one was a blur, but the second one had caught the sedan's rear end. I zoomed in on the license plate, only to see a glare where the numbers should have been. A plastic cover over the plate had acted like a mirror, bouncing back the light, making the numbers unreadable.

The evening was a bust.

Friday started out as any other day, except that I was still so keyed up from my late night adventure and my plan to catch Oliver's stalker that I downed three cups of coffee before the flower shop even opened. Grace and Lottie wanted to know what was up, so I told them about chasing the mysterious black Buick and the results of my visit with Kayla.

"How wonderful that you were able to arrange for a surgeon for the poor child," Grace said. "I'm sure she was ecstatic. But as for Oliver's mysterious stalker, I'm concerned that you're in over your head on this case, dear. You could have been injured in that car chase."

"I know, and that's why I backed off."

"Do you think Oliver's stalker is the same person who killed his mom?" Lottie asked.

"It's possible," I said. "Or he might have set this whole thing up to make everyone believe he's going to be the next victim. That was Marco's suggestion, anyway."

"Is there any possibility that Marco is right?" Grace asked. "Because if there is—"

"You shouldn't put yourself in jeopardy," Lottie finished for her. "Let Oliver pay someone else that thousand dollars he offered you. We'll find the money to pay for the cooler repair somewhere."

"I'll be careful," I assured them. "All I intend to do is to get that license plate number."

"Perhaps you should ask Marco to help you," Grace suggested, as I filled my coffee cup again. "You know he'd do anything for you."

"Not necessary," I said between sips.

"But he has more experience in these things," Lottie countered.

"I don't need Marco's help."

"Abby," Grace began, her tone lecturing, "we're quite aware—"

I looked up to see Lottie elbow her. "What was that for?" I asked.

They glanced at each other. Then Lottie said, "What was what for?"

Like I was going to fall for that. I walked around the coffee counter to confront Lottie, which was easier than confronting Grace because she could outsmart me by quoting Shakespeare. "What are you keeping from me?"

"Nothing," Lottie said, avoiding my gaze.

"Why did you poke Grace, then? You know I'm going to keep asking until you tell me."

Grace struck a statesmanlike pose. "Perhaps you should consider the words of William Shakespeare."

Uh-oh. Here it came.

" 'Where words are scarce, they are seldom spent in vain; / For they breathe truth that breathe their words in pain.' "

I sighed resolutely. "I give up. What does it mean?"

"We've become aware," Grace said, "that you've been very—shall we say mum?—on the subject of Marco lately, and we're growing concerned."

"Well, don't be. Marco's simply been extra busy lately with his bar and his PI cases. . . ."

They gazed at me with knowing eyes, as if to say, *Don't try to fool us.*

"We've split up," I said despondently.

"Why?" Lottie asked. "You're crazy about Marco."

"And he's undoubtedly crazy about you," Grace added.

"Not so much anymore," I said. "I kind of blew it."

"It's that danged Libby, isn't it?" Lottie exclaimed, looking like she wanted to punch somebody's lights out. "She wormed her way between you two."

"If our relationship had been solid, Lottie, Libby wouldn't have been able to worm her way between us. The truth is, I tried to convince Marco to give her back her retainer and her file, and he refused because he thinks I'm overreacting to her. So I threatened to walk out, and he didn't stop me." I took a breath to keep my chin steady. "So we're over."

Both women rushed to hug me. "Don't you worry, sweetie," Lottie said. "He'll come to his senses after I have a little talk with him. And if not, there are plenty of fish in the sea. You just have to get back out there and cast your nets."

"Okay, this is why I didn't tell you before," I said, breaking free. "I'm not ready to cast my nets. In fact, I hate fishing, and it isn't a matter of Marco coming to his senses. He doesn't trust my gut feelings. How can I be with a guy who doesn't trust me? That's why our getting back together is highly doubtful."

"Listen to me, dear," Grace said. "You've known Marco for a short six months. It takes a long time to build a solid relationship, and I guarantee that there will always be setbacks along the way. You mustn't think of this as the end but as merely a bump in the road. Don't close any doors on Marco just yet."

I appreciated Grace's advice, but she really couldn't understand because she hadn't been there. "Thanks, Grace. Whatever happens, I'm fine with it. But I don't want anyone talking to Marco about this. Now let's get to work."

I took a deep breath, then turned and marched toward the curtain, hoping that they'd drop the subject so I could get on with my day. Unfortunately, Grace's quotation kept echoing in my head: *For they breathe truth that breathe their words in pain.*

She'd nailed it. Speaking those words out loud—*We've split up*—had been excruciating. Before I started to feel sorry for myself, I snatched an order from the spindle and pulled the flowers for it. There wasn't any better medicine than an armful of fresh blossoms.

At eleven thirty that morning, I reviewed my plan to find Oliver's stalker with Lottie and Grace. While Grace kept an eye out for suspicious-looking people from the parlor window, Lottie would make sure Oliver got in and out of the shop within five minutes, leaving with a small bouquet of mums. Meanwhile, I would be eating my lunch on a bench in the middle of the courthouse lawn where I could watch Oliver's progress as he walked to Bloomers and back.

At eleven forty-five, I bought my usual turkey sandwich at the deli, added an apple to the order—apples took time to eat, giving me more reason to linger outside—and strolled across the street to the courthouse commons. I found a cement bench that didn't have too much bird poop on it in a central location, then made myself as comfy as possible, readied my cell phone, and unwrapped my sandwich.

Exactly at noon, Oliver stepped outside Blume's Art Shop and glanced cautiously in both directions. Wearing his olive drab long coat over camouflage pants and army boots, he skulked along the sidewalk heading toward Lincoln Street. I didn't see anyone following him.

As Oliver crossed the street at the light and proceeded east on Lincoln, he kept darting glances over at the courthouse lawn as though searching for me. I saw him put his cell phone to his ear and a second later my phone vibrated. "Is the coast clear?" he asked quietly.

"I haven't spotted anyone following you, Oliver.

Don't look over here. You're being too obvious. Just keep moving."

"He's here, ma'am."

"Where?"

"I feel him. He could be watching from his black sedan."

I did a slow visual inspection of the streets around the courthouse but didn't see a black Buick either in motion or parked. "If he's here, Oliver, I sure don't see him."

"He could be inside a store, watching from a window."

I studied the shop windows on Lincoln Street. The guy could be hovering overhead in a chopper, too, but he wasn't. "He'll have to come out at some point, Oliver. Maybe when you enter Bloomers."

Oliver hung up on me, but this time I didn't care. I chewed a bite of sandwich as my gaze tracked him, searching for anyone the least bit suspicious. I was beginning to think Marco was right about Oliver, and I didn't enjoy the thought that I was being taken for a ride.

Suddenly, a black sedan pulled up to a red light at the intersection where Oliver was crossing. I stopped chewing and sat forward, watching as Oliver froze like a statue in the middle of the street, his hollow eyes wide with terror. But the car was a brand-new Ford Taurus, and when the light changed, the driver had to honk to snap Oliver out of his trance. He did a fast shuffle across the street, then darted more glances my way as he slunk up Franklin heading for Bloomers. I sat back in relief. If Oliver was bluffing me, he sure knew how to put on an act.

"Abby!" someone called cheerily. I glanced around to see my cousin Jillian come prancing across the lawn. Just what I needed—someone to draw attention to me.

And draw attention Jillian did. As a personal shopper, my fashion-conscious cousin always wore the latest style, no matter how outlandish. Today she sported a long, patchwork duster made of many different colors of dyed leather, with a red beret topping her long, shimmering coppery locks, a red silk scarf flying out behind her, a black patent purse with huge gold buckles on the front, and shiny black boots.

She flopped down on the bench beside me, casting off her shopping bags like a tree shedding its leaves. "Don't you love preholiday sales?"

"What holiday? Thanksgiving is three weeks away."

"Christmas," she replied blithely, as though she thought nothing odd of it.

"A little early for a pre-Christmas sale, isn't it? Shouldn't we at least get through Thanksgiving first?"

"Abby," she said gravely, "it's never too early for a sale. Why are you eating lunch outside? No one eats outside in November."

"I wanted to get some fresh air, do some people watching, clear my head." I turned just as Oliver walked inside Bloomers.

"I'm starving," Jillian said. "What kind of sandwich is that? Turkey? Can I have a bite?" Without asking, she took half my sandwich from the wrapper on my lap and began to daintily nibble the corner.

Growing up in our close-knit family, Jillian had been, and remained, the annoying sister I never had. The fact that she was a year younger, a head taller, and wealthy to boot had only exacerbated our siblinglike rivalry.

"Are you going to eat that apple?" she asked, her mouth stuffed full with my sandwich.

"No, I'm going to have earrings made out of it."

"There's no need for sarcasm."

"Go away, Jill," I said, guarding the remains of my lunch. "I'm busy."

"Busy what—people watching?" She unscrewed my water bottle, tipped her head back, and emptied half the contents.

I snatched the bottle and cap from her hands, screwed the cap on, and put the water bottle on the bench beside me. "I'm busy working out a problem."

"Like how to get Marco back?"

"What are you talking about?"

Jillian leaned close to say in a confidential tone, "You know exactly what I'm talking about. Libby told me Marco dumped you . . . when I was still associating with her, of course. She seemed way too happy about it. Libby caused it, didn't she? I sensed she was trouble from the moment I met her. I mean, breaking up relationships and killing people? Who does that?"

"Okay, I'll admit Libby isn't one of my favorite people, but we don't know that she killed her mother, so you shouldn't go around making that kind of accusation. There are other very good suspects."

"Oh, right." She winked conspiratorially.

"Go away, Jillian."

"Want my advice on how to get Marco back?"

"Right. I want advice about relationships from the woman who jilted four men at the altar." I peered at the locket peeking from the open collar of her coat. "Is that a BFF locket? Oh, my God! Libby gave that to you, didn't she?"

"Will you look at the time!" she exclaimed, gazing at

the heavy gold watch on her wrist. "I have to get these bags to my car so I can finish shopping. Baubles is having a huge clearance sale." She stood up and began to gather her loot, partially blocking my view of Bloomers. I leaned around her to see just as Oliver came out with his wrapped flowers.

At the same time, a black Buick came down the street from the south, slowing as it approached him. Oliver saw it, too, and froze in his tracks. Clutching my apple and half-eaten sandwich, I jumped up in alarm as the Buick braked in front of him. Oliver instantly dropped the flowers and raced into the narrow alleyway alongside my shop. I shoved my food into Jillian's already laden arms, grabbed my purse, and raced across the wide lawn. I had to get that license plate number!

"Where are you going?" Jillian called. "What's wrong?"

"Bugs in the sandwich," I called back. "You can have the rest." I heard her shriek. That would teach her to steal half my lunch.

Suddenly, the Buick's taillights came on, as though it was about to back up. What the heck was the driver trying to do? Go down the alley after Oliver? Then a big SUV behind the Buick honked, and the black sedan took off. By the time I got to the curb, the car was already rounding the corner on Lincoln, heading east.

Damn! I stopped to catch my breath, then had a frightening thought. What if the driver came up the alley from the other direction? What if he really *was* planning to kill Oliver? Would there be another dead body found behind Bloomers?

CHAPTER SEVENTEEN

Quickly, I dug in my purse for my cell phone and punched in 911.

"Emergency assistance," a woman answered. "What is the nature of your problem?"

"This is Abby Knight from Bloomers Flower Shop. A car is following my friend and he's in danger. We're in the alley behind Bloomers on Franklin Street. Send help."

I darted across Franklin and ducked down the narrow passageway that gave access to the wider alley behind the shops. When I reached the alley, I glanced both ways but didn't see the Buick. To my left were rows of garbage bins, one behind each business, including the two closest to me—the Dumpsters where Delphi's body had been discovered. That was where I found Oliver, sitting between the dirty metal containers, hugging his knees, rocking back and forth.

"Do you believe me now?" he whispered, gazing up at me with a pale, gaunt face.

"Okay, Oliver, calm down. You're not hurt. Obviously

the driver only wanted to scare you. Otherwise he'd probably be coming up this alley right now."

Oliver moaned, pulling into a tighter ball. "Why are they doing this to me? Why are they hunting me down like an animal?"

I crouched down before him. "Look, I know our deal was that I'm supposed to find out who this person is before you answer questions, but we need to have that talk now. It could help me find out who's following you."

"What do you want to talk about?" he muttered, his face buried.

"Your mother's death."

He raised his head, his eyes wide and frightened. "I— I can't."

"I know it's painful, but maybe the person who's following you is connected with her murder."

"No!" Oliver sprang to his feet, causing me to fall back on my hands. He glanced around wildly, like a trapped animal. "I have to hide. They'll find me here. They'll put me away."

"Why?" I cried, righting myself. "What did you do?"

He turned on me, a feral look in his eye. "Are you with them?"

"No, Oliver. I'm with you. Remember what you called me the day you came into Bloomers to buy the bamboo plants? O.O.T.T.O.? One of the trusted ones?"

He pulled his cell phone out of his shirt pocket and tried to use it, but his hands were shaking too much. "Call Libby for me," he said, thrusting the phone at me.

I opened the phone and clicked on her phone-book entry. "Here you go," I said.

He jabbed his index finger toward the phone. "You

talk. Talk the talk. Tell her what happened. Tell her I have to hide. Hide-and-seek. Seek and ye shall find."

At that moment Libby answered with, "Where are you, Oliver? You're supposed to be helping me."

"It's Abby. I'm with Oliver in the alley behind Bloomers. Your brother had an incident and wanted me to call you. He's pretty upset."

"An *incident*? What happened?"

"Someone's been following him, and gave him quite a scare just now."

"Tell her I have to hide," Oliver said nervously.

"He said he has to hide," I repeated.

Libby sighed sharply. "Put him on."

I handed Oliver the phone and he held it to his ear, his eyes darting nervously around as he listened. "But the black car came after me again. Abby saw it, too." He listened for several moments, then straightened as though he'd been called to attention. "Yes, ma'am. Understood."

He clapped the phone shut and slid it into his chest pocket, carefully buttoning the flap over it. He held his hand to his forehead in salute. "Thank you for your help, ma'am." Then, as if nothing had happened, he pivoted, clicked his heels together, and marched away.

"Wait, Oliver. You can't leave now. The police haven't arrived yet. We need to make a report on that Buick. And we still need to have that talk."

"No time, ma'am," he called over his shoulder. " Duty calls."

Frustrated, I watched him march up the alley. What duty? What in the world had Libby said to snap him out of his paralyzing fear?

I heard a car pull into the alley from the opposite

direction and turned to see a squad car coming toward me, lights flashing but no siren on. I gave a friendly wave to let the cops know I wasn't in danger. The car stopped and one officer jumped out—Reilly. Great.

"Are you okay?" he called, his gaze combing the alley as he moved cautiously toward me.

"I'm fine, the danger is over, and before you ask how I happen to be everywhere you show up, tell me, why is it that you show up everywhere I happen to be?" The best defense was a good offense, as my dad often said.

"I heard your call come in and volunteered to take it." He glanced around. "What was the danger?"

Wow. My strategy had worked. "Someone has been following Oliver Blume, and about five minutes ago I thought the driver was going to come down the alley after him. That's why I called for help. I tried to get a license plate number, but the car sped away. It's a black Buick LeSabre, probably four years old. Wait, I have a photo of it."

I pushed buttons on my cell phone and one of the photos I'd taken the evening before appeared on the screen. "This is the car, but there's a glare on the license plate. He's got some kind of reflective cover on it."

"Did you get a look at the driver?"

"The car has tinted windows."

"Does Oliver have any idea who it is?"

"No. That's why he hired me. The Buick has been driving by his apartment every night at midnight."

Reilly glanced at me curiously. "Oliver hired *you*?"

"Is there something wrong with that?" I asked testily.

"No offense, Abby, but since Marco is already in Libby's employ, I'm surprised Oliver isn't using him."

I made a quick decision not to tell him about Marco's

opinion on the matter. There was no way Oliver had faked his terror. "Look, all I know is that Oliver offered me a thousand big ones to take the case. I don't think he trusts male authority figures."

"So why do you figure someone's following him? Is it possible that whoever killed his mother is after him, too?" Reilly glanced around. "Where *is* Oliver?"

"On his way back to Blume's. I couldn't get him to stay. I think his sister told him to get back to work, and when he gets an order, he follows it."

"Oliver gets a scare like that and Libby orders him back to work? She's real sympathetic, isn't she? You know, the way she's aping you, it still seems to me that she was setting you up to take the blame. But, hey, what do I know? I'm just a cop."

"Well, you might know if Oliver was questioned after the murder."

"Family members are usually questioned first. Why? You think he might have done it?"

"I don't have an opinion about Oliver yet. Did he have a good alibi?"

"You'd have to talk to Detective Wells about that. I wasn't a party to the interview."

"Could you take a peek at the file for me?"

"Abby, how many times do I have to remind you—"

"—that you really need this job because you have a kid to support and don't want to put your pension in jeopardy. Never mind. I'll just ask Detective Wells."

"Good luck."

"Why?"

"She's tough, that's all I'm saying." Reilly finished writing and put away his notebook. "I'll prepare a report on the Buick, but Oliver is going to have to come in and sign it."

"Thanks, Reilly. I'll let him know."

"Any luck?" Lottie asked as soon as I stepped inside Bloomers.

I was about to answer when Grace came hurrying out of the parlor. "I saw a black Buick through the window a bit ago. It stopped right out front. Was that the car that's been following Oliver?"

"That's the one."

Grace handed me a slip of paper. "I'm afraid this was the best I could do. I caught only the first two numbers on the license plate, and, as you will notice, it's an Indiana plate, but not local."

"Thanks, Grace. I'll give it to Marco. He has a source at the DMV who'll trace it."

"Tell us what happened," Lottie said as they gathered around. So I gave them a two-minute briefing on what had transpired, including Oliver's odd behavior afterward. "One minute he was stammering in fear and the next he was standing at attention."

"Is there any possibility that Marco was right about Oliver setting this up?" Lottie asked.

"When that car stopped in front of him, Lottie, Oliver looked terrified. I'd have a hard time believing he hired someone to scare him like that."

"There must be a way to find out," Grace said. "Could you have a chat with Libby? She might have some insight."

"Why don't you go talk to her right now?" Lottie suggested. "I'm curious myself, and then maybe you won't have to waste any more time doing those stakeouts.

Besides, it's quiet here. We've got a few orders to finish this afternoon, but that's no problem."

I glanced at my watch. One fifteen. I'd have time to run across the square to Blume's and still have several hours to help with the orders. "I'll take you up on it. I need to talk to Oliver about the police report anyway."

"On a related topic," Grace said, "four calls came in for you while you were gone. One was from Dave, informing you that Cora is presently being questioned at the jail. The second was from Sally Mitchum, who said she wanted to drop off something for you later today. The third was from the gent who owns the costume shop. I wrote down his name and phone number, and it's on the spindle. I think you'll be quite interested in his report." She rocked back on her heels, looking quite pleased with herself.

I knew she was dying to tell me, so I said, "What was his report, Grace?"

"He remembered selling a red wig to a stout woman with gray hair and a hard-to-understand British accent."

"Cora!"

Grace beamed. "Yes, indeed. She bought it just a few days before Delphi's murder."

"Great work, Grace. I'll tell Dave and he can pass the information on. What was the last call?"

"Your mother, dear, reminding you that dinner will be at her house tonight."

With Grace around, who needed voice mail?

Before I left, I put in a call to Dave. "Guess who bought a red wig? Cora!"

"I'll be damned. Did you get my message that she's at the jail?"

"You bet I did. And I've got a new development to

report regarding Oliver. By the way, do you know if Oliver's alibi for the time of the murder checked out?"

"I haven't heard, but I'll try to find out."

"Great. I'll see you at five o'clock."

Blume's Art Shop had a black swag across the top of the door and the sign was turned to CLOSED. No lights were on in the showroom, but when I cupped my hands around my eyes to peer through the glass pane, I could see a glow coming from behind the blue curtain. I knocked on the door, but no one responded, so I headed for the back, where I saw the Blume's van parked in a nook formed by two buildings of different depths. I rapped on the heavy fire door. "It's Abby, Oliver. Are you in there?"

In a moment I heard a bolt slide. Then the door opened a few inches and a deep-set eye appeared. "State your business, ma'am," Oliver commanded.

"My business is that I need to talk to you, and I'm not in the mood to play games."

"I'll need a password, ma'am."

What didn't he understand about not in the mood for games? "I don't know, Oliver. How about O.O.T.T.O.?"

"Not acceptable."

"You never gave me the password. How am I supposed to know?"

"You should know. But I can't talk anyway, ma'am. I'm on assignment."

He could have told me that at the start. "Well, I'm on assignment, too. I'm carrying an important message for you from command central."

His one eye blinked a few times. "You'll have to be quick about it, ma'am."

"I'll be so quick you'll hardly know I was here."

He opened the door barely wide enough for me to squeeze inside. I stood in the storage room amid huge shipping crates, some empty and others waiting to be unpacked of their art. A decorative folding screen partitioned one corner to form an office, where I could see part of a lovely antique red Chinese cabinet and desk.

"Where's Libby?" I asked, glancing around.

Oliver shifted from foot to foot, rubbing the top of his head, as though my being there made him nervous. "She went to the bank down the street. What's the message?"

"You have to go over to the police station to sign off on the report about the Buick."

"Not acceptable, ma'am."

"Why not?"

He kept rubbing his hair. "I have to get back to work."

"Would you sign it if I brought it to you?"

He thought about it, then gave a single nod. "Are you going to do a stakeout this evening, ma'am?"

I sighed inwardly at the thought of dinner with my zany family followed by hours of sitting in my car keeping watch over a garage apartment. Talk about a wild Friday night. "Sure."

He crouched on the cement floor and motioned for me to do likewise. "Here's the plan, ma'am. Park one block away from my apartment, then call my cell phone and I'll tell you where the point of contact will be."

"Point of contact?" I felt like I was in a bad episode of *Without a Trace.*

"Drop-off locale." He scowled, clearly exasperated. "The place to leave the report."

"I get it, Oliver."

"What's our rendezvous time?"

"How about eight o'clock?"

He pushed back his sleeve, revealing a large-faced watch with multiple dials on it. "Let's synchronize."

"Let's not and say we did. I have to get back to work."

He jumped to his feet, marched to the door, and opened it just a little.

"I'm not going to fit, Oliver. You have to open it wider."

He put his eye to the door to check the alley, then opened it half a foot more. "The coast is clear."

"One more thing, Oliver. Did Detective Wells ask you for an alibi for Monday morning?"

"Confirmed."

"What did you tell her?"

His gaze moved off to the side. "I told her I was sleeping, ma'am. Deep in sleep."

"Did she ask you to prove it?"

"Confirmed."

"*Could* you prove it?"

His gaze shifted again, a sign that he was thinking about his answer. "Confirmed."

"Okay, I'll see you this evening."

I got to the end of the alley just as Libby came around the corner, which was almost like walking into a mirror. Instead of her usual perky self, however, Libby seemed to be plodding along as though burdened and blue. I wanted to credit it to her having just buried her mother, yet I hadn't shaken that niggling doubt that Libby might have killed her.

"Abby," she cried, wrapping her arms around me and laying her head on my shoulder, "thanks for coming down to check up on me. When you didn't come to her funeral service yesterday, I thought . . . well, anyway, you must have been busy, so I forgive you."

She forgave me? *Bite your tongue, Abby. She just lost her mother.*

Libby released me with a quivering sigh. "I miss Mummy so much, Abby. I can't stand it. I keep expecting her to walk into the shop. . . . Losing a mother is so much worse than you could ever imagine. I feel so alone now, and Oliver doesn't even seem to notice she's gone."

"I'm sorry, Libby. I'm sure it's incredibly painful, but maybe Oliver is preoccupied because of his stalker. You know how it feels to be stalked, don't you?" I watched her expression, waiting for a flicker of guilt. Instead, she just grew annoyed.

"Don't believe everything Oliver tells you, Abby."

"In this case, Libby, there really is a car. I took photos of it."

"Why were you taking photos?"

"Because your brother hired me to find out who's been following him."

Libby threw up her hands in disbelief. "I swear, Oliver wants everyone in town to know he's crazy."

"What are you talking about?"

"Haven't you figured it out? My brother is ill, Abby. He's got a paranoid personality disorder and is on prescription medication—or at least he's supposed to be. Stupid Oliver takes it for a while, feels better, then thinks he doesn't need it and goes off of it. Then his paranoia comes back. That's why I said not to believe everything he tells you."

That would explain Oliver's ranting about having to

hide and the fear that he would be put away. But it didn't explain the car. "I photographed a black sedan driving past his apartment last night and down Franklin Street around noon today. How do you explain that?"

She sighed as though exasperated. "Was it a Buick LeSabre?"

"You know the car?"

"Of course I know the car. It belongs to one of Oliver's weirdo war game buddies. They're playing spy, Abby, and they've suckered you into it."

CHAPTER EIGHTEEN

"Wait a minute. You're saying Oliver's *friend* is tailing him," I asked Libby, "as part of a spy game?"

"His name is Tom McDoyle. He and Oliver went to high school together. He lives in Starke County now, but they're still close friends. Look him up if you don't believe me."

Tom McDoyle. I pulled out my notepad and wrote it down.

"Do you understand how crazy my brother is?" Libby asked. "These games are his entire life. He has a hard time separating them from reality. He's almost thirty years old, and I have to employ him as my delivery guy because he can't keep a job anywhere else. How pathetic is that?"

Almost as pathetic as a girl who has to take over someone else's identity.

"But if Tom is his friend," I asked, "why would Oliver be afraid of him?"

Libby shrugged. "Maybe Oliver forgot he was still playing the game. It's understandable, isn't it, given his mental condition and how our lives have been destroyed this past week? Honestly, Abby, you have no idea how bad my brother gets. When he's off his meds, he puts aluminum foil over his windows, his computer monitor, and even his TV screen, and he refuses to go outside if the sun is up. He sees enemies everywhere, and these stupid games of his only feed his paranoia. I'm afraid one of these days he'll think I'm an enemy and try to hurt me."

Libby sighed. "The truth is that Oliver's illness is getting worse, and I don't know what to do about it. Mummy always made sure he took his meds. Now I'm stuck with him, but I can't watch him every minute. What am I supposed to do, commit my brother to an institution because he forgets to take his pills?"

What could I say to that? "I'm sorry, Libby."

"Me, too," she said in disgust, walking away.

I headed back to Bloomers, mulling over Libby's revelation. Could Oliver's paranoia have caused him to kill his mother? Or would Libby exaggerate his problems for her own reasons?

As soon as I got back to the shop, I filled Lottie and Grace in on the new information, then called the operator and asked for a listing for Tom McDoyle in Starke County. She gave me two numbers, and I hit pay dirt on my first try.

"Hi, Tom, this is Abby Knight. I'm a friend of Oliver Blume's."

"No, you're not," a high, reedy, very skeptical male voice said. "Oliver doesn't have any girlfriends."

Girlfriend? *Ew.* "I'm not his girlfriend. Oliver hired me to investigate a matter for him, and I'd appreciate it if you could answer a few questions. Do you own a black Buick LeSabre?"

"Why?" he answered cautiously.

"Is that a yes?"

"That's privileged information, ma'am," he said crisply, using the same monotone inflection Oliver used.

"I'm going to take that as a yes. Have you been tailing Oliver as part of a spy game?"

"That's privileged information, ma'am."

"Well, I have a privileged message for you, Tom. The mission has been scrubbed."

"Mission?"

"Your spy game."

Silence. Then, "Are you sure you're not with the enemy forces?"

"Let me put it bluntly, Tom. Stop following Oliver or I'll sic the cops on you."

He hung up on me. I was really getting tired of that.

"Abby, dear," Grace said, coming through the curtain. "Sally Mitchum is here and she has a surprise for you."

I followed Grace through the curtain, where I found Sally standing beside a young Latina girl with long dark hair and a pretty face. I recognized the girl at once, even though this time she was smiling. "Maria," I said, giving her a hug. "It's great to see you again."

"You, too." Maria dipped her head shyly.

Sally said, "Maria has something for you, Abby."

The girl picked up a small gift bag from the floor and handed it to me. "This is to thank you for helping me, and for sending Mrs. Mitchum to me."

I was stunned. Lottie and Grace came over to watch as I opened the gift bag, unfolded the bright pink tissue paper, and removed the gift inside, a silver locket on a long silver chain. I held it up so everyone could admire the oval turquoise stone set in silver.

"I love it," I said, slipping the chain over my head, while Lottie sniffled tearfully and Grace dabbed her eyes with a tissue. "I'm so glad we were able to help you."

Now, *that* was a locket I'd wear with pride.

I didn't have to plan a dramatic entrance for our five o'clock meeting that day because Marco strode out of Down the Hatch just as I was leaving Bloomers. We walked around the square together, careful not to make bodily contact, only small talk, such as, "How's the family?" "How's business?" "Great weather for November, isn't it?" "Can I smack you upside the head for taking Libby's case?" Okay, that last one was wishful thinking.

Dave was on the phone when we arrived, but he motioned for us to have seats. "That was Sergeant Reilly," he said, replacing the receiver in the cradle. "He was good enough to let me know what's been happening with Cora. Apparently Detective Wells has been questioning her all afternoon. Cora's real name, by the way, is Corabelle Finklestein."

"I can see why she used an alias," I drawled.

"Has Cora admitted to anything?" Marco asked.

"She's maintaining her innocence," Dave replied. "On the subject of stealing money from Blume's cash drawer, she said Oliver told her to take it as a gift."

I would have laughed at Cora's lame excuse, except that after what Libby had told me about Oliver's obsession with his war games and his paranoia, maybe he *had* told her to take the money. Maybe that was part of his spy game. Or maybe he was setting Cora up as a suspect for murder.

"Does Cora have an alibi for the morning of the murder?" Marco asked.

"According to Reilly, she said she stayed at a motel on the east side of Detroit, Michigan, on Sunday night," Dave replied. "The police are sending someone up there to investigate."

"Then they're treating Cora as a serious murder suspect?" I asked.

"You bet they arc," Dave said, "because they also found a car key in her purse that appears to be for an older-model Chevrolet. Naturally, Cora is claiming not to know how it got there. She also claims she never got a driver's license here because we drive on the wrong side of the street, and she can't manage that."

"Here's another piece of evidence." I handed Dave the paper with the costume-shop owner's information on it. "That man will testify that Cora bought a red wig a week before Delphi was murdered."

"A red wig, a Chevy key, a theft, and a flight to Canada," Marco said. "That should be enough to get an indictment."

"Let's hope you're right," Dave said. "Then Libby will be off the hook. I'd better call Lisa Wells and let her know about the red wig."

While he made his call, Marco said quietly, "I hear you talked to Libby about her brother this afternoon."

"She sure got that news bulletin to you fast. Did she tell you that Oliver is paranoid?"

"Libby mentioned it, but she didn't seem to want to

discuss it. My understanding is that Delphi worked hard to keep it quiet. She worried that her reputation would suffer."

"That's cold."

"No one ever accused Delphi of having a heart," Marco said.

Dave hung up and turned back to us. "Detective Wells will get a statement from the costume-shop owner. Good work, Abby."

"Actually, it was Grace who got that information. I'll pass along your thanks."

"Anything else to report?" Dave asked, looking from me to Marco.

"I have news," I said, "but first, were you able to find out if Oliver had a good alibi?"

"Phooey," Dave said. "I forgot to ask. I'll make a note of it right now."

He took notes as I told him about the black Buick, my follow-up phone call to Oliver's friend, and my subsequent discussion with Libby about Oliver's paranoia.

"Libby says the stalking is part of a spy game," I said, "and that Oliver simply forgot about it. But how could Oliver forget what his friend's car looked like?"

Marco stretched out his legs. "I still wonder if Oliver didn't scheme with his buddy to fool Abby so she'd back him up when he claimed he was being stalked by his mother's killer. He probably wasn't counting on Abby finding out who the stalker was."

"Hey!" I said, giving him a glare.

"I'm not saying you're not capable," Marco said, "just that Oliver might have been counting on your inexperience."

"Is there a way to find out if Oliver truly has been diagnosed with paranoia and is on medication?" I asked Dave.

"You know the rules about doctor-patient confidentiality," Dave said.

"I was hoping you'd have a way around it," I answered. "I guess I'll just have to break into Oliver's apartment and take a peek inside his medicine cabinet."

At the look of incredulity on Dave's face, and the scowl on Marco's, I quickly added, "Just kidding." I'd only take a peek if I was already *inside* his apartment.

"What are you thinking?" Dave asked me. "That Oliver might have committed the murder in a paranoid state?"

"I don't have a strong gut feeling about him, but he has to be considered. If he's supposed to be on medication to control his paranoia, then his mental state at the time of the murder would probably be influenced by whether he actually took his meds that day. It would help to know if he had been prescribed medication. I'll try to sound him out about that this evening when I drop off the police report. Obviously, I won't be filing the report now that we know who the Buick belongs to, but it'll give me an excuse to meet with him."

"You're going there tonight?" Marco asked.

"That's my plan."

"Then I'm going with you."

"Thanks, but Oliver won't cooperate if you're there."

"I'll stay out of sight."

"Let him go with you," Dave said.

Great. Another torturous car ride with Marco.

Dave pulled a piece of paper from his file. "This is a

copy of the report from the state crime lab. Their finger-print analyst identified Libby's, Oliver's, and Delphi's prints inside Delphi's house—no surprises there, since they all had access. The wine bottle that they believe is the murder weapon was too smudged to print."

"What makes them believe the wine bottle is the mur-der weapon?" I asked.

"The blow to Delphi's head was made by a curved ob-ject, and the bottle was on the floor near the body. DNA testing is ongoing, and as you know, the results can take weeks, sometimes months, to get back. There's no report from the trace analysts yet, either. I'm assuming they're still combing through all the evidence they collected." He closed the file. "That's all I have. Is there anything else to report?"

"Did you ever ask Libby about Roshni Shah and that restraining order?" I asked.

"Yes, and Libby said Roshni was aware that the order had been falsely filed, but apparently there's animosity between them, so Libby wasn't surprised by Roshni's claims. As for the restraining order, Libby said Nolan Grant had made suggestive comments while she was babysitting, and when she threatened to tell his wife, he turned it around to say that she had been the aggressor, then filed a restraining order the next day to validate his claim."

I knew I shouldn't question Libby's assertion in front of the two men who were hired to defend her, but I just couldn't help myself. "If Nolan Grant was the aggressor, why would Libby make herself over to look like his wife? Or buy a car like his wife's? Why would she e-mail her roommate asking for photos and news on

Nolan Grant after the restraining order had been issued? Come on, guys, does that sound like a woman who wanted to keep a man away?"

"I could easily come up with a defense for each one of your points, Abby," Dave said, "but the only thing I needed to know to defend my client was about the existence of the restraining order. The rest isn't important to the case."

Not to the case maybe, but it was to me. "So you believe Libby's version?"

"It's not my job to judge her, Abby. You know that."

Yeah, yeah. That was a defense lawyer's cop-out. And I knew better than to ask Marco. Neither one would tell me his true feelings. Was it possible that they were confused, too?

Marco glanced at me. "Do you want to fill Dave in on Kayla Olin?"

Kayla! So much had happened since I'd talked to her that I'd almost forgotten. "Thanks for the reminder."

The corner of his mouth curled up in that quirky, adorable way of his, making my heart go *twang.* It had to stop doing that!

I told Dave about my visits to Kayla's hospital room, and how I'd managed to get her to talk to me by enlisting the help of a generous plastic surgeon friend of my brother's. I couldn't help bragging a bit; it wasn't often that my way succeeded where Marco's failed, so I took the opportunity to shine. Then I explained why Kayla had walked out of the hospital and how she had ended up at the funeral home for Delphi's viewing.

"The first time I spoke with Kayla's doctor at the hospital," I said, "she told me she didn't believe Kayla had

ever been a danger to anyone but herself. And now Kayla
seems to have passed that danger point. She's very excited about the upcoming surgery and is anticipating a
bright future. I think we can safely cross her off our list
of suspects, especially in light of the evidence the cops
have against Cora."

"Abby, you did a good thing for that young woman,"
Dave said.

"Thanks," I said, beaming.

Dave turned toward Marco. "Do you have anything
you want to report?"

"Not yet," he said cryptically.

"Okay, then," Dave said, closing the file, "let's hope
Cora's alibi doesn't hold up and the prosecutor files an
indictment next week. Tomorrow is Saturday. Should we
leave it that we'll meet Monday unless something comes
up in the meantime?"

Marco gave a nod.

"Works for me," I said. "I have a *biz-zee* weekend."
Right. Real busy. Dining with my parents, doing laundry,
and trying to get Oliver to talk. I needed a social life—
desperately.

Outside Dave's office, Marco fell into step beside me.
"What time are you planning to go to Oliver's place?"

"Eight o'clock."

"Then I'll pick you up at seven forty-five—if that's
okay." He was so stiff and formal with me. Was that how
people acted when they'd broken up? Like they barely
knew each other?

The anger I'd felt at first had faded enough that I
wanted to say, *I understand this is an awkward situation,*

but can't we still be friends? Instead, I said, "On a busy Friday night, don't you have to be at the bar?"

"Chris can take over for me for a while." He was quiet for several minutes, then asked, "So, are you heading for the country club for your family dinner?"

"Not this week. Mom wants us to come to her house instead."

"What's the occasion?"

"Nothing special. She's waiting for a delivery and doesn't want to leave the house."

"What kind of delivery?"

"A truckload of yarn is my best guess."

"Couldn't the package be left on her porch?"

"This is my mom we're talking about, Marco. We don't question her reasons. We just show up and shut up."

After a stop at the police station to pick up the report for Oliver, *show up* was what I did, arriving at my parents' old-fashioned, two-story frame house just as my oldest brother, Jonathan, and his wife, Portia, pulled up in their Jag. I watched as the passenger door opened and Portia wafted out, which is how one exits a car when one is five feet seven and weighs only ninety-three pounds. I had secretly dubbed her Partial Portia.

Having grown up in a wealthy home in the Gold Coast area of Chicago, Portia was something of a snob. If a piece of clothing didn't have a Parisian designer label inside, it wasn't fit to hang in her closet. If her food wasn't cooked to a certain temperature, her minuscule stomach held a protest rally. And if, like today, I was sporting a garden-variety pair of jeans with a generic, long-sleeved cotton T-shirt, her tiny nose would wrinkle like a prune.

For those and other reasons I'd appointed myself Minister of Keeping Portia Humble.

"Hey," I called from the porch as they came up the sidewalk, "where's the beer?"

Portia gave my brother an alarmed glance. "We're having *beer*?"

"Didn't Mom tell you we're having a beer-and-brats night?" I asked.

"Jonathan," Portia said with rising panic, "why didn't you tell me?"

"Tell her you're joking, Abby."

"Fine. I'm joking, Portia. We're actually having Polish sausage and sauerkraut."

With a huff, Portia tossed her long, pale blond hair and marched past me into the house.

"Why do you do that?" Jonathan asked me.

"It's fun." I stepped inside and sniffed the air. There was a peculiar odor inside the house, and it wasn't coming from the kitchen. "Do you smell that?" I asked my brother.

"Why am I thinking of the county fair?" Jonathan asked.

"Hey, kids," my dad called from the back of the house, "come back here."

Dad was in his wheelchair in the kitchen with my brother Jordan, his wife, Kathy, and their only child, Tara, a somewhat gawky but utterly precocious thirteen-year-old who had inherited the Knight family's red hair and freckles.

"Grandma has a surprise for us," Tara announced. She tried to act indifferent, but there was a sparkle of excitement in her eyes.

"Does this surprise have anything to do with her knitting?" I asked Dad.

His eyes twinkled. "You could say that."

"Please prepare us, Dad," Jordan said. "We're begging you."

"I'm not sure that's possible," Dad replied, clearly enjoying the role of insider.

All but Portia groaned. She was too busy sniffing the contents of the pots simmering on the stove. "Are these organic beets? Does anyone know?"

"Are you ready?" Mom called from behind the closed door of her studio.

"Yes, Grandma," Tara answered, rolling her eyes.

I heard odd clicking noises on the other side of the door, like tap shoes on ceramic tiles.

"Okay, come in slowly, one at a time, and keep your voices down."

We left Portia inspecting the food and filed into Mom's spacious studio.

"Everyone," she said, stroking the neck of a six-foot-tall, slender, silky-coated llama, "meet Taz."

For a long moment no one uttered a word. We merely gaped. Finally Jonathan found his voice. "You bought a *llama*?"

"They make great pets," Mom said, holding on to Taz's leash so he didn't shy away. "They're very affectionate and quite intelligent, as intelligent as some dogs. Isn't he beautiful? His coloring reminds me of a calico cat. Tara, do you want to pet him?"

Tara stepped behind her dad. "He might bite me."

"Taz is very gentle," Mom explained. "And his teeth are flat, designed for chewing grass. He even has an under bite. Want to show off your teeth, Taz?"

The llama regarded us warily through his big brown

eyes, obviously preferring not to bare his teeth to perfect strangers.

"Approach him slowly," Mom said, drawing Tara toward the animal. "He's very timid. In llama years, he's still a teenager."

"You're not going to keep him in the house, are you?" Jordan asked.

"Of course not," Mom said with a laugh. "We're having the toolshed turned into a stable, with a heater and an air conditioner inside, although we won't use the heater much because llamas prefer the cold. See how much luxuriant fur he has, except around his middle? We have to keep that area clipped so he won't overheat. Then I can send the fleece out to be carded and woven into yarn so I can knit with it."

"Are we to understand," Jonathan asked, using his official doctor's voice, "that you bought this llama so you can knit sweaters?"

"Not just sweaters, Jonathan. Scarves, hats, mittens, shawls, even throws. Llama fur doesn't contain lanolin, you see, so it won't make you itch. The problem is that you can't find yarn made from llama fleece, so I decided to go right to the source. Isn't that clever?" She gazed around at us. "Isn't anyone going to say anything?"

Couldn't Mom feel the air in the room vibrating from all of our silent screams?

"I think it's awesome, Grandma," Tara said, fearlessly stroking the animal's soft fur. "I like Taz. How did you think of his name?"

"He was already named," Mom said. "Actually, Taz is short for Catastrophe."

"Which is what this is going to be," I muttered to Jordan, "a catastrophe."

He snickered.

"What did you say, Abigail?" Mom asked. She had ears like a bat.

"I said, 'Welcome to the family, Catastrophe.' "

"I'm glad you approve, honey," Mom said to me, "because I'd like to sell my knitting projects at Bloomers."

I bit my lip to keep my scream from going public.

"What's this big surprise that kept us from dining at the club tonight?" Portia asked in a snippy voice as she joined us. I stepped aside to give her a clear view of the llama. She took one look at the furry beast and staggered back against Jonathan. "What is *that* thing doing here?"

"I was wrong about the sauerkraut and Polish sausage," I told her. "We're having roast llama for dinner."

Portia wafted to the floor like a feather from a nest. My job there was done.

"Did your mother get her delivery?" Marco asked later as he drove me out to Oliver's apartment.

"Um—" Did I really want Marco to know that my mother bought a llama so she could have her own supply of yarn? He'd already witnessed many of her other strange projects, including the neon-hued Dancing Naked Monkey Table, and the seven-foot palm-tree coatrack, made up of many green hands on the ends of bark-coated, curving arms. Weren't those bad enough?

Then again, what did it matter? It wasn't like he was planning to marry into my family.

"Yes, it did arrive, or I guess I should say Catastrophe arrived."

He glanced at me in concern. "A catastrophe? What happened?"

"Catastrophe is the name of her pet llama."

Marco nearly blew a stop sign. "Did you say *llama*?"

"You heard me right. Mom bought it for its fleece. She'll have to shear it, then send the fleece away to be turned into yarn."

"How do you take care of a llama? Aren't they like camels?"

"More like alpacas, kind of a cross between a deer with long, soft fur and a small camel with a sparkling personality. They eat grains, but not a lot, so it doesn't cost too much to feed them, and they're really very gentle. Mom fully believes Catastrophe will behave like a pet dog."

Marco shook his head in disbelief. "I can't believe she's going to keep a llama in town."

"Yep. In the toolshed, which they're turning into a stable."

"What does your dad have to say about it?"

"I think he likes the idea. He left the dinner table early so he could spend time with Taz. That's the llama's nickname."

"Aren't there laws about what kinds of animals can be kept in town?"

"I'm assuming my dad would know about that. But you haven't heard the best part. I get to sell Mom's knitting projects at Bloomers."

"I don't know what to say except I'm sorry. I can guess what you'll be getting for Christmas this year."

"And probably for the foreseeable future." I sighed. "Knowing Mom, she'll slipcover everything in her house with Taz's fleece. Then we can call it the catastrophe house and mean it."

"It could be worse. Remember the mirrored tiles?"

I groaned at the recollection. A trip to the bathroom at my parents' house had been like a visit to the House of Mirrors at the fair. Some body parts just didn't warrant that much reflection.

Marco turned onto the road that intersected Delphi's street and pulled over to the curb beneath a huge maple tree that blocked most of the streetlight. From there, I had a good view of Oliver's apartment while still being hidden from view. I noticed the Blume van wasn't in sight.

I pulled out my cell phone and punched in a number, explaining to Marco, "I have to call Oliver so he can tell me where to meet him."

Marco kept watch over the apartment and surrounding street while I made the call. It rang five times, then went to Oliver's voice mail. "It's Abby," I said, "O.O.T.T.O. I have the report. I'm here. Call me back."

"What's O.O.T.T.O.?" Marco asked.

"One of the trusted ones. That's what he calls me."

Marco rolled his eyes. I glanced away, wishing I were one of Marco's trusted ones.

We waited for ten minutes; then I called him again and left a second message.

"Did he know what time you were coming?"

"I told him around eight."

After another ten minutes, I phoned Blume's Art Shop, but no one answered there, either.

"Maybe Libby knows something," Marco said, dialing her number, which I noticed he'd memorized. "Hi, it's Marco," he said when she answered. "What's Oliver up to this evening?"

He listened, then said, "So you haven't seen him since five o'clock? Did he mention what he was doing tonight?" He listened again, then said, "It's nothing important. There's no need for you to worry. He's probably asleep or out with his buddies. I'll catch up with him tomorrow."

Another pause, then he said, "Okay, I'll talk to you later."

Later, huh? As in, while on a date?

Marco closed his phone. "Libby doesn't know where he is, and now she's worried. Apparently, Oliver didn't say anything about going out with his friends this evening. In fact, he told her he had a headache and was going straight home after he finished at Blume's."

"Great. Now what should we do?"

Marco checked his watch. "Let's give him another ten minutes. If we don't hear from him by then, we'll investigate."

We sat without talking for ten long minutes, having exhausted all the filler conversation earlier. It was impossible to sit that close to him, almost touching, and not wish he'd pull me into his arms, apologize for being an idiot, and smother me with kisses. But it was not to be.

"That's it," he said. "Let's go check it out."

We got out of the car and started up the block. Marco had dressed all in black, making it easy for him to blend in, but I had worn my navy coat with jeans and brown boots, my red hair uncovered, thinking this was going to be a straightforward meeting. Luckily, there was a thick gray cloud cover that obliterated the moonlight.

"I'll wait across the street," Marco said, pointing to a tall shrub border that ran along the edge of a neighbor's driveway. "Approach his apartment as though you were expected. Ring the doorbell, if there is one, or knock. If he doesn't answer, use your phone to call him again and let him know you're at his door. If he still doesn't answer, come back, and I'll take it from there."

I continued the rest of the way alone, entering the yard through the back gate and climbing the stairs leading to the apartment above the garage. There was no buzzer, so I rapped on the door. No lights showed from behind the blinds, but I would have expected that if Oliver was out or sleeping.

I rapped again, waited another minute, then phoned him. I didn't hear any ringing coming from inside the apartment, and when the call went once again to his voice mail, I hung up. Had Oliver forgotten our meeting? Had he taken something for his headache and gone to sleep?

I started to turn away, ready to give up, then, on a whim, tried the doorknob. To my surprise, the door opened. Well, that was convenient. But it was also odd. People didn't leave doors unlocked anymore, especially not people who were paranoid.

Okay, Abby, this is where you're supposed to go back downstairs and let Marco take over.

Fat chance.

CHAPTER NINETEEN

"O liver? Hey, it's Abby." I stood just inside the open doorway and listened for a reply. Hearing nothing but the distant hum of a refrigerator, I stepped farther into the apartment. A fresh cedar scent filled the air, bringing back not-so-fond memories of the hamsters my brothers owned briefly. I still had nightmares about those few frightening months of listening to hamster wheels turn all night. I'd hardly slept a wink, fearing human mothers ate their young, too.

"Oliver! Hey!" I rapped on the doorframe. "Are you sleeping?"

Silence. I felt for a light switch beside the door and flipped it up. A table lamp turned on, illuminating the living room. Across from me were two blue recliners on either side of a white leather sofa that faced a giant-screen TV. In the middle of the polished wood floor was a blue and white area rug, with blue miniblinds over the windows. The room was immaculate, symmetrical, and sparsely decorated. No photos, knickknacks, or magazines were to be seen. Also no aluminum foil.

"Okay, Oliver, I'm inside your apartment now. If you're here, please come out. I'd hate to walk in on you naked, or . . ." *Dead?*

I shook off my trepidation. If something had happened to Oliver, surely I'd have seen signs of a disturbance by now. As I tiptoed across the wooden floor to peek around a doorway into the kitchen, my cell phone buzzed in my purse. About time, I thought, fully expecting to see Oliver's name on the screen. But it was Marco.

"I can handle this one myself," I muttered, and slid the phone back inside my purse.

"I'm stepping into your kitchen now, Oliver," I called. Somehow it was reassuring to keep up a running monologue. I felt for another light switch and a row of overhead lights came on. "This is some setup you have," I said aloud.

The kitchen had a black granite countertop, cherry cabinets, a wood floor, and stainless steel appliances. Against a side wall beneath a window was a glass-topped pedestal table with four chairs. Once again, the room was spotless, almost sterile.

I peeked inside a kitchen cabinet and saw stacks of dinner plates, dessert plates, cups, and saucers, everything symmetrically placed, with all the handles on the cups pointing in the same direction. I was betting Oliver had an obsessive-compulsive disorder on top of his paranoia.

Suddenly, I heard the floor creak in the living room. Oops. Marco must have figured out what I was up to. Or was that Oliver?

Or the killer?

I glanced around for something to use as a weapon, then opened a cabinet under the sink and grabbed the window cleaner. My boot slid on a small pile of black dirt on the floor, which seemed odd in light of the cleanliness of the place.

"Hello?" I called, moving toward the doorway, my finger on the bottle's trigger spray.

Marco stood in the center of the living room looking decidedly peeved. This called for a defensive strategy. I hoped it worked on Marco as well as it had on Reilly.

"Where have you been?" I asked, putting one hand on my hip.

He glowered, clearly not as gullible as Reilly. "Don't give me that. You were supposed to come back down and let me take over."

"Yes, but we made that plan before I knew the door was unlocked."

"Which is an even greater reason for you to get the hell out of here. You could have been attacked."

"Could have, would have"—I shrugged—"all water under the bridge. Anyway, I'm armed." I held up the spray bottle. "Besides, no one's here. I've been calling Oliver's name for the past five minutes. If he were sleeping, he would have heard me by now."

"You still shouldn't have taken the risk."

As Marco gazed around the living room, taking in the big television, I said, "Nice digs for a deliveryman. A little too blue for my tastes, but I'm sure Delphi provided the furnishings. And wait till you see the kitchen. It's a cook's dream."

"What's up that hallway?"

"I was just about to investigate."

Marco put a hand on my arm to stop me. "Would you allow me go first, please? You don't know what you'll find up there."

I wouldn't find anything if *he* went first. But I stepped back graciously and let him proceed. He stopped at the first doorway and turned on the light, revealing a luxurious bathroom. I followed him inside, staring around at the marble sinks, gold fixtures, bidet, Jacuzzi, and walk-in shower.

"Wow," was all I could say.

I opened the mirrored medicine cabinet and found four bottles of saline nasal spray, four boxes of bandages, four tubes of antibacterial ointment—but no prescription medicine. "If Oliver is on meds, he must have them with him," I told Marco.

There was one more doorway to investigate at the end of the hall, most likely opening up to the bedroom. Marco approached cautiously and used his penlight to do a quick visual sweep of the interior. I stood just behind him, peering over his shoulder, but it was clear at once that Oliver wasn't there. Behind a drapery of gauzy mosquito netting, the queen-sized bed was neatly made.

Marco flipped a switch on the inside wall and a black light attached to a ceiling fan came on, throwing the bedroom into total weirdness. The cedar scent was stronger here, I noticed. I followed Marco inside and glanced around, expecting to see a hamster cage, but there was none in sight.

Two posters on the wall entitled, EXTREME MARINES glowed incandescently with steroid-fueled males clad in war gear. Twin saber swords, their blades forming an *X*, hung above a low dresser. Army helmets made the bases for twin dresser lamps, and a collection of old army medals filled two shadow boxes. Everything in the room was perfectly symmetrical.

Marco found another light switch and the dresser lamps came on. He opened a sliding door, exposing three sets of camouflage fatigues hanging neatly on the rod. Three pairs of army boots were lined up underneath. I was guessing Oliver was wearing the fourth outfit. There were also four black cardboard boxes on the shelf above the pole, but it was the laptop computer sitting on the large, black metal desk nearby that caught my attention. What would Oliver's laptop reveal about him?

Suddenly, we heard Libby call, "Oliver? Hello?"

Marco headed for the living room, calling, "Hey, Libby, I'm here with Abby."

Great. Let Marco deal with her. I was more interested in the laptop. I lifted the lid and moved the roller ball to activate it. Instantly, a huge photograph of a brown and cream snake's head filled the screen, its opened mouth poised to strike, its long, curved fangs gleaming menacingly. There were no icons, just a cursor blinking beside the words *Enter Password.*

If you insist.

I glanced around to make sure no one was watching, then typed *Oliver* and hit Enter. *Invalid Password* appeared, although I had expected as much. *Hmm.* What might Oliver use? I tried the easy words—*spy, army, Delphi, Blume,* and even *Libby*—with no luck. They'd been long shots anyway. Oliver wouldn't use a word or phrase someone could easily guess.

"Honestly, I don't understand where he could be," Libby said, coming up the hallway.

I shut the cover and turned just as Libby came into the bedroom. Seeing me standing beside the laptop in her brother's room, she cast me a suspicious look.

"He's not in here," I said with a shrug, edging away from the desk.

"You talked to Oliver this afternoon," she said. "Didn't he tell you where he was going?"

"No. Why would he tell me?"

"You seem to be his new confidant," she replied in a snippy tone, almost as though she was jealous of me.

"Believe me, Libby, he doesn't confide in me."

Libby turned to Marco. "I'm really worried. He's not even answering his cell phone."

"Did Oliver seem anxious or upset when you talked to him?" Marco asked me.

"I wouldn't say upset, but he was definitely edgy. I figured it was because he was supposed to be unpacking crates, not wasting his time talking to me."

"Wasting time has never bothered Oliver," Libby said sarcastically.

"Does he have the company van?" I asked her.

Libby shook her head. "If he went somewhere, he either walked or got a ride with one of his friends."

"I'll call his friend in Starke County," I said, pulling my phone out of my pocket. "Maybe he knows where Oliver is."

I called information and asked for a number for Thomas McDoyle. This time I recognized the first number the operator gave me, and quickly dialed it. "Hi, Tom, this is Abby Knight again. Do you know where Oliver is?"

"Why?" he asked warily, his reedy voice breaking like a preteen's.

"Because his sister is here with me and she's worried about him. Oliver didn't say where he was going and he's not at home. So do you know?"

"That's privileged information, ma'am."

Not the military act again! Marco was standing with his arms folded, waiting, so I whispered, "Tom is playing hard to get. Want to persuade him?"

Marco held out his hand for the phone. "I'm going to say this once, Tom, so listen up." He was using his gruff cop's voice. I loved it when he talked tough. "If you don't tell me what you know about Oliver's whereabouts in the next ten seconds, you'd better expect me at your door—" He paused, listening, then said, "Where?"

Libby tugged on Marco's sleeve. "Is Oliver okay? Does Tom know where he is?"

Marco gave her a thumbs-up. "Can you get in touch with him? Cool. Call him and tell him no one is after him. The game is over, and it's safe to go home."

"Tell him the coast is clear," I whispered.

Libby groaned, dropping her head into her hands. "He's off his meds. I know he is."

"Okay, listen, Tom," Marco said. "I'm going to be expecting you to call back as soon as you speak to Oliver. Got it?"

Marco ended the call and handed me my phone as he said to Libby, "Oliver phoned Tom shortly after five o'clock today and asked him to come pick him up because *they* were after him. Tom says he dropped your brother off at the edge of a forest preserve around seven o'clock. Oliver had a backpack with him. Tom promised he'd try to get him home tonight."

"So what am I supposed to do now?" Libby said petulantly. "Wait here all night for him to come home? What if he hurts himself out there in the forest? What if Tom can't reach him? Should I call the police and report him missing?"

"Oliver isn't a child," Marco said. "Besides, I can tell you from experience that the police won't search for him until he's been missing for forty-eight hours."

"Forty-eight hours?" Libby cried. "Do you know all the things that could happen to him in forty-eight hours?" She sank down onto the end of the bed, covered her face, and wailed, "Mummy would be so upset with me. If anything happens to Oliver, it's all my fault."

"Oh, for heaven's sake, Libby," I snapped. "Stop that. You're not your brother's keeper. You can't control his life. That's what your mother did. Is that how you want to be, too?"

"Don't you talk that way about Mummy," she cried, jumping to her feet. "Everything she did was for our benefit."

"Ladies," Marco called, "we've got more important concerns right now." He was standing in front of a door in the corner of the bedroom. "Libby, where does this lead?"

Still glaring at me, she said, "That's a walk-in closet."

"Do you know why it's locked?" he asked.

"Oliver told me it was private. He's always been very secretive about it. I figured it had something to do with his stupid army games."

"Let's find the key," Marco said.

While he checked the tops of the doorframes and window frames, Libby pulled open the dresser drawers, searching through neat rows of brown socks and boxer shorts. I went back to the desk and pulled open the top drawer. Inside was a shallow black metal storage container with four identical black pens lined up neatly inside. Another container held four erasers, and another, four boxes of paper clips.

I opened the second drawer and found four sleek black staplers and four boxes of staples. The third revealed four new ink cartridges. Clearly, Oliver had a thing for the number four. By all that I'd seen so far, my amateur diagnosis of OCD seemed to be right on target.

While I was at it, I also checked around for eavesdropping devices, remembering that Oliver had been certain someone had gotten inside his apartment to bug it. But I couldn't find anything the least bit suspicious.

I turned around to see Marco remove a thin strip of metal from his wallet and crouch in front of the closet door. He inserted the strip into the lock and carefully worked it until the bolt slid back, then cautiously opened the door, using his penlight to look around. He spotted a chain hanging from an overhead light and pulled it.

Immediately, he jumped back with a muttered, "Shit," and pulled the door shut.

"What is it?" Libby asked as Marco hurriedly punched in numbers on his cell phone.

"Hello, Sean? It's Marco."

He was calling Reilly? What the heck was behind that door?

CHAPTER TWENTY

"Listen, Sean, I need you to get someone from animal control out to the Blume residence right away," Marco said. "Tell them we've got a snake on the loose"—at that, Libby let out a scream that could have peeled paint off the wall—"and judging by the size of the aquarium tank, he's a big guy."

Libby scrambled onto the bed and pulled the mosquito netting around her. Taking advantage of her hysteria, I climbed onto the desk, pretending to be frightened so I'd have a reason to be near the laptop. No need for them to know I wasn't afraid of snakes.

"Tell them I'm inside the apartment over the garage," Marco continued. "The door is open." He listened a moment, then said, "No, I'm not alone. Abby and Libby are with me."

Why did I suddenly feel like half of the Doublemint gum twins?

"Is the s-snake inside the c-closet?" Libby asked as Marco took one of the saber swords from the wall.

"All I know," Marco said as he prepared to open the closet door, "is that the top is off and the glass tank is empty. And by the way, that was one pampered snake. Oliver has quite a setup in there."

"Now I know why I smelled cedar," I said. "There must be shavings on the bottom of the tank—except how do you know it's a snake tank if there's no snake?"

He paused to glance back at me. "Do you really care to know?"

"Don't I?"

"Trust me. You don't."

I wasn't sure what that meant, but he was right; I didn't care. I was more interested in the laptop.

"Marco, I'm afraid," Libby whined. "Don't go in there."

"Just stay where you are," he cautioned, which I deemed a completely unnecessary warning, given the way she was clinging to the netting.

Marco eased the door open and peered inside. Using the tip of the sword, he poked around, then stepped inside and shut the door behind him. I would have used that opportunity to work on the password for the laptop, but Libby was staring at me through the holes in the netting like a frightened bug about to be devoured by a spider.

Marco emerged moments later with the news that the snake was no longer in the closet. Hearing that, Libby's skin turned the exact color of the netting, giving her the appearance of a beeswax candle with a flame on top.

"Where would a snake hide?" Marco mused, gazing speculatively around the room.

"Under the b-bed," Libby whispered, pulling her knees up to her chest.

Marco crouched down at the foot of the bed and shone

his penlight underneath the box spring, then checked beneath the dresser and desk.

"They like to curl up in small spaces," I said. "Don't people find them in their bathtub drains and toilets and wastebaskets?"

At that, Libby let out a gasp of alarm. "M-mailbox," she whispered, staring at us with saucer eyes.

Marco and I both glanced around the room, looking for the mailbox in question.

"N-not in here," she said. "I mean Oliver m-must have put his snake in my m-mailbox."

"Why would Oliver want to scare you?" Marco asked.

"I d-don't know. He knows how snakes t-terrify me."

"Would that mean your stalker is out of the picture?" I couldn't help asking, although I did manage to keep the snide tone out of my voice.

Suddenly Libby's eyes got even wider, which I hadn't thought was humanly possible. "M-maybe he was trying to kill me."

Somehow I found that hard to believe. Oliver wouldn't kill off an ally. "Come on, Libby," I said. "We don't know that the snake in your mailbox was poisonous, or if it was even your brother's snake. A lot of people keep snakes."

"N-name one," she said, rubbing her arms.

She had me there. Still, the reptile had shown up in Libby's mailbox days ago. Would Oliver have been able to keep a cool head around Libby after having sicced his snake on her? And if he was truly concerned about spies watching him, would he keep the empty snake tank in his closet as evidence?

Marco sat on the end of the bed. "Do you believe Oliver is a threat to you, Libby?"

"I don't want to believe it, but . . ." She hunched her shoulders forward and pressed her lips into a flat, blue line, as though she couldn't bring herself to finish the sentence.

Her consternation certainly seemed genuine, but I couldn't keep myself from doubting her. I pivoted around and opened up the laptop. "Remind me what the snake-in-the-box looked like."

"B-big, b-brown, s-scaly, long f-fangs." Her teeth were clattering against one another.

I turned the laptop so she could see the photo. "Did it look like this?"

Libby took one look at the hissing-snake photo, then hid her face in her hands. "Yes."

"If this snake," I told Marco, pointing to the picture on the screen, "is the same one that was in the closet, and the same one that was put into Libby's mailbox, then I doubt it's in the apartment. I'm sure it escaped soon after she opened the mailbox."

"It's the s-same s-snake," Libby muttered from behind her fingers. "I'll never forget that hideous face."

I heard a car outside, so I swung around to look out the window. "It's Reilly. Animal control just pulled up, too."

"Stay here," Marco said, "until we know for sure that the snake isn't in the apartment."

"Marco, don't leave me," Libby called, stretching out her hand for him, but he was already out of the room. She immediately curled up in a fetal position. I frowned, studying her. Was her fear real or was it an act?

"Police," I heard Reilly call. "We're coming in."

I turned back to the computer, mulling over the snake situation. By the photo on Oliver's laptop and the evidence Marco had seen inside the closet, my guess was that the snake was a pampered pet. So why would Oliver put his spoiled serpent in Libby's mailbox, knowing it would escape when she opened the box? If Oliver had wanted to frighten Libby—or kill her—he'd had plenty of better opportunities. Was it possible that, while in a paranoid state, he'd believed Libby had become his enemy? Could he have turned on his mother for the same reason? I eyed the blinking cursor. Did his laptop hold the answers?

Enter Password, the cursor beckoned.

I could hear Marco having a discussion with Reilly and another man somewhere in the apartment, probably in the living room, so after making sure that Libby was still curled up, her face turned away from me, I tried once again to gain access to the computer. *Military*, *espionage*, *war*, *battle*, *saber sword*—none of them worked.

I heard footsteps in the hall outside, so I quickly turned away from the computer and donned a concerned expression. Seconds later, Marco strode into the room followed by Reilly and a man in a protective jumpsuit, his head encased in a hood with a clear face shield on it, his hands in thick gloves. He carried a long-handled hook in one hand and a sturdy butterfly net in the other. Marco showed them to the closet, then came back to us.

"How about if I escort you out now?" he said to Libby.

"Are you sure it's safe?" she whimpered.

At Marco's nod, she uncurled her legs, peeled back the netting, took his hand, and allowed him to lead her out of the room. Quickly, I swiveled back to the laptop to try a new password: *snake*. Damn. It didn't work, either. *Viper*? Nope. *Serpent*?

"What are you doing?" Reilly asked, peering over my shoulder.

Yikes. I shut the lid and turned my back to it. "Waiting for my escort."

"Sure you are. What were you looking at?"

I opened the lid for him and the snake photo appeared. "That."

"Huh," was his comment. "Looks to me like you were snooping in Oliver's computer."

"No, I wasn't. I don't have the password."

"What a shame," he drawled.

"I know. So let's say that you were going to guess a password for a guy who's into military games and snakes, and may have put his snake in his sister's mailbox to kill her, and has now gone into hiding. What would it be?"

Reilly folded his arms and gazed down at me. "Marco didn't tell me that part. When did Oliver go into hiding?"

"Sometime after five o'clock this evening. According to his buddy Tom, he's in a forest preserve in Starke County. So . . . passwords?" I positioned my fingers over the keypad.

"Do we know *why* Oliver went into hiding?"

"Because he believes someone is after him, which is another reason I need a password. There might be a clue inside." I raised my eyebrows, my fingers poised.

"Forget it," he said.

"Listen, Reilly, this is me being serious now. Something strange is going on with Oliver that needs to be investigated. According to Libby, Oliver is paranoid and, as a result, sees enemies everywhere. He's supposed to be on meds to keep the paranoia under control, but Libby said he keeps going off them. She believes he's off them now, and that his condition is worsening, and that one day he'll mistake her for an enemy and harm her. I checked his medicine cabinet and didn't see any prescription bottles, but he could be carrying them with him."

I paused as the man from animal control stepped out of the closet. "All clear," he said.

As soon as he left the room, I said to Reilly, "Are you with me so far? Okay, then, if we're to believe Libby about Oliver's paranoia getting worse, then we have to believe that Oliver may be dangerous, and if we take that a step further, then he could have been dangerous enough last Monday morning to kill his mother. But the bigger question is, do we believe *Libby*?

"For instance," I continued, "Libby said that when Oliver is off his meds, he covers his windows with aluminum foil. Look around. Do you see any foil? So is he off his meds and dangerous, or does he really take meds at all? Do you see why I want to get inside this computer? I'll bet we'll find things in here that will tell us whether Oliver's mental state is as bad as his sister wants us to think it is."

Reilly cast a quick glance over his shoulder, then said in a hushed voice, "Look, I don't trust Libby any more than you do, and I can understand why you have your suspicions about Oliver, but, well, I probably shouldn't be telling you this yet, so you didn't hear it from me. Don't waste your time on Oliver or Libby."

"Why not?"

"Because neither of them killed Delphi Blume."

CHAPTER TWENTY-ONE

"**D**on't keep me in suspense, Reilly. Was it Cora?"

"You got it. She lied about everything. There's no record of her staying at the motel she claims she was at, or at any other hotel or motel in that area, and no one recognized a photo of her, either."

"What about the key they found in her purse? Did it fit Libby's Corvette?"

"It sure did." Reilly began to list items on his fingers. "Cora had the Corvette key, she was tall enough to have needed to move the car seat back, and she had purchased a red wig—which we learned thanks to your help. Means, motive, opportunity—a slam dunk case."

Reilly hooked his thumbs in his thick black leather belt and rocked back on his heels. "She was indicted an hour ago and is now an inmate of the county jail. So that's why I'm telling you not to waste your time on Oliver or Libby."

I should have felt relieved—after all, my goal had been to make sure every possible suspect was considered until the true killer was caught—but somehow this development wasn't sitting right with me . . . that old gut feeling again. The evidence was simply too neat. I wondered if Reilly felt the same way. "Did the detectives verify that Cora never got a driver's license?"

"I don't know, but she did take a bus to Michigan. Why?"

"Because if she lied about everything, including the driver's license, plus had the stolen cash on her, you'd think she would have rented a car to drive to Canada. It would have been a heck of a lot faster than taking the bus."

"The murder happened early in the morning. Maybe she didn't want to hang around until the car-rental agencies opened."

"Or maybe Cora was telling the truth about not being able to drive in the U.S., in which case she wouldn't have used Libby's car to dispose of Delphi's body, would she? And she wouldn't have needed a key, either. So maybe she didn't lie about *everything*."

"She's a thief, Abby. Why would we believe anything she tells us?"

"I don't know, but I'd sure like a chance to find out. Am I able to visit Cora in jail?"

Reilly looked surprised. "Are you *able* to? Well, sure, but—"

"Awesome." I hopped down from the desk. "How soon can I get in?"

"Whoa. Slow down. I just got done telling you she's been charged with murder. That means you don't need to talk to Cora. If there are any loose ends, Detective Wells will see to it."

"Yeah, right. After deciding Cora is the murderer, do

you think either Detective Wells or the prosecutor will spend time trying to prove Cora *didn't* do it?"

"No, but that's why she'll have a defense attorney."

"Who may or may not be able to convince a jury that she's not guilty. Tell me something, Sarge, are you one hundred percent satisfied that Cora's the killer?"

"Listen to me, Abby. She's been indicted. The investigation is over. *It doesn't matter.*"

"Not to you maybe, but I have to be satisfied in *here*." I tapped my stomach.

He sighed in resignation. "You never give up, do you? Fine. Talk to the matron at the jail. See if she'll get you in. Otherwise, you'll have to wait until visitor day next Tuesday—*if* Cora agrees to see you."

"Talk to the matron?" I shuddered, recalling the harsh, pug-faced woman who'd let me out of lockup. "Well, that's out, then."

"Matron Grody is on vacation this week. Patty is there. Go see her."

That was a different story. Patty had been very fond of my dad and always kind to me. "Thanks for the tip, Reilly."

Hearing footsteps coming up the hallway, Reilly put his finger to his lips. "If it's Marco, I'll fill him in about Cora. You don't know anything about her being charged, got it?"

"I won't say a word about Cora—as long as you don't tell Marco I'm going to visit her."

He knew there was no time to negotiate with me, so he said gruffly, "Deal."

I started to give him a high five, but then Marco strode into the room. Noticing that I was off the desk, he said, "I take it you don't need an escort?"

"No, but thanks anyway."

"I'm still not clear why you were on the desk in the first place," Marco said, giving me one of his inquisitive gazes. "You're not afraid of snakes."

I put a hand on my hip. "How do you know I'm not?"

"Because you told me."

"When?"

"About a week after we first met. We drove out to the dunes to hike through the woods, remember?"

How could I have forgotten such a romantic moment? It was my first clue as to what a gentleman Marco could be. He'd gallantly stepped in front of me when a snake took exception to our crossing his path. I started getting all misty-eyed thinking about it. Boy, how time changed everything. "I remember."

"The maple trees?" he asked huskily.

Another moment I'd never forget. I'd leaned against the trunks of two entwined crimson maples to gaze up at a hawk overhead. Marco had put his arms on either side of me and kissed me like I'd never been kissed before. I used to picture us as those two trees, united for eternity. I was surprised he remembered, though.

I gave him a nod, and he smiled at me with his eyes, as though it was our secret.

The sound of Reilly clearing his throat brought me back to reality. "Sorry to interrupt, but I've got to get going. If you two are going be at the bar tonight, maybe I'll come by with Karen and we can hoist a few brewskies together."

Talk about an awkward moment. Marco glanced down at his shoes, so I said, "I've got something going on tonight. Sorry."

Reilly's gaze moved from me to Marco, his brows drawing together.

"I'll be at the bar all evening," Marco said. "Bring Karen by."

I could tell by Reilly's expression that he knew something wasn't right. But, conveniently, my cell phone rang, so I left, hurrying out of the bedroom as I slipped my phone from my pocket. The man from animal control was standing in the living room, so I stepped into the kitchen to take the call.

"This is Tom McDoyle," the high, reedy voice on the other end said. "I was supposed to call this number after I talked to Oliver."

He was? Oh, wait. Marco had used my phone to speak to him. Amazing how cooperative Tom had become since his little chat with Marco.

I was about to have Tom hold while I located my erstwhile boyfriend, but then I reconsidered. I was pretty sure Reilly was filling Marco in about Cora's indictment, and once Marco knew, he wouldn't feel the need to investigate Oliver any further. I, on the other hand, *did* feel the need.

I moved to the far side of the kitchen and stood by the sink, talking softly so I wouldn't be overheard. "This is Abby Knight. Are you with Oliver now?"

"No, I couldn't find him—it was too dark and he doesn't have his cell phone on. I didn't want that dude I talked to before to think I'd forgotten, so just tell him I'll go back to the forest preserve in the morning. Then I'll call this number again after I find Oliver. Okay?"

"Sounds like a plan, Tom."

I put my phone away and as I turned, my boots made a crunching sound. I glanced down and saw that I'd stepped in the dirt I'd noticed earlier. Hmm. Where had it come from? There were no pots of flowers or herbs in the kitchen that I could see. No signs of dirt being tracked in, either.

I opened the double cabinet doors beneath the sink and saw a tidy row of plastic bottles—four dish detergents and four glass cleaners, lined up like soldiers. Behind the glass cleaners I saw something that looked like sticks poking in the air, so I crouched down for a look. At that moment I heard Reilly and Marco talking as they came down the hallway, so I went absolutely still, hoping they wouldn't catch sight of me.

They continued through the living room, exiting through the front door and pulling it shut behind them. Knowing it wouldn't be long before Marco realized I wasn't waiting for him by his car, I pushed aside the bottles for a better look. There I saw a twelve-inch clay pot with a leaf design carved into the rim. I knew that pot. It was from Bloomers.

I tugged it toward me and saw the reason for the dirt spill. The pot was badly damaged, with huge cracks down its sides and half of the rim broken off, as though the container had tipped over and fallen onto a hard surface. Inside were the remains of a bamboo plant, the reedy stalks broken off a few inches from the base.

Now I knew where the fourth bamboo plant had gone. Had Oliver broken it, then stashed it away so his controlling mother wouldn't drop by and discover his misdeed? But wait. Oliver wouldn't hide a fractured, messy pot in his neat cabinet. And he'd certainly never let a pile of dirt sit on his spotless kitchen floor. Red flags were waving all over the place, but what did they mean?

"Abby?"

I almost fell over. "Marco, don't sneak up on me like that."

He knelt down beside me, sending wafts of musky aftershave over me, stirring embers deep inside that I didn't want to be ignited. "What are you doing?"

"I saw a pile of dirt on the floor and wondered where it came from." I shrugged. "Just call it my natural curiosity at work."

"Is that the same curiosity that conveniently found a snake photo in Oliver's laptop? Yeah, I knew what you were doing. Don't give me that innocent look."

Innocent? Not at that moment. Lustful was more like it. "Never mind the laptop. Look what I found in this cabinet—one of the bamboo plants I sold Oliver for Blume's Art Shop—or I guess I should say the remains of the plant. Someone did quite a number on it. Look at these broken stalks. The leaves have been stripped off, too."

"So?"

"So look around, Marco. This apartment is spotless. It would be totally out of character for Oliver to stuff a broken pot under his sink and leave dirt on the floor. So who did, and why?"

"You're assuming that Oliver cleans his own apartment. A better guess would be that a cleaning service takes care of it, courtesy of Delphi. Besides, it's a moot point. Cora has been indicted in Delphi's murder."

I tried to look shocked. "No kidding?"

From behind us Reilly said, "Hey, you two, this is no place for a romantic rendezvous. . . .What have you got there?"

"A broken pot," Marco said, rising and brushing off his jeans.

"It's not *just* a broken pot," I said. "It's one of the four bamboo plants I sold Oliver for Blume's Art Shop. It was stuffed in the back of a cabinet. I noticed this pile of dirt and took a peek inside."

"Imagine that," Reilly drawled.

"You've seen how neat this apartment is," I said. "Don't you think it's suspicious that Oliver hid this in his kitchen cabinet? Wouldn't you think he'd at least have cleaned up the dirt on the floor?"

"Maybe he was in a hurry to leave and didn't have time," Reilly replied.

"But Oliver is compulsively neat, Reilly. Look in any cabinet and see for yourself. He wouldn't have left without cleaning it up. I think someone else put it there after Oliver left home this morning."

Reilly scratched the back of his neck. "For what reason?"

"I don't know, but it should be investigated, don't you think?" I asked.

"You'd better say yes if you want to get out of here anytime soon," Marco joked.

Reilly pursed his lips. I could tell he didn't think the damaged container was any big deal, yet he wasn't ready to ignore it, either. "It wouldn't hurt to take it into the station, I suppose, to see what the detectives want to do with it."

"Thank you," I said. "That's all I wanted. Now I'm ready to go."

"So, what do you have going on tonight?" Marco asked as he drove me home.

I gave him a puzzled glance. "Tonight?"

"You told Reilly you had something going on."

"Oh, that." I didn't want Marco to know that I'd made up an excuse to cover the awkward moment with Reilly.

In truth, the only thing on my agenda that evening was a pedicure. "I'm meeting up with some old friends. They've been complaining about feeling closed in lately, so I'm going to help them paint the town red, so to speak."

"College friends?"

"We go back a lot farther than that."

"Well, then, I hope you have fun."

"Oh, we will." All eleven of us. Great fun.

As soon as Marco pulled up in front of my apartment building, I opened the car door and started to scoot out, leaving him with nothing more than a quick *buh-bye*, as befitted a former girlfriend. But then I paused.

Dumped or not, I couldn't leave it at that. It just wasn't right. So I turned back. "I appreciate your going with me tonight, Marco. I know you had better things to do, but it was comforting having you there as backup. I couldn't have handled that creature by myself."

"Luckily, we didn't have to deal with the snake, but you did keep a calm head, and that's what's important in any investigation."

That wasn't the creature I meant, but no sense bringing up a sore subject. "Well, anyway, thanks for your help."

His face was hidden in shadow, so I couldn't see his expression, but his voice was warm and husky. "I was glad to be there—Abby—so I'll see you around, then."

I forced myself to say cheerfully, "You bet."

Marco waited until I'd let myself into the apartment building; then I gave him a wave from the doorway, and he pulled away. With a sigh, I plodded up the stairs to the second floor. My sunshine days were gone.

CHAPTER TWENTY-TWO

"I'd like to see Matron Patty, please," I said to an armed guard at nine o'clock the next morning. "She knows I'm coming."

The guard was sitting at a counter behind a window of bulletproof glass inside the main entrance of the county jail. The old brick building, a stark box of a structure five stories high, was situated two blocks east of Bloomers, an easy walk even in the chill autumn air. Luckily, it was my Saturday off, so I didn't have to feel guilty about leaving Lottie and Grace in the lurch. I'd taken the precaution of calling Patty earlier to ask if I could see Cora. I wasn't about to visit the jail unless I had a very good reason to do so.

"Sign in," the guard said, pushing a form through an opening in the window. "I'm gonna need some ID, too."

I printed my name, then took out my driver's license and slid it through the opening. He looked it over, then pushed it back. "Stand over there by the wall."

I did as told, then had to wait ten minutes before a thick security door opened and Matron Patty came out.

"Great to see you, Abby," Patty said, shaking my hand with a grip that could have bent metal. She was a dishwater blond, five-foot-four spitfire in a cop uniform, with a fully equipped police belt around her tiny waist.

"You've been busy, haven't you?" Patty said as she took me through the first security door and had me hand over my purse and shoes and empty my pockets. "There's a congressman who's trying to get some federal money allocated for a courtroom here in the jail, and I understand we have you to thank for that."

"That's great news, Patty, but you should thank that state trooper who mistook me for someone else and stuck me in lockup. That was when I realized the problem existed. And it's not an experience I'm in a hurry to repeat. No offense, but I wouldn't be here now if I didn't have to be."

"You're lucky Cora agreed to talk to you. She hasn't been real friendly."

I couldn't blame Cora for that. The jail wasn't exactly a social club.

"How's your dad doing? He used to come by to visit us, but he hasn't been here in a while. I always got such a kick out of him, with his quick Irish wit." As Patty talked, she patted me down, then ran a wand over me. Afterward she pressed a button, and a buzzer loud enough to shatter glass sounded. A second steel door opened, so I followed her through it down a hallway to a row of identical doors. We stopped at the third one.

"You've got fifteen minutes, honey." She opened the door, and I stepped into a cubicle that was barely big enough for a wooden chair and me. The closet-sized space smelled of old wood, pine disinfectant, and nervous sweat. Good thing I'd had a light breakfast.

I sat at a counter facing a pane of glass with a speaker in it, giving a start when the door shut behind me with a loud click. Through the thin, paneled walls on either side of me I could hear the murmurs of voices, and from somewhere in the bowels of the building I heard the hard clang of steel that sent a shudder through me, as memories of my few hours there flooded back.

A few minutes later the door on the opposite side of the glass opened and Cora shuffled in. She was wearing the putrid orange jumpsuit that looked no better on her than it had on me, disproving the fashion myth that tall people could wear anything. Her short, iron gray hair was combed off her face, giving her a manly appearance, and her face, devoid of makeup, showed pockmarks and purple veins.

She sat down in the chair opposite me and folded her arms, fixing me with a fierce scowl. "Wotcher want, then?" she snarled.

"I need some information."

"Wot? I was told you wanted ter 'elp me. Aren't you me free counsel?"

"I'm not your public defender, but I do want to help you."

"Unless you can spring me, there's no reason to talk to you." She stood up and called to the guard standing just outside, "I'm done 'ere."

"Wait, Cora. I'll give you a reason to talk to me." I leaned toward the speaker. "I think you were framed."

Cora turned back toward me, her hostile expression changing to one of wariness. "Wot makes you think so?"

"A gut feeling."

"Gut feeling, my arse. Why would you believe me when the coppers don't?"

"Does it matter?"

"'Ow do I know yer not a jail snitch?"

"Well, you don't, really. You're going to have trust that I'm not here to hurt you."

"Wot's in it fer you?"

"I don't like to see an innocent person pay for a murder she didn't commit, which is what will happen to you if someone doesn't find the real murderer soon."

She frowned at me for a few moments, then sat down and waved her hand impatiently. "Get on wif it, then."

I got out my notepad and pen and set about to watch her for any signs of nervousness or anxiety, anything that might indicate she was lying. "Did you take a bus to Detroit, Michigan?"

"I did , an' I 'ave the ticket stub to prove it. It's in me purse. Ask the coppers."

"Why did you lie to them about staying in a motel up there?"

"'Oo you calling a liar!" she cried, banging her large hand on the counter. "I told them coppers I din't use me real name and that I wore a knit cap on me 'ead to keep warm, so wot use was there of showin' me mug shot to anyone, askin' if Corabelle Finklestein 'ad checked in? But d'yer think they listened? If yer don't believe me, check fer yerself that I was there. I'll give yer the name of the place and the name I used for meself, too."

I wrote down the information as she dictated. "Thanks, Cora. I'll check it out. Next subject. Tell me about the red wig."

"Wot about it?"

"Why did you buy it?"

"It weren't fer meself. All I did was go into the costume shop to pick it up. Oliver drove me there and gave me the money fer it, too."

Oliver? I hadn't expected that. "Did Oliver say why he wanted the wig?"

"A secret mission 'e called it, the barmy swine. And there's another thing—me pocketing money from the cash drawer. I'd just taken payment from a bloke and was tuckin' it inside, 'n'all, when Oliver says to me, 'You've got three hundred dollars comin' t'you, Tilly.' 'Wotcher talkin' about?' says I. 'Me mum shortchanged you,' says 'e. 'It's owed you, but she'll never admit it. Take it while you can. The coast is clear.' So I did, din't I? Next thing I know, Delphi is screamin' 'Thief!' and threatenin' to 'ave me deported."

Her story sounded far-fetched except that she had used Oliver's favorite phrase: *The coast is clear.* How would she have known that unless she'd heard him say it? But what did that mean? Was it possible that my gut feeling was wrong? That Oliver had plotted to kill his mother?

"Why do you think Oliver told you to take the money?" I asked.

Cora leaned closer to the glass. "I think 'e wanted to set orf 'is mum, to tell yer the truth. 'E got a bang out of it, 'e did. 'E stood there watchin' 'er scream 'er bloody 'ead orf at me, gettin' a good larf from it. 'E's tetched in the 'ead, if you ask me."

I remembered that scene. I also remembered that Oliver had seemed to enjoy watching Delphi chase Cora through the shop. I'd even had to prompt him to phone the cops. Perhaps I hadn't given Oliver enough credit. Perhaps he was shrewder than he let on. Surprisingly, Cora seemed to be on the level. She had a bus ticket stub, she'd given me the motel name and her alias, and she knew Oliver's favorite phrase.

"Do you know anything about the bamboo plants Oliver brought to the art shop?"

"All I know is Delphi 'ad a fit 'cause she wanted only three and 'e got four, so she told 'im to take one 'ome. 'E was all flustered-like and said 'e couldn't 'ave it at his place, so she said she'd take it, then."

So Oliver hadn't wanted the fourth bamboo in his apartment. That made the pot under his sink even more suspicious. "Did Delphi take the plant home with her?"

Cora shrugged. "Couldn't tell yer that. All I know is that Oliver moved it out o' the shop."

"Do you drive, Cora?"

"Not 'ere, I don't. Back 'ome I did, when I 'ad me own car. Cor, that were a long time ago."

"Could you drive a car here if you put your mind to it?"

"Suppose I could, but I wouldn't want ter be another driver on the road wif me." She cackled at her stab at humor, and it wasn't a pretty sound.

"Have you ever driven Libby Blume's Corvette?"

She puffed up like an outraged pigeon. "Wot? Me drive that fancy machine? Are you crackers? I'd 'ave smashed it all to pieces."

"Then why was the Corvette key in your purse?"

"Summin' put it there, that's why. I told those coppers I din't know it were there. Wot reason would I 'ave for it when I don't drive?" She leaned toward the glass. "I'll tell you just 'oo put it there. It were Oliver!" She sat back with a firm nod of her head.

Cora seemed sure Oliver was behind everything. "Why do you think he put it in your purse?"

She narrowed her eyes into slits of outrage. "To pin the murder on me, that's why."

"You think Oliver killed his mother?"

"'Oo else?"

"Libby?"

"Oliver was the evil one. I could see it in 'is eyes, always makin' 'is evil plans."

"Yet you took the cash when he told you to. Didn't that make you wonder if he was up to something?"

She gave me a canny glance. "I didn't say I was an angel, now, did I?"

Fair enough. "What about Libby? What's your impression of her?"

"Spoiled rotten an' always under 'er mum's thumb. She couldn't take a piss wifout askin' permission first. Oliver did 'er a favor, din't 'e?"

"Are you saying he did her a favor by killing their mother?"

"Wotcher think?"

At that moment the door behind me opened, and Patty stuck her head in. "Time's up."

Damn. I quickly finished making notes, then put my notepad away. "Thanks for agreeing to see me, Cora. If I have more questions, would you let me come back?"

She rose from her chair as the guard came to get her. "Long as yer keep yer word about 'elping me. But yer'd better 'urry. I don't fancy sittin' in front of no judge anytime soon."

"Trust me, Cora. With our legal system, it'll be a good while before that happens."

"There's someone waiting outside to see you," Patty told me as she walked me through the security doors. She whispered in my ear, "Detective Wells."

"Did she know I was here visiting Cora?"

Patty nodded. "She knew."

Great. Now the detective probably wanted to know why I was poking around. Well, too bad. I needed time to sort through Cora's surprising revelations before I gave anything away.

I slipped on my boots, donned my peacoat, put my purse over my shoulder, and walked out the front door of the jail, instantly experiencing that heady rush of freedom. At once, Detective Wells came toward me. She wore an open trench coat, a stylish black suit, a colorful silk scarf at her throat, and two Oriental hair picks through the blond bun at the nape of her neck.

"Abby," she said, sticking out her hand. "Lisa Wells."

"I remember, Detective," I said, shaking her hand. It was firm and confident, a no-nonsense grip.

"Call me Lisa." She smiled as though trying to befriend me. "I'd like to ask you a few questions regarding the Blume case. Why don't we go back to my office and talk?"

I glanced at my watch. "Can we make it another time?"

"I'd really like to talk to you now."

There was something in her tone that made me uncomfortable. "I thought you had the case sewn up. I heard Corabelle Finklestein was indicted for the murder."

"Actually, Cora was indicted for theft. You'll have to tell Sergeant Reilly to be more careful with his information next time."

Yikes. Lisa knew about Reilly. But how had Reilly gotten the wrong information?

"So why do you want to talk to me about the Blume case?" I asked lightly. "Am I a suspect now?"

She smiled, revealing an attractive set of white teeth. "Not if you can explain why your fingerprints are all over the murder weapon."

CHAPTER TWENTY-THREE

My heart began to race with panic. "My prints can't be on the murder weapon. I've never even been inside Delphi's house."

"Do you know what the murder weapon was?" Lisa was watching me closely, trying to detect signs of nervousness.

"The wine bottle?"

"It was the clay flowerpot that you removed from beneath Oliver Blume's sink. I understand it came from your shop."

My mouth fell open. Oh, dear God. *That's* why the pot was broken. But did Lisa actually believe I had used it to kill Delphi? "I think I should have a lawyer present before I answer any more questions."

"If you'd feel more comfortable, Abby, please do. But if you've got nothing to hide and can clear this up with a few simple answers, then why bother, especially when you know the ropes? You've got a year's worth of law school under your belt, don't you?"

Very clever of her to appeal to my vanity. Well, fine. Let her bring those questions on. I'd sat in on enough interviews to know how to handle myself. But it would be better to be on my own turf. "Why don't we go back to my flower shop, then? I can offer you gourmet coffee in a cozy Victorian tea parlor."

"I wouldn't mind good coffee for a change. I've heard your scones are to die for, too."

That was a phrase I could have done without.

As we walked the two blocks to Bloomers, Lisa asked me questions about the floral business, which I was guessing was her way of getting me to let down my guard. But I wasn't about to let that happen. That year at New Chapel Law School hadn't been a total bust.

Lottie and Grace were at the cash register when we strolled in. After introducing them to Lisa, I said, "Detective Wells wants to interview me about Delphi's murder, so I convinced her to come here to sample your delicious coffee and scones, Grace." It was my way of letting them know what was going on.

"Of course, dear," Grace said as she and Lottie exchanged concerned glances.

I led Lisa into the parlor and we sat at the corner table near the bay window that Reilly always preferred.

"This is charming," Lisa said, glancing around admiringly.

"It was Abby's idea to add the parlor onto Bloomers," Grace said as she set out place settings and a basket of scones. "She always strives to please her customers."

"And talk about honest!" Lottie exclaimed, pouring our coffee. "Why, Abby's as honest as the day is long." She stroked the top of my head as if I were her pet.

"Honorable is how we describe our Abby." Grace struck her theatrical pose, raising her voice to say, "*'Honor virtutis praemium.*' 'Honor is the reward of virtue.' "

"And you want to talk about someone who fights the injustices of the world," Lottie said, "well, you're looking straight at her."

"*'Justitia omnibus,'*" Grace cried dramatically. " 'Justice for all.' "

"Ladies," I said quietly, "thanks for your testimonials, but it's not necessary. Lisa just has a few questions for me."

Lottie and Grace exchanged worried frowns, then slipped away. I knew they'd be hovering outside the doorway, though, ready to swoop in if the situation warranted it.

"This coffee is delicious," Lisa said, sipping the brew straight, while I doctored mine with half-and-half. She took a bite of scone, chewing with her eyes closed. "M-m-m. Heavenly. I can see why they're so popular." She reached into her large leather purse and pulled out a thick notebook. Flipping to a fresh page, she got down to business.

"Why don't you tell me how your fingerprints came to be on that broken pot?"

"That's easy enough. Oliver Blume showed up here one day asking for four bamboo plants for his sister's art shop. I rang them up and helped him carry them to his van. The other three pots should still be at Blume's."

"Let's talk about the one you found under the sink. How did you know it was there?"

"I saw dirt spilled on the floor and thought it was out of place in his spotless apartment."

"How did you happen to be inside Oliver's apartment? Did he invite you in?"

Oops. Nice move, Abby. "He was supposed to meet me at eight o'clock last night and he never showed up, so I decided to investigate and"—I shrugged—"his door was unlocked."

"Was it standing open?"

I had a feeling I was digging myself into a hole. I prayed there was no tombstone above it. "No, just unlocked. I turned the knob and it opened."

"So you let yourself inside?" she asked, writing.

"Absolutely not! I phoned Oliver first, several times, in fact. Then I went up to his door and knocked. When I found the door unlocked, I started to worry that something had happened to him. People don't usually leave their doors unlocked, especially not paranoid people. Under those circumstances, wouldn't you have gone inside and looked around?"

She smiled. "What happened next?"

I decided I'd better condense it. Less to get me in trouble. "Marco helped me look for Oliver. Then Libby showed up because she was concerned about him, too. Then I called Oliver's friend Tom, who told me Oliver had gone into hiding. As we were leaving, I noticed dirt on the kitchen floor, so I opened the cabinet to investigate and pulled a broken pot from beneath the sink. And that would be how *more* of my prints got on the pot."

She wrote it down, checked back in her notes, then glanced up at me. "Why did you insist that Sergeant Reilly bring the pot in to be tested? What made you think it was important to our investigation?"

"I didn't know it had anything to do with the murder investigation. I just thought it was odd because after seeing his apartment, it's obvious that Oliver has an obsessive-compulsive disorder. He wouldn't leave dirt on his floor or keep a broken pot stuffed inside his cabinet. Someone else had to have put it there, and it must have happened after Oliver left home yesterday, because someone with his compulsions would have had to clean up the spilled dirt before he left. And, by the way, if I had killed Delphi, I certainly wouldn't have volunteered that pot for testing."

That seemed to score a point in my favor. "Did you notice anything unusual about the pot, other than it being damaged, I mean?" she asked.

"Only that the bamboo shoots were broken. Why? Should I have?"

"We found blood and pieces of scalp on the edges," she said, making my stomach churn. "I thought you might have noticed that." She waited a beat, then said, "How well do you know Oliver?"

"I have a business relationship with him. He hired me to conduct a private investigation."

"Why did he hire you? You're not a licensed PI."

If Lisa knew that, she'd done some checking up on me. "Oliver knew that I'd helped solve a few murder cases, so he felt safe asking for my assistance, I guess."

As Lisa sipped her coffee, I asked hopefully, "So, have you heard about those cases I helped solve?"

"Yes, I have."

And was obviously not impressed. She took another bite of her scone, wiped her fingers on a napkin while she studied her notes, then glanced up at me. "Marco Salvare was hired by Libby Blume for another investigation. Since he was already employed by a family member, can you explain why Oliver didn't use Mr. Salvare's services?"

"Oliver has trust issues."

"Yet he trusted you. How did that come about?"

"When he came to Bloomers to buy the plants, he told me I was *one of the trusted ones*. That was his phrase. I'm not sure how he came to that conclusion. He did say he saw in Libby's scrapbook—which is another story in itself—that I'd helped solve murder cases." I shrugged. "Or maybe I just have one of those faces."

"A face that looks remarkably like his sister's."

Ouch. That struck a nerve. The bell over the door jingled out in the shop, signaling an incoming customer. From the corner of my eye I saw Lottie scurry away from the other side of the parlor doorway, but I was more concerned with convincing Lisa that she was questioning the wrong person than with who had entered Bloomers.

"Look, I had this face before Libby did. She came back to New Chapel, asked to be my intern, and when I said no, she began to copy everything about me and worm her way into my life in every way possible, even showing up for a family dinner. Ask around. People in town can't tell us apart. And FYI, Libby did the same thing to one of her professors at school, trying to steal the professor's husband."

"So do you believe Libby's aim was to take revenge on you?"

"Why else would she go to all that trouble—unless she had another motive?"

Lisa gave me a piercing look. "By another motive, are you implying that Libby might have copied you so she could kill her mother and blame you for it?"

Damn. That was the dilemma that got me involved in the investigation in the first place. Very cautiously, I said, "I'm not implying that."

"Then, if I understand you correctly, you think she

went to all that effort—and that truly was a hell of an effort—simply to get even with you for not hiring her? Even though she had the means to open her own shop? Doesn't that strike you as highly improbable?"

Was Lisa trying to get me to say I thought Libby was the murderer? "Maybe you should ask Libby why she did it."

Lisa tapped her pen against the table. "Could she be protecting someone?"

"Like who? Her brother?"

Lisa pounced on that at once. "Why did Oliver come to mind?"

"Because Libby doesn't have anyone else to protect."

"Do you think it's possible that Oliver killed his mother?"

I rubbed my temples, feeling a headache coming on. "Anything is possible, right? You're not dealing with rational people. Libby goes around stealing people's identities, and Oliver dresses like a solider, plays war games, and imagines that enemies are spying on him. And I won't even start on the obsessive control Delphi had over her children. The Blumes aren't normal, which is probably one reason why Libby wormed her way into my family. She needed some normalcy in her life."

"Excuse me, honey?" I glanced over at the doorway and there was my mom waving at me. "I'm sorry to interrupt, Abigail, but could I ask you a quick favor?"

Lottie stood just behind Mom, shrugging apologetically.

"I'm kind of busy right now, Mom."

"That's okay," Lisa said. "It's your mother. Go ahead."

"Oh, good," Mom said, then hurried across the room to shake Lisa's hand. "Hi, I'm Maureen Knight."

"Lisa Wells."

No mention of her being a detective, I noticed. Was that a strategic move to keep Mom from interjecting herself into the interview in order to protect me—or was Lisa trying to save me from a second interrogation—from my mother? "What did you need, Mom?"

"Your father and I are going to a meeting tonight and I don't want to leave Taz alone. Can you come over for a while?"

Oh, no! I'd just told Lisa my family was normal. *Please don't say anything about the llama!* "I'll check my schedule and call you in about an hour, okay?"

"Okay, honey. Don't forget." Then to Lisa she said, "Taz is a teenager, and you know what mischief teens get into."

"Lottie, do you want to show my mom those new roses that came in today?" I said, giving Lottie a look that said, *Get Mom out of here!*

Lottie tried to steer her out of the room, but Mom held her ground. "So you can only imagine the mischief a teenaged *llama* could do," she finished.

Too late. I cringed as Lisa asked in amazement, "You have a llama?"

"Would you like to see a picture of him? Taz is such a sweet animal, and his belly can be shaved to produce knitting yarn."

I dropped my forehead into my hands as Mom proudly displayed the photo she'd snapped with her new cell phone. So much for the normal family.

"You know, Mo, my boys would love to meet Taz," Lottie said, ushering Mom out.

I darted a glance at Lisa, who was writing in her notebook. I could only imagine what her notes said. "My mother is a kindergarten teacher," I said, trying to smooth things over. "She took up knitting as a hobby and thought it would be novel to grow her own yarn. She's always trying new ideas. Just ask my dad. He was a cop, by the way. You probably knew him. Sergeant Jeffrey Knight? He was wounded in the line of duty and had to retire."

Lisa took a sip of coffee. My pedigree was clearly not impressing her. "I'd like to talk more about your impressions of Oliver. You mentioned he liked to dress like a solider and play war games. Do you know how realistic he got? Did he use guns, swords, or maybe instruments of torture?"

Instruments of torture? "I honestly don't have a clue. Why?"

"We found tiny shards of bamboo stalk under what remained of Delphi's fingernails. I don't know if you're aware of this, but bamboo shoots have been used as—"

"Yes, I know," I said, cutting her off as the blood drained from my face. *"You just jam those suckers right under the fingernails. The pain is unbearable."* I took a deep breath and explained, "When Oliver came down to buy the plants, he asked if I knew that bamboo shoots had been used to torture people in World War Two, but I never thought he intended to . . ."

I couldn't finish the thought. It was too gruesome. I grabbed my coffee cup with both hands and took a drink, thinking over what I knew about the murder. Yet what I knew still didn't convince me that Oliver was the killer. "All this evidence—the red wig, the planted car key, the body left behind my flower shop, the bamboo plant under the sink, and the shoots under the fingernails—wouldn't that indicate the work of a cold, calculating murderer? Because I don't think Oliver could pull that off."

"Oliver's fingerprints weren't on the pot, Abby. The only prints on the pot were yours."

I gaped at her. What did that mean? Had I been set up? Was my prediction coming true?

Your arrest was a mistake, Abby, Dave had assured me. *You're not a suspect.*

I will be, Dave. Trust me. It's all part of her plan.

"Look, Lisa, I told you how my prints came to be on that pot. I didn't kill Delphi, and if you're going to keep insinuating that I did, then I *am* going to call a lawyer."

"I'm not insinuating, Abby, only trying to figure out what happened."

"Well, so am I, so instead of putting me on the defensive, why don't you let me help you find the real killer?"

She seemed taken aback. "That isn't necessary."

Not necessary for whom? I wracked my brain for a way to turn the focus off me. *Think, Abby. Pump those brain cells! Why aren't the killer's prints on the pots? Because . . . ?*

I had it! "When Oliver came into Bloomers asking for the bamboo plants, he was wearing a camouflage outfit that included a pair of gloves. If he always handled those pots with his gloves, that would explain why his prints aren't on them, right? So it stands to reason that the killer was wearing gloves, too."

Lisa leaned toward me, her gaze sharp and focused. "You're sure he had on gloves?"

"Yes. If you check his bedroom closet, you'll find

three camouflage outfits, including gloves. He's probably wearing the fourth. He buys four of everything."

She wrote it down. "Did Oliver ever say anything about or against his mother? Ever hint at a reason why he might want to kill her?"

"Not that I recall. I heard her yell at him once for dropping an art print, but I can't imagine that triggering her murder."

"What was his reaction to her yelling?"

"I don't know. Oliver speaks very softly, and I wasn't in the room with them. But I never heard him refer to his mother in a negative way. Whenever I saw Oliver, he was behaving as a soldier and didn't seem to mind taking orders. I know he was rejected by the army, so obviously he never got it out of his system."

"Do you know why he was rejected?"

"All I remember is that he broke into the high school computer lab and destroyed the computers. I'm sure you've come across that in your investigation."

Lisa didn't answer, only kept reviewing her notes. "Oliver's sister claims that he tried to kill her by planting a poisonous snake in her mailbox. What's your take on that?"

Lisa must have interviewed Libby before coming to see me. At least I'd managed to shift the focus off me. "My take is that Libby is jumping to conclusions. She seemed as surprised to learn about the snake's existence as we were, so how would she know whether it was poisonous? Conveniently, the snake is gone and so is Oliver, so there's no way to verify her claim.

"And here's another thing that puzzles me," I continued. "Oliver told me that Libby was his ally, so why would he want to harm or possibly kill her? If he really wanted to kill Libby, putting a snake in her mailbox wouldn't be a very effective method."

"Not for a rational person."

I couldn't argue that point.

"I understand that Oliver is hiding in a forest preserve in Starke County, and you've been in touch with the friend who took him there. Want to tell me about that?"

I gave her the rundown on Tom McDoyle, his black Buick, the spy game that Oliver forgot, and the phone call to Tom in which we learned Oliver's whereabouts.

"Do you expect to hear from Oliver or Tom?"

"Tom is supposed to call when he finds Oliver, but I haven't heard from him yet. I *hope* to hear from Oliver. He owes me a thousand dollars."

"That's a pretty hefty fee for an amateur PI."

"That's what he offered to pay me."

She pulled out her business card and handed it to me. "If you hear from either of them, will you let me know?"

"Sure." In my own good time.

Lisa finished her coffee, put away her notebook, and stood up. "Thanks for your cooperation, Abby."

"Can I ask you something?"

"Of course."

"Am I still a suspect?"

She smiled cannily. "I haven't ruled anyone out."

I stared out the parlor window, thinking about what to do next. Damn Libby for entangling me in her life. Now look at the mess I was in.

The bell over the door jingled and a moment later I saw Lisa pass by on her way back to the police station.

At the same time, Lottie and Grace came rushing over to the table.

"Are you okay, sweetie?" Lottie asked, taking my hand in hers and rubbing it. "She really put you through the wringer."

"The nerve," Grace huffed. "Grilling you as though you were a common criminal. Clearly, all signs point to Oliver as the killer. Why isn't the detective out searching for him?"

"I think she will search for him," I answered. "But I don't think it's clear that Oliver killed his mom. Whoever did it planned it very carefully, setting others up to look like suspects, and I don't think Oliver is capable of that."

"Do you think it was Libby?" Lottie asked.

I rubbed my throbbing forehead. "Libby could have stashed that pot in her brother's kitchen cabinet, I suppose, and planted the key in Cora's purse. But why would she need to purchase a red wig? Her hair *is* red. And she wouldn't have had to move her car seat back, either."

"Then perhaps it *was* Oliver," Grace said. "Perhaps he hides his cleverness behind his so-called paranoia."

"Grace is right, sweetie," Lottie said. "Oliver has been playing military games for a long time. He might be very smart when it comes to planning and carrying out missions."

"He *has* used the term *mission*," I said. "But our speculation is moot because *my* prints were on the murder weapon. Not Libby's, not Oliver's, not even Cora's. Mine. And not only did I handle the weapon; I also supplied it. If no other evidence comes to light, I'm afraid it could come back to who held that bamboo plant."

"Can I get you anything?" Grace asked. "Calming tea, perhaps?"

"No, thanks." I rested my head in my hands. "Can the day get any worse?"

"I'm sorry your mom interrupted," Lottie said. "I tried to stop her without letting her know what was going on, but you know how she can be."

"I appreciate the effort. I'm just thankful she didn't recognize Detective Wells and figure out I was being interviewed by the police. I'd hate to worry her or Dad for no reason. At least I hope there's no reason."

I got up and started to stack the cups and saucers, but Grace stopped me. "We'll see to that. Go do what you need to do."

Which was what?

I could call Marco. He'd know what to do next.

Out in the shop I hit speed dial number two and Marco answered in one ring. "Hi, it's Abby," I said. "Are you busy right now? I'd like to run something by you."

There was a moment of silence. Then he said, "Hold on."

In the background I heard Libby ask, "Who is it?"

I ended the call. Who needed Marco anyway?

CHAPTER TWENTY-FOUR

My cell phone rang and I checked the screen to be sure it wasn't Marco calling back, but it was Tom—at last!

"I found Oliver," Tom said, "but he won't leave the forest preserve until he talks to you."

"Why?"

"He's scared. He said the cops are looking for him."

"Did he say why they were looking for him?"

"He's not saying much of anything. He's sitting on the ground with a blanket wrapped around him, rocking back and forth and making moaning sounds. He's really freaking me out, man. I've never seen him like that. You've gotta get out here soon."

It sounded like Oliver was coming unhinged. "Do you know if he's contacted his sister, or heard from her?"

"I don't think he talked to her, because he won't use his phone. He told me he had to bury it in the woods because the cops were listening in. He says you're the only one he can trust . . . well, besides me."

I debated about whether to go. If Oliver had murdered his mother, then he was dangerous. If Oliver was in a bad way because he was off his meds, he could also be dangerous. If the two were both true, he was definitely dangerous. But if he hadn't killed Delphi and was hiding simply because his paranoia had kicked in again, then maybe I could calm him down enough to get some answers. Because, boy, did I have questions. But should I go or not?

Oliver trusts you. Why would he hurt you? my little voice of reason said. *Besides, do you really believe he's a ruthless killer?* No, I didn't. No matter how the evidence appeared to point to Oliver, I couldn't shake the growing feeling that Libby was the culprit after all.

"Tell me how to get there, Tom. I'll leave right now." I grabbed the message pad off the counter and wrote down his instructions. Then I dropped the piece of paper and my phone in my purse and headed for the door.

"You're not going out to the forest preserve alone, are you?" Grace asked, standing behind me.

"Tom will be there." Before she could argue, I grabbed my peacoat and flew out the door.

As I hurried to the parking lot, shivering as I shrugged on my coat, my cell phone rang and I foolishly answered it without checking the screen. *Damn.* It was Marco.

"Hey," he said. "We must have been cut off earlier. What did you want to run by me?"

"Nothing. It's not important now. Besides, you have company."

"I don't have company. Libby stopped by briefly, but she's gone now, so tell me."

"Really, Marco, it was nothing. I have an appointment, so I have to run." I hung up, slid into my Vette, and took off. I followed Route 30 east to 39 and headed south, following the directions Tom had given me. Within forty minutes I had located the forest preserve and pulled into the parking lot beside Tom's Buick. Other than our two cars the lot was empty, which wasn't odd for a chilly November day. I glanced around but didn't see anyone.

My cell phone rang again and I answered it, expecting to hear Tom's voice, but it was Marco. I *had* to start checking that screen.

"Abby, what the hell are you doing? I called your shop and Lottie said you were on your way to Starke County to talk to Oliver."

"So?"

"So turn around and come back. An APB was just issued for Oliver. The cops recovered a pair of men's camouflage gloves from his apartment half an hour ago. The gloves were wrapped in aluminum foil and left in the back of the cabinet where you found the pot. The gloves had blood on them, Abby, and the blood type matches Delphi's. Do you understand what I'm saying? Oliver is the killer. Don't even think about trying to talk to him alone."

Bloody gloves near the bamboo plant. Dirt on the floor. Obsessive-compulsive disorder. Paranoia. My mind raced to make sense of it all. "How do they know Oliver wore those gloves, Marco? Couldn't someone else have used them? Couldn't someone have planted both the gloves and the pot under his sink?"

"Abby, come on. I know what you're thinking, but I'm telling you that Oliver ditched the gloves and the pot and went into hiding because he knew the cops were getting close."

"I know it looks bad for Oliver, Marco, but I just don't think he could have pulled it off."

A shadow fell across my lap. I glanced out my side window to see a guy with a round, red face standing beside my car. He was short, squat, and about thirty years old. He was wearing a hooded parka, pants, and hiking boots all in olive drab. I rolled down my window. "Yes?"

"Are you Abby?" the guy said in a high, reedy voice that I recognized at once.

"Yes. Are you Tom?" At his nod I said, "Would you give me a minute, please?"

"Make it quick. Oliver is really losing it."

"Tom's there?" Marco asked as I quickly rolled up the window. "Abby, for God's sake, stay in your car. Don't do anything stupid."

"Thanks for the vote of confidence. Maybe you should take your own advice and have some trust in *me*." So take *that*, PI Salvare!

"Okay, look, I deserved that. Just please don't let your feelings for Libby cloud your judgment. Stay where you are. I'm on my way. I should be there in—"

"I'll be fine, Marco." I hit End, put my phone in my purse, and got out of the Vette.

"Oliver is about half a mile into the woods," Tom said as we started across the lot.

"That far? Can you convince him to come here? I'm not really dressed for a hike."

"Are you kidding? He's curled up into a ball with the

blanket over his head. In about ten minutes he's going to start drooling all over himself."

I glanced down at my good boots with a regretful sigh. "Lead the way."

As we tromped through bramble and a thick carpet of wet leaves, I said, "Tom, how well do you know Oliver?"

"About as well as anyone, I guess. We've been friends since grade school."

"What was Oliver like back then? Was he mistrustful? Fearful?"

"No way, man. Oliver was fearless. It was his idea to get a group together to play war games. He was crazy over anything military. He couldn't wait to graduate so he could enlist."

"Being rejected by the army must have been quite a blow to him."

"Hell, yeah. He was ready to jump in front of a train. I mean, it wasn't like we robbed a bank. A couple of us guys got high one night after a football game and thought it would be funny to break into the school. We had this computer teacher who was a real ballbuster, so we decided to get even with him by smashing up the computer lab. I know it was a terrible thing to do, but we were stupid back then.

"We got away before the police arrived, and made a pact never to talk about it to anyone. But somehow the police found out that Oliver was in on it, because they picked him up after school the next day. He never ratted us out, though, even though they offered him a deal. Poor guy, he never thought it would ruin his chances of getting into the army, but when he went to the recruiting office, they checked his records and that was the end of that. He tried the navy, the marines, even the police department, but no one would touch him.

"Oliver was never the same after that. He lost interest in everything but our war games. Most of our friends went away to college, but Oliver and me, we kept them up. I do it for him mostly. I mean, I still enjoy the games, but if Oliver wasn't so into it, I wouldn't be, either."

"Has Oliver ever said anything about his mother's death?"

"What do you mean? Like who did it? Nah. I told him I was sorry about it, and all, but he just shrugged it off. He isn't really much of a talker. He mostly likes action."

"What about snakes? Has Oliver ever mentioned that he had one?"

"Yeah, he said he got one from his sister for his birthday. He showed me some photos he took of it."

Well, wasn't that interesting? Libby bought him the snake, then pretended to be surprised about it. "When was his birthday?"

"Maybe a month ago?"

Perfect timing for a mailbox trick.

Tom came to a stop and pointed to a thicket of pine trees. "He should be just beyond those pines." He cupped his hands around his mouth and called, "Oliver? Hey, buddy, Abby is with me and she came alone." Tom glanced at me. "Can you hear that?"

I listened closely, trying to shut out the chattering squirrels and cawing blue jays, and finally heard a low moaning sound. "Is that Oliver?"

"Creepy, isn't it? Talk to him as we get closer so you don't spook him."

"Are you sure this is safe?"

At Tom's nod I said, "Okay, then, let's get on with it." As we pushed through thorny branches, I called, "Hey, Oliver, it's Abby." We emerged from between two towering pine trees and there, under the drooping branches of another huge pine, I saw a large, quivering lump covered by an olive drab blanket. Next to the lump was an army canteen with its cap off, as though it was empty, and the discarded wrapper from an energy bar.

Stopping a few feet away, I said, "Oliver, I'm here."

A scrawny hand emerged to grasp the edge of the blanket and peel it back, revealing two sunken eyes and a pathetic-looking face. "Is the coast clear?" he rasped.

"All clear." I crouched so I could look him in the eye, putting my purse on the ground beside me. "What happened to you last night, Oliver? You didn't show up."

"I had to leave, ma'am. They're after me. They know what I did." He hugged himself, rocking, as he muttered, "It's bad. Real bad. *Bad News Bears.* Bare it all now. Time to bear it."

Tom was right. Oliver was losing it. Whatever he'd done, the guilt was eating him up. I didn't want to think that he was talking about murder, but what else could it be?

Suddenly, his hand shot out and grabbed my wrist, nearly yanking me off balance. "You have to make them understand that I didn't want to do it, ma'am."

"Of course you didn't want to," I said soothingly, darting a concerned glance at Tom.

"Tell us what happened, buddy," Tom urged.

"I had no choice," Oliver said, his sunken eyes holding a deep inner anguish. "No say-so. No rights. No wrongs. No in between. Over and done with. Over and out." His grip grew tighter. "Do you see that I had to do it?"

"Absolutely." I gently tugged on my hand, but his grip was firm.

"You're the only one I can trust on this, ma'am. The only one not in the game. No game, no shame. Do I have your word on that? Are you as good as your word?"

He was squeezing harder now. I glanced over my shoulder for help. "Tom?"

Tom knelt down beside me. "Hey, buddy, don't cut off her blood supply or anything."

Oliver instantly released my hand. "You understand what I'm saying, don't you, ma'am?"

"I'm trying, but I'm still a little confused. You've got to tell me very clearly what happened."

He pressed his fingertips into his eye sockets and began to rock. "I killed Delphi."

CHAPTER TWENTY-FIVE

The shock of Oliver's confession hit me like a punch in the gut, but I had to pretend to be calm. The last thing I wanted to do was to lose his trust. I glanced at Tom and he gave a shrug, as if to say he hadn't known, either. *Damn!* How had my gut feeling been so wrong?

Quickly, I reached into my purse to find my cell phone. I wanted Marco to hear the conversation so he could call the Starke County cops and get them out here. The tactic had worked before; I was desperately hoping it would work now.

"I didn't want to do it," Oliver moaned, holding his head.

"Did your mom hurt you, Oliver?" I asked. I felt for the buttons on my phone to speed-dial Marco, then hit Send.

Oliver began to rub the top of his head, rocking faster and talking louder. "You know what she did? She reported me to the cops. Her own son, ma'am. *Delphi* was the snitch."

"Holy shit," Tom murmured out the corner of his mouth. "His mom was the one who turned him in for breaking into the computer lab."

"She said it was for my own good," Oliver continued, "that I might get killed in the army, but she just wanted to control my life. It wasn't about my safety—it was about Delphi's *control*."

Poor Oliver. His own mother had shattered his life's ambition. How telling that he used her first name, as though to depersonalize her. Judging by his reaction, I was betting Oliver hadn't known about Delphi's betrayal until recently. But who had told him? Who would know?

"How did you find out, Oliver?" I asked. "Who told you, and when?"

Tears spilled out of Oliver's eyes and rolled down his cheeks. "Delphi always said I didn't get into the army because I didn't measure up. That I would never be good at anything. But she lied! She knew why they wouldn't take me. She knew I would have been the best soldier they'd ever seen. Heads above the rest. Best of the rest. 'I know what you did,' I told her. 'Now you apologize for it.' But all she said was to get out. It's over and done with. Grow up. Then she reached for the phone. She said she was calling the police, but I knew what she was planning—to put me into a mental hospital, just like Libby said she would."

I darted a glance at my phone and saw that I was connected. I hoped Marco was listening.

With his emotions running high, Oliver began to speak in a falsetto voice, as though imitating his mom. "See? I'm dialing the cops, Oliver, just like I told you I would."

"Stop her!" Oliver cried suddenly, flailing his arms as though reliving the scene. The blanket fell away to reveal his camouflage fatigues complete with a leather belt full of army implements. "Stop her, Oliver. Stop and drop her!" He clutched my hands, his expression imploring. "I had to do it, ma'am. I had no choice. You see that, don't you?"

Then his arms went limp at his sides. "She had such a surprised look on her face, like she didn't believe I would hit her. Then she just—collapsed." Oliver clapped his hands to his ears and began to rock. "Sorry, sorry, sorry. Didn't mean it. Didn't mean it. You brought this on yourself. You should have apologized. See what happens? See?"

"What did you hit her with, Oliver?" I asked gently.

He kept talking as though he hadn't heard me. "She was trying to tell me something, so I got down beside her and smoothed back her hair. 'What, Mummy? What is it?' I couldn't hear her, but I knew what she wanted to say. She wanted to say she was sorry for what she did, so I told her I forgave her. There was dirt all around her and I knew that would upset her, so I went to get the hand vac from the pantry. She wouldn't like all that dirt in her kitchen. No dirt for Delphi."

"Where did the dirt come from?" I asked.

"The pot!" he cried, becoming agitated again. "It came from the pot when I hit her! When I came back to clean it up, she was grabbing on to the bamboo shoots and trying to pull herself over to the counter and making funny sounds, and there was blood on her fingers and dirt everywhere. No place to walk. Can't walk the walk."

I glanced down at my phone again and saw that my call had disconnected. I hoped that meant that Marco had heard enough and called the cops. Now I had to keep Oliver talking so he'd stay put until they got here.

"Did you try to help her?" I asked, hoping that maybe he'd at least made an attempt.

"Yes, ma'am. I cleaned up the dirt and took the pot to the garage."

"What I meant was, did you *get* help for her?" I asked.

"What was the point? Dead is dead. Time is meaningless. Death needs no time." As he talked more gibberish, he pulled the blanket over his shoulders and hunkered down again, rocking and muttering to himself, "Mission accomplished. Over and done. Time to move headquarters. All we can do now is wait. Wait and bait."

So far what Oliver had described was an accident, a reaction to being deeply hurt, not a calculated attack. But then what about the wig and the planted key? There were so many questions yet to be answered, but I wasn't sure how much more probing he could tolerate.

I glanced at my watch, wondering how much time I had before the cops arrived. I wanted to get as much information as I could before they took Oliver into custody. I decided to change topics and come back to the murder later.

"Oliver, do you remember the clerk Tilly? I talked to her this morning and she said that you told her to take money from the cash drawer because it was owed to her. Is she right?"

Oliver shrugged one shoulder as though he didn't care, so I pressed on. "Did you mean for Tilly to steal from your sister's shop?"

"It wasn't Libby's shop. It was Delphi's. Everything was Delphi's. Ask Libby for verification. Delphi would have screwed Tilly out of her salary just like she screwed that kid—Kayla. Just like she screwed me. So I told her to take it. Justice served."

"I agree. Justice is very important," I said to mollify him. "But Tilly also said someone put a Corvette key in her purse, which doesn't seem very just to me. Is she right about that?"

He shrugged again. "The end justifies the means."

"Did you put the key in Tilly's purse, Oliver?"

"What if I did?" He rearranged the blanket to cover his head, his movements jerky.

Tom whispered, "Let me try. I think your questions are making him jittery."

I gave Tom a nod, so he said, "Hey, buddy, were you pulling a joke on the lady? Is that why you put the key in her purse?"

"It was part of the game," Oliver said, peering at us with hollow eyes from beneath his hood. "Part and parcel."

"That wasn't part of any game we played," Tom whispered to me.

"Oliver," I said, "was part of the game taking Tilly to a costume shop to buy a red wig?"

"True lies," he muttered to himself. "Truth or consequences. Truth or dare."

"Truth," I said. "Why did you need a red wig?"

"It was a covert operation. That's the way it's done. Ask Tom. He knows."

"Whose covert operation?" I asked. "Did someone order you to buy the red wig?"

Oliver rubbed his head and began to mutter, "Name, rank, and serial number."

Was Oliver afraid to tell me the truth? "I can't help

you if you're going to pull that, Oliver. I'm trying to make sense of what you've told me, but some things don't add up, like the bamboo plant. You said you took it to the garage. So who put it under your sink?"

He wouldn't look at me. Instead, he pushed his fists against his head. "Stop hounding me! Hounding and pounding. I can't do this anymore."

"You'd better back off," Tom whispered. "You're wearing him down."

"Good. Maybe he'll stop lying." To Oliver I said, "Your gloves were there, too, wrapped in foil. Do you remember putting them there?"

"Yes, yes, yes!" Oliver cried, glaring at me. "Why do you keep hounding me? It's over and done with."

"You're right, Oliver. It is over, and that's a big relief, isn't it? But there are a few minor details I still don't understand, like about driving Libby's car. Did you have two keys made for the Corvette, one to put in Tilly's purse and one for yourself?"

Oliver began to hit himself on top of his head. "Name, rank, and serial number. Name, rank, and serial number."

"I'd stop if I were you," Tom whispered. "He's gonna bolt any minute."

"I need to ask one more question," I whispered back. Then, practically holding my breath, I asked, "Oliver, did you put on the red wig and drive your mother's body to the alley behind my flower shop?"

"Name, rank, and serial number!" he shouted, saliva spewing as he threw back the blanket, revealing a face red-hot with rage.

"Okay, calm down," I said, holding up my hands. "I didn't mean to upset you."

At once he grabbed my wrist, and before I had time to react, he pulled me toward him, turning me so my back was against his chest, one of his arms around my neck. At once Tom jumped to his feet and backed away, clearly frightened by the way Oliver was spiraling out of control. By the looks of things, I doubted that I could count on him to tackle Oliver for my sake, but I still needed his help.

"Tom . . ." I was thinking as fast as I could. "I brought some bottled water for all of us. It's in my car. Would you get it for us? Please?" I hoped by playing it cool I could regain some control over the situation. And with a great deal of luck, Tom might be at the car when the cops arrived, so he could lead them right to us.

Tom gave me a surprised look, then nodded and jogged off. I turned my attention back to Oliver, who was holding me much too tightly for me to even hope I was still O.O.T.T.O. "Oliver, why don't we sit down and relax until Tom gets back with the water? We can chat about whatever you want."

"Shut up!" he snarled in my ear. "I'm sick of your questions, sick of you hounding and pounding me until my head is ready to explode. I killed Delphi. *I* did it. It was *my* mission and I executed it perfectly."

I swallowed hard, my throat suddenly dry as I realized the true danger of my situation. I had expected him to run, not turn on me. "I—I'm glad you explained it, Oliver," I rasped, trying to sound calm and commanding, even though he was squeezing my throat. "Now please let go. You're cutting off my air."

Instead, he got to his feet, dragging me with him. I tried to twist around so I could use my hands and feet as weapons, but he clamped his other arm around my body and, in the process, squeezed my neck tighter. What was taking the cops so long?

Choking, I tugged frantically on his arm with my one free hand and pinched his skin, but he only pulled me deeper into the forest. I felt myself starting to faint from lack of oxygen and forced myself to go limp, hoping my deadweight would make him drop me. Then I heard a metallic *scritch*, and suddenly the point of a long knife was at my throat.

My heart raced in terror as I eyed the double-edged blade of a bayonet. "What are you doing?" I whispered, afraid to move.

"You're not fooling me," Oliver sneered. "I know you're with *them* now. You went over to their side. Libby was right. I told her you were one of the trusted ones, but she said she was the only one I could trust." The pitch of his voice had changed; he sounded now like a man possessed. "And you've got Tom, too. You *conspired* against me."

"No, Oliver," I whispered, trying not to jar his hand, "I'm on your side."

"You're lying. Lying and spying. A lying traitor!"

"I'm not a traitor. I came here to help you. You don't want to hurt an ally, do you?"

"Libby's my only ally now. You want to control me just like Delphi did. Libby was right. She said you were both traitors. She said you couldn't be trusted."

"Please, Oliver," I cried hoarsely as tears sprang to my eyes, "let me go. Don't hurt me."

"I have no choice. You see that, don't you? Do you see that I have to do it?"

Was he talking about killing me? "You have free will, Oliver. You don't have to do anything. Please let me go!"

"Don't you get it yet?" he cried, pushing the tip of the knife against my throat. "There is no free will!"

I flinched as I felt a sharp sting, then something warm and wet began to trickle down my neck. Oh, God, he'd punctured my throat.

"No will!" Oliver ranted. "No say in the matter. Over and done with. Over and out."

My heart was pounding so hard that the world began to spin around me, but I felt no pain, only a slow slide into darkness as my body sagged against him.

"It's time to go," he said in my ear. "Time to go where Delphi went."

CHAPTER TWENTY-SIX

Somewhere far away I heard the crunch of boots on brittle twigs. Then suddenly I was jerked upright. "Stay back!" Oliver cried, and at once the pressure on my neck eased enough for me to drag air into my lungs. I forced my eyes to focus, needing to know what was happening.

There stood Marco, tall, straight, steely-eyed, and iron-jawed, his dark gaze fixed solely on Oliver.

"I said stay back!" Oliver cried, pushing the sharp tip against my neck once more, only this time he was trembling as much as I was.

"Take it easy, man," Marco said in his deep, husky voice. "I'm not here to hurt you."

"Liar!" Oliver shouted. "You're one of them. You want to lock me away, too."

Marco took a step forward, hands outstretched, palms facing us. "I'm unarmed, troop. Your mission is over now. It's time to stand down."

Oliver dragged me back a step. "Stay away or I'll use this bayonet on her!"

"Listen to me," Marco said in a firm, compelling voice. "You know we soldiers have a strong moral code. You know that, right?"

"What do you know about soldiers?" Oliver spit out.

"Army Ranger, Third Battalion, Fort Benning. We talked about it at the bar, remember?"

Oliver's trembles ceased. Marco had his attention.

"You know civilians are not to be harmed," Marco said, "and Abby is a civilian."

"She's a traitor!" Oliver yelled.

"She's a civilian first, troop. She mustn't be hurt. That's our way. Our code of honor. You know we live by that code. We soldiers always obey the law, troop, so it's time to give it up now. You've got to let her go."

Oliver didn't move. He wasn't buying it. Tears blurred my vision and I blinked them away, praying the sting of his blade would be quick when it sliced across my throat. For several long, tense seconds I waited, my gaze on Marco, and his gaze on Oliver. Then, miraculously Oliver took the knife away and shoved me forward. I was free.

As I stumbled toward Marco, holding my hand against the cut on my throat, weakened by the feel of the sticky blood on my hand, he motioned for me to keep back, his commanding gaze never leaving Oliver's face. "Put down your weapon, soldier, and stand at attention."

At once, Oliver dropped the bayonet and drew himself up to salute. "Yes, sir."

I sank to the ground, shaking so hard my teeth were clattering, and watched in awe as Marco walked over to

Oliver and kicked the weapon out of his reach. "The authorities are on their way," he said, putting his hand on Oliver's shoulder. "Let's walk out together as men of honor."

"Yes, sir."

As they started toward the parking lot, a swarm of cops in blue uniforms, helmets, and flak vests surrounded them, weapons drawn. "Hands in the air," one of them shouted to Oliver.

Marco stepped back as they put Oliver on the ground and cuffed him. Then Marco turned, searching for me, and saw me huddled among the leaves. In a few long strides he was on his knees beside me, his arms around me, holding me tight as his strong hands stroked up and down my back. He rested his chin on top of my head and sighed, "Abby."

I wept tears of gratitude as I slid my arms around his waist and laid my head against his chest, soaking up his heat and strength. The feel of him, the scent of his clothing and skin, were safe and familiar. Boyfriend or not, Marco was still my hero.

When the worst of my trembling had subsided, he held me away to examine my neck. When he saw the cut, he immediately pulled a tissue from his pocket and pressed it against the wound. "It's not deep," he assured me. "You were lucky. Bayonets are sharp and deadly."

I couldn't think of anything to say in reply. My brain felt foggy and my muscles lethargic, as if my body had been drained of energy. Marco searched my eyes, then said, "Come on. Let's go back to the parking lot. The medics should be there by now. I want them to bandage that puncture wound and check you over."

"Oliver was going to kill me."

Marco peeled back one side of his leather jacket to show me his gun in its shoulder holster. "I was prepared to take him down." He let his jacket drop back in place, then put an arm around my shoulder.

"Aren't you going to say 'I told you so'?" I asked.

Marco said nothing, just helped me to my feet. The cops were in front of us, leading Oliver away. He marched stiff and straight between them like a well-trained soldier.

As we stepped out of the forest, Reilly came toward us. "Are you okay?" he asked me.

"She's got a wound on her throat," Marco said, "and I think she's in shock."

"There's the medics' van," Reilly said, pointing to a red, blue, and white vehicle.

"Where's Tom?" I asked, glancing around. "I sent him out here to find you."

"He was waiting by your car when I got here," Marco said. "He's giving a statement to the cops now."

I sat on a bench in the medics' van as the EMT cleaned the wound in my neck, covered it with a bandage, and checked out my blood pressure, temperature, and heart rate. I kept trying to sort through everything that had happened, but my thoughts felt disjointed. I glanced out the back of the van where I could see Marco talking to Reilly.

"You're good to go," the medic said. He handed me some bandages and a bottle of water. "Drink plenty of fluids today so you don't get dehydrated, and change the bandage every day until it forms a scab. My advice is to go home and eat something right now, then get some rest. You should be fine by tomorrow."

I stepped down from the van on legs that felt like wet noodles just as Marco came toward me. "I'm going to drive you home in your car and Seán will bring my car back. Is that okay?"

As if there was any doubt.

As soon as I got into the passenger side of my Vette, I put my head against the back of the seat and closed my eyes. I was emotionally exhausted and my body felt as though it had been run over by a steamroller. Marco seemed to understand and let me doze on the ride home. I heard him talking quietly on his cell phone to Nikki, and sure enough, when we reached my apartment building, Nikki was waiting at the front door to take over for him.

"I'll see you tomorrow, okay?" Marco said, cupping the side of my face.

I gave him a hug, unable to find the words to express my gratitude.

He hugged me back, gazed down at me for a moment, then turned and strode over to the curb, where Reilly was waiting in the Prius. As I watched him drive away, I said to Nikki, "It's been one freaky day, Nik."

"So I've heard," she said, putting an arm around my shoulders, "but we can talk about that later. Right now you need some food. I've got scrambled eggs and toast waiting for you."

Up in our apartment I sat at the table and forced myself to eat, but I felt no hunger. I was oddly numb, the events of the past hours seeming more like a dream. I gave Nikki a condensed version because that's all my brain could handle. Afterward, I lay down on the sofa with Simon curled up beside me and watched a home-decorating show until I began to drift off. Halfway between wakefulness and sleep, Oliver's voice began to float past me, bits and pieces of things he'd said.

I had no choice. . . . Delphi was going to put me into a mental hospital, just like Libby said she would. . . . Libby was right. She said both of you were traitors. . . . I had no choice. No say-so. No rights . . . Stop her, Oliver! Stop and drop her! . . . Those are my orders. . . . There is no free will. . . . Name, rank, and serial number. . . Mission accomplished. Time to move headquarters. All we can do now is wait. Wait and bait. . . . Those are my orders.

I sat up with a start as everything crystallized in my mind. Oliver hadn't planned the murder. He'd merely followed orders. Libby was the mastermind.

Mummy always made sure he took his meds. Now I'm stuck with him, but I can't watch him every minute. What am I supposed to do, commit my brother to an institution because he forgets to take his pills?

That was exactly what she'd intended to do. So she ordered him to kill Delphi and left him to take the blame, which he'd done willingly, as any good soldier would. Then no more mother to control Libby and no more crazy brother to hold her back. Talk about killing two birds with one stone. But how could I prove it?

I checked my watch and saw that it was only four o'clock in the afternoon, perhaps early enough to catch Libby in her office at her art shop. I jumped up, startling Simon and making myself dizzy. "Nikki?"

A note on the table said she'd gone to work. I splashed water on my face at the kitchen sink, grabbed my keys and my purse, and took off. I still felt off-kilter, but my adrenaline was so high I barely noticed.

Ten minutes later I turned onto Washington Street and pulled into an empty parking space near Blume's. I tried the yellow door first, but it was locked. I cupped my hands against the glass and peered inside, stunned to see that the shop had been emptied out, every piece of art and every stick of furniture gone. I ran to the deli next door and asked when Blume's had closed. The woman behind the counter said she'd seen workers wheeling large crates through the alley into trucks all morning.

Suddenly Oliver's cryptic words came back to me: *Mission accomplished. Time to move headquarters.* Libby was leaving town!

I ran to the Vette and took off, driving a little too fast as I headed for her subdivision, hoping she hadn't already packed up her condo and left. Surely Libby wasn't that fast.

I pulled up to the curb in front of the town house, jumped out of the Vette, and jogged up her long, curving driveway, then came to a sudden stop. Lisa Wells's green Volkswagen was parked in front of Libby's garage. Lisa must have figured it out, too.

At that moment Lisa came out of the garage carrying a leather case. She was wearing her black trench coat with a bright scarf and signature chopsticks through her blond bun. She shoved the case into the backseat of her Volkswagen, then headed toward the garage again. Was she removing evidence?

"Lisa? What's going on?"

She swung toward me, and my mouth fell open. Libby!

"You're just in time to say good-bye," Libby said.

I circled around her, staring in disbelief. She had dyed her hair back to blond and styled it just like Lisa's. A casual observer wouldn't be able to tell them apart. I peered into the garage bay. The yellow Corvette was gone, replaced with a green VW like Lisa's. How clever. If the police came looking for Libby, she could drive out of town right under their noses and everyone would assume she was Lisa.

"Mission accomplished?" I asked, standing in front of her.

"I don't know what you're talking about."

"Give me a break, Libby. You're not fooling me this time. You accomplished what you set out to do and now it's time to move headquarters."

"Honestly, Abby, you're beginning to annoy me. I'm merely taking a trip to Pittsburgh to visit my college roommate. Roshni's been bugging me to come see her."

"*Honestly?* You haven't been honest with me since the day I met you, Libby, so cut the act. I know what you did. Oliver told me all about how you planned your mother's death."

"Don't be crazy, Abby. I've had my fill of crazy people." She picked up a suitcase from inside the garage and shoved it in the backseat of her car next to the leather case. "And by the way, it's Leeza now. Libby is so—yesterday."

She started to get into the car, but I grabbed her arm. "You stole my identity, Libby, but you're not going to get away with murder."

"Let go of me!"

"What kind of monster are you to plot your mother's death, then use your own brother to carry it out? And

then, to make sure he was caught, you planted the broken pot and bloody gloves under his sink."

"Again, Abby, you're really annoying me."

"Then, just to confuse the picture, you set Tilly and
me up as suspects, too. Don't deny it, Libby. I know you
sent Oliver with Tilly to buy a red wig, and had him plant
a key in Tilly's purse to make *her* look guilty. Then you
had him wear that wig and drive your Vette to drop the
body behind Bloomers to make *me* look guilty.

"And all the while you played the victim role to the hilt.
You even bought Oliver the snake as a birthday present,
then ordered him to put it in your mailbox. The only surprise was Kayla showing up at your mom's viewing, but
that only reinforced everyone's belief that you were a victim. Poor little Libby. And all the while you orchestrated
everything, down to the last detail—sending Oliver running
into the woods to hide, telling him the cops were on to him."

Libby gave me a smug glance. "Too bad you can't
prove any of it."

"Were you at your mother's house the morning she
was killed? Did you tell Oliver that Delphi snitched on
him back in high school in order to make him angry
enough to hit her? Did you tell Oliver she was going to
commit her to a mental hospital, then give Oliver the
order to stop her from making that phone call?"

Libby jerked her arm away and got into the driver's
seat, but I held open the door.

"Did your mother beg you to help her, Libby, or did
she crawl over the bamboo plant to get away from you?
She was still alive when Oliver took the broken pot to the
garage, wasn't she? What did you do, hit her with the
wine bottle to finish her off?"

Libby started the engine and put it in gear. "Like I said, prove it." She gunned the engine, so I jumped back.

"Your brother is going to stand trial for murder because of you," I called, following her down the driveway. "You're crazier than Oliver is, *Leeza*."

At the bottom of the driveway, she rolled down the window. "Oliver won't go to prison. They'll commit him. It's where he belongs anyway. He'll get good care there."

"While you drive off with your half of the inheritance and guardianship over Oliver's half. How convenient."

She shrugged. "I learned everything at my mother's knee. So good-bye again, Abby. It's been fun being you."

She rolled up the window, then drove away, and all I could do was stand there with my hands curled into fists of helpless rage because, as she'd pointed out, I couldn't prove a thing.

Suddenly I heard sirens and saw three cop cars race up the street and form a blockade to stop her. Marco pulled up behind them and got out of his car as the cops cautiously approached the Volkswagen with weapons drawn, shouting orders. I watched as Libby emerged from the car with her hands in the air, a look of shock on her face.

"What did I do?" she cried. She spotted Marco and called, "Marco, do something! Tell them I'm innocent."

"I doubt they'd believe me," he replied, coming to stand beside me. He gazed at me in concern. "Are you all right?"

"Probably not, but seeing that"—I pointed toward Libby, who was being handcuffed and tucked into the backseat of a police car—"makes it worth the effort."

"How did you figure it out?"

"Just call it a gut feeling," I said, giving him a pointed glance.

Marco got it. "I guess I had that coming."

"Take the *guess* out of it. So how did *you* figure it out?"

"I remembered Lisa Wells telling me about a conversation she'd had with Libby a few days ago. It seems Libby was blaming her brother for planting his snake in her mailbox *before* we found the snake tank that she claimed to know nothing about."

"Very good, PI Salvare."

"Yeah, well, don't give me all the credit. The real clincher was the DNA evidence. It came back today." He gave me that captivating half grin that made me want to melt inside.

I didn't let him see it, though. I played it cool. "What did the evidence show?"

"Scrapings from under Delphi's fingernails placed Libby at the murder scene." Marco shook his head in amazement. "She and Delphi must have had quite a struggle."

"Hard to believe, isn't it? Libby planned her mother's murder, had her brother carry out the execution, and set up others to take the blame. I knew Libby was up to no good, but I never thought she was that evil."

"She fooled me at first," Marco said ruefully. "I really bought into her innocent act. But once I started investigating Libby's stalker and dug up her former college roommate, I caught on." For my benefit, he added, "According to her roommate's story, Libby stalked her professor's husband and was nearly thrown out of school."

I didn't mention that I'd talked to the roommate, too. Sometimes it was wiser to leave people in the dark.

"All those threatening e-mails Libby got," Marco continued, "she sent to herself from a computer at the library. A trace on the phone messages led right back to her art shop, and I'm guessing she also wrote letters to herself and mailed them from out of town. It defies belief that she thought she could fool everyone. I don't know what that says of her opinion of my detective skills." He paused, then said, "I'm sorry I couldn't talk to you about the case. You understand why, don't you? You were too close to the situation."

Too close to the *situation*? That's how he viewed what Libby had done to me?

At that, the hurt feelings that I'd been nursing for weeks gushed out. "Of course I was close to the situation, you jerk," I cried, smacking his arm. "Libby was stealing my life right in front of my eyes, and you wouldn't believe me. Then I poured my heart out to you, pleading with you to stay away from her, and you *still* took her side—because she'd hired you."

I tried to smack him again, but he caught my wrist in midair and pulled me close, wrapping his arms around me. It was the nearest I'd been to him in a long time. "Why would you do that to me?" I asked against his jacket, almost in tears. "Is your PI work more important to you than I am?"

He merely continued to hold me, his chin resting on top of my head, leaving my questions unanswered. Or maybe not answering was his answer. Maybe he was trying to figure out how to break it to me that his work came first.

I heard the squad cars pull away, taking Libby with them. Then Marco said quietly, "It's over, Abby. Now you can get your life back."

Most of it, anyway. I pulled away from him, and without meeting his eye, I said, "So I guess that wraps it up." With a lift of my shoulder, I added, "I'll see you around, then."

"Before you go, would you walk over to my car with me? I have something for you."

I gave Marco a skeptical glance, but he wouldn't say anything more, so I followed him along the curb to his car, and waited while he opened the trunk.

"Go ahead," he said, gesturing. "It might be a little painful, but it won't bite."

A little painful? Curious now, I stepped forward and peered inside—and there lay my mom's beaded jacket that had been on display at Libby's shop. I didn't know whether to be pleased or horrified. "How did you get it? Libby packed up everything yesterday."

"I found it on top of a pile of crates in the alley behind her shop, waiting for garbage pickup."

"When?"

"A few days ago."

Which meant Libby had never actually wanted my mom's artwork at all. She'd taken it just to torture me. "I'm so glad Mom didn't see it there. She would've been humiliated."

"Yeah, I kind of figured that."

I gazed at Marco with deep gratitude, and despite my hurt, I could feel myself falling in love with him all over again. "That was very kind of you."

He picked up one of my hands, smoothing the skin on

top with his thumb. "I don't want to lose you, Abby. We had something special, something I've never had with another woman. I don't know where it might lead us, but I do know that I sure as hell don't want to let it go."

I gulped back tears. "Me, neither. But the thing is, if you don't trust me—"

"Who said I don't trust you?"

"You, by not trusting my gut feelings about Libby."

"That was a mistake, and I'm really sorry about it, but it had nothing to do with my trust in you."

"It does, Marco. Don't you see? You brushed off my concerns as though they were silly, and that told me you didn't trust my judgment."

"Maybe so, but you sent me the same message, Abby. You didn't trust my judgment, either."

"That's because you were wrong."

I heard the words come out of my mouth and had to laugh at myself. "Okay, we both goofed on this one, but if we want to get back that something special, we've got to do better next time."

"What can I do to make it better right now?"

"Well, for one thing, don't let me walk out of your office in a snit again. Come after me. Bar the door. Whatever it takes to show me you care. And if I should ever give you another ultimatum, just say the word *Libby*. That'll snap me out of it. Also, a few more apologies and maybe a little groveling wouldn't hurt. Oh, and one more thing—"

Marco cupped my face in his strong hands. "God, how I've missed you, Abby."

Ah-h. Music to my ears.

He traced a line down my jaw to my chin and around

my lips, then dipped his head to kiss me, his mouth sweet and seductive against mine. I closed my eyes, feeling the firm texture of his lips, breathing in his clean, lightly musky male scent.

"I was a stubborn ass," he murmured, his lips moving to nibble my ear, "and I'm sorry."

"I'm sorry you were a stubborn ass, too," I breathed on a sigh.

"We've got a lot of making up to do," he whispered, sending tingles of pleasure through every nerve ending in my body.

"What did you have in mind?"

"Well," he said, leaning back to gaze at me, "since you've had a rough day, how about that foot massage I promised you?"

Oh, baby, a foot massage.

Are you going to let him off the hook so easily? that little voice of reason whispered in my ear, fighting against my urge to completely abandon myself to the pleasure of being in Marco's arms again. But the voice was right. No way was Marco getting off with only a foot massage. I wasn't a pushover.

"Excuse me, but I believe there was a bottle of wine and chocolate truffles in that offer?"

Marco grinned that quirky, adorable grin that made my heart flutter, then dipped his head to kiss me again. "That's my Sunshine."

Read on for an excerpt from the next
Flower Shop Mystery by Kate Collins

Evil in Carnations

Coming soon from Obsidian

"Isn't there a law that says public hallways have to be lighted?" Marco complained. "This bulb was out last week. How are you supposed to find your key in the dark?"

I stopped rummaging through my duffel bag to whisper, "Keep your voice down. You'll wake the neighbors."

In a complete change of mood, my hunky, ex–Army Ranger boyfriend swept one side of my hair back to press hot kisses against my neck. "You didn't seem to mind waking the neighbors yesterday."

"I didn't *know* those neigh—" *Oh, baby.* His kisses were sending tingles to erotic zones I didn't even know existed—and I thought he'd found them all.

Where was the damn key? I really had to get a smaller bag.

"Why don't we go back to my apartment," Marco murmured in my ear, "and extend our trip another day?"

Now there was an offer that was hard to refuse. Who wouldn't want to prolong a romantic weekend with a hot, handsome hunk like Marco Salvare? He was all man, all the time, a guy who was both tough *and* sensitive, who could cook up a mean omelet and take down a killer all in the same day.

After our seven-hour red-eye flight back to Indiana from Key West, I wasn't exactly looking forward to putting in a long day at the flower shop—I don't do well on only a few hours' sleep. But as Bloomers' owner, I couldn't ignore my responsibilities, either. So, as much as it pained me, I had to decline.

Abandoning my key hunt, I wound my arms around his neck and gazed up into those sexy dark brown eyes. "I really, *really* wish I could, Marco, but you know how hectic Mondays are, and besides, Lottie and Grace are expecting me. But it's a nice thought." Almost too nice to let go.

"Yeah, I figured as much."

Reluctantly, I released him to start rummaging again. "What time is it, anyway? Is it six o'clock yet? I still have to unpack, shower . . ."

Marco ran his hands over my shoulders and down my arms, his body close to mine, the seductive aroma of his spicy aftershave calling forth sweet memories of our weekend. "How about that?" he murmured in my ear. "I was planning to shower, too."

My fingers closed around the key at last and I pressed it into his palm. "You know what they say? Two can shower cheaper than one."

"I think we should test that theory right now." He started to unlock the door, then paused. "Nikki will be asleep, right?"

"Déjà vu. You asked me that same question last Sunday night."

"And the answer was?"

"Nikki's depressed and dateless, remember? She'll be sound asleep until noon."

"*Sound* asleep . . . as in, nothing will wake her?"

"Except for smoke alarms."

"Then we'll have to be careful not to set them off."

"Like we did Saturday night?"

"Like we did *twice* Saturday night." Marco tilted my chin up and kissed me, a deep, hot, stirring kiss that made me glad there were no smoke alarms directly overhead.

Somehow he managed to unlock the door, back me inside, drag our bags in with his foot, close the door *and* lock it without breaking our kiss. I dropped my peacoat and purse on the floor and we began fumbling at each other's clothing, still kissing hot and heavy.

All at once, someone pounded on the door, shouting, "New Chapel Police. Open up!"

With a gasp I jumped away from Marco. Our watch cat, Simon, who had just come around the corner to greet us, arched his back menacingly at the disturbance, then changed his mind and fled the scene, his claws skittering on the hallway tile. Some protector he was.

"What the hell?" Marco exclaimed, buttoning his shirt as he started for the door.

"I'll bet it's Reilly playing a joke," I said, following him. "I wonder how he got into the building."

Marco peered through the peep hole. "It's not Reilly." He opened the door, leaving the chain in place, so I ducked beneath his arm to peer through the crack.

Two men in blue uniform stood outside, neither of whom was our buddy Sergeant Sean Reilly. One appeared to be in his mid-thirties, about five years older than Marco. The other had a boyish build, a smooth, baby face, and a belligerent stance that young cops often adopted to make them seem experienced.

Instantly I stepped out of sight. Great. What had I done this time?

"What's up?" Marco asked nonchalantly. Men in uniform didn't intimidate him. He'd served on the New Chapel police force for about a year after his Army Ranger days—until all the rules and regulations, as well as a vindictive watch commander, got to him.

"We're looking for Nikki Hiduke," a deep voice said. I was guessing it was the older cop.

Nikki? That was novel. I was usually the one in trouble.

"What business do you have with Nikki?" Marco asked.

"Is she here or not?" a tenor voice demanded. The younger officer was clearly unwilling to divulge any info. He probably had no clue he was talking to an ex-cop.

"She might be here," Marco replied coolly.

Just to be sure, I looked around and spotted Nikki's keys on the table.

"Is it all right if we step inside?" the deep voice asked politely. "You might not want the neighbors in on this."

Yikes. That didn't sound good.

Marco unchained the door, pulled it open, and stepped back to allow them to enter, putting me in full view. Out in the hallway, Mr. Bodenhammer, the building superintendent, tried to get a peek inside before Marco shut the door. Now I knew how the police got in.

"How's it going, Pete?" Marco said, obviously recognizing him from his time on the force.

"Business as usual. That's why we're here."

"Are you Nikki?" the rookie asked me. He was definitely

new in town, because only a stranger would see my bright red hair and freckles and not know who I was. Not that I was a celebrity or anything. More like the town's trouble magnet.

"I'm Abby Knight," I said. "Nikki's my roommate."

"You're the florist, right?" the cop named Pete asked.

It was such a pleasure to hear myself labeled as something other than "the troublemaker who flunked out of law school" that I nodded eagerly. In a college town like mine, a flunk-out was the equivalent to being the village idiot.

"Yeah, I thought that was you." To his partner he added, "She's the one who keeps sticking her nose into police business."

"Excuse me," I said, taking exception to his snide remark. "I helped solve a few murder cases by sticking my nose into police business. And I'll have you know that my dad was a sergeant on the police force before a drug dealer's bullet put him out of commission."

"Abby," Marco said quietly, laying a hand on my arm as though he feared I might take a swing at the guy. Although I measured in at a mere five feet two inches, Marco knew that I knew how to throw a punch.

At that moment, Nikki came around the corner, sleepily rubbing her eyes, her spiked blond hair sticking up more than usual. She'd tied her purple robe tightly around her tall, slender body, and stuck her feet into giant dark purple slippers, making her long legs look like cocktail toothpicks capped by kalamata olives.

"What's all the noise about?" she asked with a yawn.

Marco glanced around in surprise, then gave me a pointed look, obviously remembering my comment about the smoke alarms. Okay, so it was smoke alarms *and* police raids.

"Nikki Hiduke?" the younger cop tried again.

She squinted at him, unable to see anything but blurred shapes without her contacts. "Yes?"

He showed her his badge, which she had to bring up close to her face. "Would you get your coat and come with us to the police station, please? We have some questions we'd like to ask you."

She looked from one to the other in confusion. "In my pajamas?"

I knew Nikki wasn't completely awake or she would have asked a far more pertinent question, which is exactly what Marco did. "You want to tell us what this is about?" he said.

I stepped in front of Nikki in a valiant act of self-sacrifice. "And why does she have to go with you to answer questions? Why can't you talk to her here?"

"We need to talk to her," the rookie said immediately, thumbs hooked in his thick leather belt, "down at the *station.*"

"I got that part the first time," I said. "But about what? She has the right to know."

"I don't hear *her* asking," the rookie fired back. He was starting to get on my nerves.

"Nikki, ask them why they want to talk to you," Marco instructed.

As she opened her mouth to speak, the rookie said, "She's wanted for questioning in a homicide."

At that, Nikki and I both opened our mouths, but only to gasp. Were they insinuating that my dearest friend had something to do with a murder? I turned and met her shocked stare, and she gave me a look that said, *I don't have a clue what's going on.*

"Do you know a man by the name of Jonas Treat?" Pete asked her.

"Yes," she answered.

"He was murdered during the night," the rookie announced, looking very pleased with himself.

Nikki gasped again. The man's name was unfamiliar to me, but she obviously knew him.

"How was he murdered?" Marco asked Pete.

"You know I can't give you that information, Salvare," Pete said. "You're a civilian now."

I quietly asked Nikki, "Is Jonas Treat the guy with the Ferrari from the speed-dating event?"

She gave me a quick nod, which left me wondering how she'd learned his last name, since no personal information was supposed to be given out.

"I told you that speed-dating thing was a bad idea," Marco murmured in my ear.

"Nikki doesn't need to go down to the station to answer your questions," I told the cops. "She met this man only briefly last Thursday night at a social event. Tell them, Nikki."

My roommate merely put a hand over her mouth, as if in shock.

"Nikki," I urged, "tell them."

"Yes," said the younger cop, with a sly gleam in his eye, "and while you're at it, tell us where you were last night."

Bewildered, I glanced at her and noticed that her face had taken on an ashen hue, as though she might throw up. What was going on?

"Nikki, you don't have to answer any questions," Marco said quietly. "Just state that you want your lawyer present."

"Were you with a man named Jonas Treat yesterday evening?" Pete asked anyway.

When she merely stared at them, I whispered, "What's wrong with you? Tell them no."

She hung her head. "I'm sorry, Abby."

Sorry?

"Okay," Pete said, stepping toward Nikki, "get your coat and let's go."

Suddenly I got it: Nikki *had* gone out with Jonas—in spite of my best efforts to warn her away from him. "Oh, Nikki, you didn't!"

"I couldn't help it, Abby. Jonas was—"

"Nikki," Marco snapped, causing her to jump, "don't say another word."

She looked perplexed. "I was only going to say he was—"

Marco put up his hand to stop her. "*Anything* you say can be used against you. Abby is going to call Dave Hammond for you now and have him meet you at the station." Marco turned toward Pete. "Is it okay if she puts on some decent clothes first?"

"And my c-contact lenses?" Nikki asked, visibly trembling.

The younger cop tapped the face of his watch. "We'll give you five minutes. I'll be right outside your door, so don't even think about sneaking out a window."

As if Nikki would ever do that. Now me, that was a different story.